Promise of the Rainbow

By Ms Randa Lynne Zollinger

Dedication

I would like to dedicate this book to two of my favorite people, who were both school librarians/media specialists. The first is my aunt, Justine Zollinger, (November, 1917) who has used her love of words to become a well-known Scrabble player and has entered in competitions across the nation.

The second is my friend, Gene Kilpatrick, (January 31, 1944 –January 2, 2014) whom I worked with at school for thirty-five years. Gene's broad base of knowledge and love of culture led him to frequently tease me about being a "philistine".

My love for them continues and extends beyond this life.

Acknowledgements

I would like to thank all my students through the years, who have brought me to the point in my life where I have something to write about, as well as all the others who have encouraged me. I would also like to thank Susan Datson, who cheerfully helped me edit and proofread. In addition, I give my thanks to Darla Todd for helping with the cover, as well as sharing her knowledge about photography.

Prologue

In Jaden's first week home from the hospital, he didn't have much energy, and he didn't do anything other than lie around. It wasn't that he was tired physically; he had slept almost around the clock for a couple of days. But, he just seemed to be drained emotionally and was beginning to wonder if he would ever feel normal again. He awoke one morning to find his twin, Jenny, sitting on the end of his bed.

"Geez, Jaden, get up! It's already the middle of June! You've been doing nothing for way too long. Don't you at least want to go swimming? You're wasting the whole summer!" Jenny had been worried about him for days and was still feeling guilty that she had let him down when he needed her. If she could just get him going again, maybe they would both feel better.

"I do want to, Jen, but I just don't much feel like it."

"Come on, Jaden. You have to start doing something. Have you even texted Trevor since you've been home?" Jenny asked.

"Oh, yeah. Lots. But, as much as I want to see him, I'm afraid to ask if he can come over. Dad's been being so nice, and it seems like he's been going out of his way to make sure I'm okay. I hate to make waves or do something to mess that up. Do you know if Dad's started going to counseling yet? I sort of want to have him start that before I ask to do stuff with Trevor."

"I don't really know. I don't think Mom and Dad would tell us that, do you?"

"Probably not," Jaden said thoughtfully. "Did you know Mom told me I had to go to counseling, too?"

"Yeah, she said it would help with your depression. If you'd start going now, maybe you can be done by the end of the summer." Jaden drummed the fingers on his left hand in frustration.

"I wouldn't be depressed if Dad would just let me be friends with Trevor and if people wouldn't make fun of me," he said vehemently. "At least

Brandon's being really nice now. He comes in my room and talks for a few minutes every day."

"He really does care about you, Jaden. He's your big brother, and he feels horrible about what happened."

The night before, when Jaden's parents, Donnie and Alice, had settled into bed, the very issue of Jaden getting counseling had come up indirectly.

Alice had said, "Donnie, when are you going to make an appointment with that psychologist?"

"I thought we'd wait until Jaden feels a little stronger," he had replied.

"Not for Jaden, for you!" she had answered.

"Alice, I'm going to; I said I would. But you know the doctor said Jaden needed to start right away because of his suicide attempt. We need to get him help first. I can wait, because we can't afford both of us going to therapy at the same time."

Knowing that was financially true, Alice agreed, but she didn't like it. She knew the longer Donnie waited to make a counseling appointment, the less likely he would go at all. She knew he needed to talk to someone, and he knew he needed to talk to someone, but he was reluctant, at best.

Chapter 1

"I can't believe school starts tomorrow," Jaden was excitedly saying on the phone to his best friend, Devon.

"I know, dude, it seems like the summer just flew by. And starting high school rocks! There'll be so much more to do, and sports to play! I can't wait!"

Brow knitted with concern, Jaden asked, "Are you still going out for the swim team?"

"For sure, buddy, at least this year. We made that pact years ago, and football can wait."

Jaden couldn't help but grin at the news. Devon was such a good athlete, and in particular, such a good football player. The coaches had been watching him since he had been in middle school, but Devon was going to stick to his vow that they would both swim in the ninth grade.

"I'm glad they had early sports physicals last week, so we can swim the first day of practice. Did you get that notice from the coaches saying the first practice would be Wednesday for everybody who already had their physicals? The others don't get to start until the next week, because the regular fall physicals aren't until Friday."

"Yeah, I'm glad, too. I guess we also have that meeting with the coaches after school tomorrow. Wonder what that's about."

Jaden answered, "Oh, I think that's just when they give us the paperwork for our parents to sign, you know, and turn in our insurance and stuff. Jenny had to do that in middle school when she played softball."

"Oh, yeah, come to think of it, I did, too, for middle school sports. Okay, sounds good. Gotta go. See you tomorrow before school."

Jaden couldn't believe how relieved he felt that Devon was being true to his word. After all the trauma and drama that Jaden had been through in the last four months, he was so glad that Devon really seemed at ease with him again and truly meant what he had said.

The next day all three of the Hansen kids headed off to school together. They hadn't all been in the same school since when they were in elementary. This year Brandon was a senior, and the twins were starting the ninth grade. Before the last summer, in fact ever since Brandon had become a teenager, he wouldn't have been caught dead having anything to do with his younger siblings. Now, however, he was including them in discussions about the upcoming school year, encouraging them to ask questions, and in general, being a great older brother.

Once they arrived at school, though, Brandon split off from the twins to go talk to his friends. Jaden and Jenny were trying to look cool, but were wide-eyed at the new school and nervous about not knowing many people and maybe not being able to find their classes. Jaden was looking in every direction, searching for Devon, while Jenny was scanning for her friend, Sarah. There would be strength in numbers, they were sure.

"Jaden, I've been looking for you!"

Jaden turned quickly to see, not Devon, but Trevor.

"Oh, wow, am I ever glad to see you!" Jaden exclaimed. "I didn't think you'd be here the first day." He stood up and impulsively hugged him with excitement, but stepped back quickly when he realized they were in full view of everyone. But Trevor didn't seem to be bothered.

"My parents cut our trip short, so that I wouldn't miss the first day. You don't know how glad I am, because I've really missed you!"

Trevor and Jaden had secretly been boyfriends for about a year and a half. They felt that secrecy was forced upon them, because Jaden's dad had repeatedly insisted he wasn't going to have a son that was a "fag". After Jaden had attempted suicide last spring, his dad had lightened up quite a bit, but still didn't know the complete story about Jaden and Trevor. Jaden continued to be nervous about the whole situation, and even though his therapist had encouraged him to talk to his dad, he hadn't yet broached the subject.

"Hey, Trev, have you decided if you're going to be on the swim team yet? I know you want to keep your job at the Y, but can't they just let you work on weekends, like you did last year?"

"Yeah, I finally talked to the head lifeguard about it, and it's all good. It's just weekends for swim season."

"Cool! We have a meeting right after school in Coach Swartout's room. See you there," he said, lightly touching Trevor's arm, as the first bell was ringing.

The day passed quickly, finding new classes, running into friends, and trying to get used to high school. Once again, Jenny and Jaden had math together. Jaden was relieved, because Jenny was a lot stronger in the subject than he, and she enjoyed helping him. Other than lunch, that was the only time in the day they were together. Devon and Jaden found they didn't have lunch together, but they had the same English, art, Freshman Foundations, and social studies classes. They had hoped to have P.E. together also, like they did the year before, but no luck. When it was time for P.E. and Jaden went to his class, his dismay about not being with Devon evaporated when he saw Trevor walk into the gym. A big smile lit up his face. Jaden had never thought he would get to have a class with Trevor because he was in tenth grade, but P.E. was one of the few classes that had multi-grade levels.

After listening to the instructor drone on and on about policies, uniforms, and attitude, gratefully, the period was over. Since it was the last class of the day, Jaden and Trevor walked down to Ms. Swartout's room together. When they got there, Jaden eyed a special friend.

"Ricardo! Mi amigo! I'm so glad to see you!" Jaden had neither seen nor talked to Ricardo since his own attendance at school had ended so abruptly the previous year, two weeks before the term was officially over. Trevor raised one eyebrow and hung back with his lips pressed together as the two friends hugged each other. As Jaden and Ricardo were catching up on the past few months, the room was filling with potential swimmers. Devon walked in just as Coach Swartout was rapping the desk and calling for attention in the crowded room. There were no seats left, so Devon stood by the door with a couple of other kids. Jaden and Ricardo had managed to find a seat, but Jaden didn't notice right away that Trevor had wandered to the back. He had been engrossed in what Coach was saying, and when she stopped talking to pass out a form, Jaden finally realized that Trevor wasn't sitting with them. He craned his head around and saw Devon at the door and then spotted Trevor in the back, but Trevor either didn't see him looking, or intentionally wouldn't make eye contact. When the meeting was over, both Devon and

Trevor exited quickly, while Jaden was caught in the throng of the other swimmers. Neither was in sight when he finally got out of the room.

As he walked out of the school building, Jaden texted Trevor.

"Where r u? R u gonna take me home so we can ride around some?" Trevor texted back.

"I didn't think u wld want to go w me. U were too involved w Ricardo." Oh, no, thought Jaden. I thought we had worked out Trevor's jealousy about Ricardo last spring. Thinking that texting wasn't a good way to communicate about this, Jaden wrote, "I'm calling u."

When Trevor answered with only a "Yeah", Jaden thought, oh brother, here we go again.

He said, "I wasn't involved with Ricardo! Just talking to him. He didn't even know what happened to me at the end of school last year. He's my friend. I can't just ignore him. Besides, you're the one I love and want to be with."

"Well, I don't know how all of us, Devon, Ricardo, you, and me being on the swim team together is going to work. Maybe I should just go ahead and work during the week."

"No, Trevor! Don't be like that! I really want us to swim together. Ricardo doesn't mean anything to me. Please?"

"I'll think about it and let you know tomorrow." The line went dead.

All of Jaden's excitement about the new school year and the swim team, and about getting to see Trevor a few days before he thought he would, fizzled and left him feeling some of the old despair of last year. As he trudged home, he thought, I don't believe this. I was so looking forward to starting a new school year and having my problems under control. Now, it doesn't seem like much has changed.

Jenny had decided to concentrate only on Young People's Theater and softball this year, so she was already home talking to Alice when Jaden walked in.

"Hey, Jay, how was your day? Wait, what's wrong?" Jenny knew her twin too well, and when she saw his face, she knew something was up. Alice, too, was more attuned to her son than she had been in the past.

"Why the long face, honey? Did something go wrong in school?"

Turning away to hide the tears he knew were building, Jaden said, "Nah, I'm good. Just tired from a long first day." Then he went to his room.

Following right behind him, Jenny said, "Tell me the truth, Jaden Hansen! Did something happen at the swim team meeting?"

"Yeah, everything was great at first. I have P.E. with Trevor, and we went to the meeting together. He told me he was definitely gonna swim this year, so I was psyched. But when Ricardo showed up, Trevor walked away, and when I texted him later, I could tell he was pissed. And, Devon showed up at the meeting, but I didn't get to talk to him at all. No telling what he's thinking, because I'm the one who talked him into swimming in the first place. It seems like everything's going downhill right from the first day."

"Try not to be so pessimistic, Jaden. You know your therapist told you to think of positive ways that things could work out when you start to feel depressed. We both know Trevor can be jealous, but he gets over it after a while. I'm sure he'll get over this like he has before."

"I hope you're right, Jen, I sure hope you're right."

As Jaden lay in bed that night, he tried to figure out how he could be friends with Ricardo, but not make Trevor jealous. And now that Devon accepted him for who he was, could he also accept Jaden's gay friends? He guessed he would talk to Dr. Lewis about it at his next therapy session.

The following day at school Jaden ran into Ricardo on his way to second period. They were pleased to find out that, even though they didn't have the same classes, their classrooms were close, so they could walk together like they did the year before.

"Ricardo, are you excited about swim practice starting tomorrow? I can hardly wait!"

"Si, I am happy, too. I hope all the kids are nice to us. I am nervous some."

"Well, at least there's you and Trevor and me and Devon. We all know each other." Jaden was trying his best to be positive, but Ricardo looked doubtful. He and Jaden had both been harassed continually the year before for being "different", and he had no reason to think things would change. Jaden gave Ricardo an encouraging clap on the back and went into his math class.

"Jaden, you'll never guess who I saw!" Jenny had a big smile on her face and an impish look. "Mr. Anthony got transferred here from the middle school!" Mr. Anthony, a towering six-foot-five former professional basketball player, was Jenny's favorite administrator and had helped Jaden and her when they had some issues with other students a couple of years before. Mr. Anthony had also gone to all of Jenny's softball games. He had been the team's biggest fan. "I saw him at the end of the hall and talked to him. He's going to be here permanently."

"That's awesome, Jenny. I hope we don't need his help any more, though," he said with a rueful smile.

Chapter 2

It was kind of cool to walk down the halls of the high school when you had a brother who was a varsity letterman in two sports, football and baseball. The football banners were already up, and Brandon's name was prominently displayed. The first football game would be in two weeks, and he was known all over campus as a player to watch. At dinner the second night of school, the Hansen family was talking about the upcoming game.

"Dad, one of my teachers asked me today if I was Brandon Hansen's sister," Jenny said proudly, smiling at her brother. "When I said yes, all the other kids looked at me like it was a big deal."

"It is a big deal, sweetheart. Your brother is a great athlete, and I'm sure he'll be recruited by lots of colleges this year," Donnie replied. Donnie had really been through it with Brandon the year before when his son was unknowingly taking steroids and had an intolerable attitude. But Brandon had made a great effort all through the summer to change his behavior and get along with his parents. The self-discipline he had learned through playing sports paid off in this respect, and he was a pleasure to be around again, just like when he and his dad were so close as he was growing up. Donnie couldn't be happier.

"And now I'll have a brother on varsity swim team, too. Don't you start practice tomorrow, Jaden?" Jenny asked. Jaden nodded and beamed at Jenny's acknowledgement of his being on a team, too.

Brandon uncharacteristically added, "Yo, Jay! That's right. When will your meets be? I hope I can go to cheer you on!" Donnie and Alice exchanged glances and smiled widely. It had been torture last year when Brandon had been at odds with everyone. This new Brandon had been worth waiting for.

Jaden, who was as thrilled as his parents about how Brandon was acting, reached across the table to high-five his brother. He had always looked up to him, but Brandon's previous behavior toward him had been more than a little painful.

He said, "We don't have our schedule yet, so I don't know what day of the week the meets will be. I sure hope you can come, though."

Donnie interjected, "We'll all come to as many of your meets as we can, Jaden." Turning back to Brandon, he asked, "Are you going to be playing offense, as well as defense next week?" From there the conversation went back to football, as it always did.

The next day dawned clear and blue, and Jaden was geared up for swim practice to begin that afternoon, albeit somewhat nervous about how the social aspect would go. At school the day before, Trevor had petulantly agreed to continue his plans to be on the team. That same night, Jaden had decided to face things head-on, so he had asked Devon and Ricardo to meet Trevor and him at the gym before practice. They would walk the short distance to the pool together.

Thankfully, when they met up, another small group of swimmers joined them as they walked, and talk was all about the upcoming season. There were a couple of kids in the group who had been on the team the year before, so they had the benefit of knowing what to expect at practice and were glad to share that information with the newcomers. When they arrived at the pool, the new kids looked at it with awe.

"Wow! This is a cool pool, isn't it? It's not as big as the pool at the YMCA, but it still has six lanes, and look! It has bleachers. Do a lot of people watch the meets?" Jaden asked the group.

Chelsea, a returning swimmer, said, "Mostly just parents and friends come, but at double-dual meets lots of people are here."

"What are double-dual meets?" wondered Jaden.

"That's when we swim against two other schools at the same time. Those meets are cool, but the downside is that each team gets fewer lanes to compete in."

Coach Swartout met them on the pool deck and introduced Coach Staley, her assistant. After that, she told all the returning swimmers to get in lanes one and two and swim ten laps free, the equivalent of the 500-yard freestyle event.

"All swimmers who are new to us, but have been on a team before, do the same in lanes three and four. The rest of you get in lanes five and six, and start swimming freestyle while Coach Staley and I watch to see how you do," instructed Coach Swartout. The swimmers, standing there in the heat, could hardly wait to get in the water. They quickly split up and got into their respective lanes. As Jaden swam in lane five, he heard Coach Staley call out corrections and encouragement to the other swimmers and was hoping he would impress Coach Swartout with the skill he had developed in all his previous practice. After watching his lane for quite a while, she switched over to watch the other rookies. After they had swum freestyle for what seemed like a very long time, they were told to swim two hundred yards each of the backstroke, breaststroke, and butterfly. Most of the rookies could do the backstroke and some semblance of the breaststroke, but many didn't have a clue as to how to do the butterfly. "We'll save the fly for another day," laughed Coach as she watched them. "Now let's do some work on turns."

At the end of a hard, but satisfying, practice, the swimmers assembled on the deck for instructions before getting dressed and leaving.

Coach Staley started by saying, "I see a lot of you wearing board shorts and two-piece suits. It's okay for practice, but for competition, you'll be wearing Speedos. We'll be ordering them next week, when the team is finalized."

Groans from some of the guys were heard, and Devon whispered to Jaden, "I wouldn't be caught dead showing my junk in those little suits. They're so gay! I didn't know we had to wear those!" Immediately Devon felt awkward having used the term gay, but Jaden didn't seem to care.

"Hold it down, guys. You'll find out that those board shorts add so much time to your events that you'll be glad to wear something else. Besides, we have to wear suits alike as a team. But, you don't have to wear the short Speedos. You can wear jammers, if you prefer. When I swam in high school, that's what I wore," continued Coach Staley.

"What are jammers?" one of the new guys asked.

"They're like the short suits, but go down to your knees." A few guys looked relieved, while others looked doubtful. None of the returning swimmers had on such a thing. The girls pooh-poohed the boys' fears and made fun of their insecurities. When the discussion finally ended, all of them went to the change rooms and got ready to go home. Jaden was anxious to get feedback from Trevor and Ricardo, because not much talking had gone on in practice.

As they dressed, Jaden asked, "What did you guys think of practice? I thought it was fun!"

Ricardo quietly responded, "Si, very fun. I think of Brownsville when I swim there." Ricardo didn't like to draw any attention to himself, although he was very cute. His dark hair and eyes set off a previously effeminate body that had filled out somewhat over the summer and hardened a bit working with his dad in the vegetable fields. Trevor had argued with Jaden more than a few times last year about his jealousy of Ricardo.

"I thought it was cool," came from Devon. "It's actually really hard work. The guys who think swimming is a girls' sport probably couldn't keep up the pace." Last to speak was Trevor.

"It was pretty good. Not as hard as lifeguard training, but pretty good." Trevor had been a lifeguard at the YMCA the previous year.

"I'm sure it'll get a lot harder," defended Jaden. "This was just the first day!" They all agreed and left to go home.

Chapter 3

Before he could start football, Brandon had been told he had to go to his baseball coach and apologize for his behavior during the season the year before. Brandon had been suspended from school near the end of the year and hadn't been able to play in the final tournament. When Lake Griffin Mustangs lost, he hadn't even gone to talk to Coach Cushing about his suspension. So, before football practice started, Coach Cushing and Brandon had a long talk about a lot of things, including steroids, responsibility and attitude. Afterward, Coach Cushing told Brandon to write a paper reflecting upon what had gone wrong last year and what he had been doing to change since then. Brandon put a lot of time and thoughtfulness into his essay, and it had cleared the way for him to play football again with a fresh start.

Football was going great. Brandon's work ethic had always been a strong point, and the other players were trying to equal his effort. The coaches were all pleased and were looking forward to a great winning season. The team had been strong last year, and with most of the starters returning, everyone knew they would probably be district champs. By popular vote, and with the endorsement of the coaching staff, Brandon was chosen captain the first week of school. He didn't tell his dad, because he wanted to surprise him when he went out on the field for the coin toss at the first game.

The team wasn't the only place Brandon's popularity was soaring. All the popular girls on campus, including the cheerleaders and the dance squad, were speaking to him in the hall and flirting with him whenever they got the chance. He enjoyed the attention, but didn't let his guard down. He had been stung badly the year before by Kristin, one of the cheerleaders, who had just used him to make her boyfriend jealous. He wasn't as naïve and trusting as he had once been.

He was ready, though, to apologize to Emily, his girlfriend from last spring. He had treated her abominably, causing her to break up with him, and he still really cared for her. She certainly wasn't the most beautiful girl in school, but she had an adorable cuteness about her, and they had really hit it off and enjoyed great times for a few months. They didn't have any classes together this year, but they did have the same lunch. Brandon had been observing whom she had been sitting with and was grateful it hadn't been with any guys. He knew that didn't mean anything, though. If she did have a boyfriend, he could just have a different lunch period. Despite his apprehension, he thought he would try to talk to her before the week was out.

He stalled until Friday, and when lunchtime came, Brandon was nervous about seeking Emily out. He had been such an ass to her last year, and he wasn't sure how she would respond. He stared at her table for quite a while before getting enough game to go talk to her. He tentatively approached the table. She wasn't looking his way, but something made her turn. However, as she did, her look became veiled.

"Hi, Emily. Um, can I talk to you for a minute?" asked Brandon. Suddenly he was not the self-confident football star, but a meek boy with downcast eyes.

"Hello, Brandon. Long time. What's up?" Emily wasn't hostile, but her eyes weren't warm, and she seemed wary.

"I was hoping we could go somewhere and talk." No answer was forthcoming, so Brandon mumbled awkwardly, "Not necessarily right now, just sometime." Thoughts began racing through Emily's mind, and she was unable to respond to his request. She had suffered all summer about the breakup and was just getting to the point where she thought she might date again. She had really loved Brandon until he had gotten mixed up with the steroids. He had turned into a different person, aggressive and mean, and she couldn't think about dealing with that again. She had even started talking to a guy in her English class. Brandon persisted, his voice low so that the others couldn't hear.

"Emily, I know you have every right not to want to speak to me, but I've truly changed. If you'll just give me a chance to explain and prove to you that I'm different," he paused, "I'll make it up to you." Emily knew she couldn't just sit there and say nothing forever, so she broke her silence.

"I don't know, Brandon. I'm getting my life straightened out right now. I don't want to get hurt again, and besides, I've been talking to a guy that I like in one of my classes." Although Brandon's very essence seemed to sink into the cafeteria floor, with all the dignity he could muster, he stood bravely in front of her and nodded.

"Well, then, all I can do for now is tell you how sorry I am for how I acted and how sorry I am for hurting you. I hope things go well for you, and I want you to know that I'm putting my life back together, too." Then, he turned and left.

As he walked away, Emily lost it. Tears began trickling down her face, and she hoped he didn't look back. All her old feelings for Brandon were back. He was her first real boyfriend and the only one she had ever slept with. He had told her she was his first, too, and she had believed him. Her friends at the table got up and hugged her and told her to just forget him. She had been moving on, and she could continue to do so.

Chapter 4

The previous year Alice had been part of a women's lunch group that, in addition to being social, discussed women's issues, as well as community issues. The group had no particular agenda, and Alice enjoyed the spirited conversations about the chosen subject in each meeting. She had taken the summer off, though, because the kids were home from school, and she had wanted to keep a watchful eye on Jaden. Now that school had started again, she had been debating with herself about returning to the group.

Taking the trashcan to the curb one morning after getting the kids off, she saw that her neighbor and friend, and Jaden's good friend, Miss Bonnie, was doing the same. Miss Bonnie was an older lady who had retired years before and who loved to spend time working in her yard. She had befriended Jaden when he was very young and had expressed an interest in flowers and landscaping. As Jaden had grown from a small child to a student in middle school, Miss Bonnie had been his biggest supporter as he struggled with his sexual identity. In addition to her support, she had lent her expertise to him in many areas, such as gardening, food preparation, grilling, and even swimming. Because of the hours spent in her pool, Jaden was as good a swimmer as he was today, even though he had never been on a team.

"Good morning, Alice, how are you doing today?" Miss Bonnie spoke in a neighborly way. "Got the kids and Donnie off to their respective arenas?"

"Yes, it's always a whirlwind in the mornings, but now I have a little time to myself."

Miss Bonnie casually asked, "How would you feel about the two of us taking a class at the community college one morning a week?" Alice's heart immediately took a little jump. She had an AA degree, but had always wanted to pursue more education. Her parents had discouraged her, and her mother had told her the only other degree she needed to get was her "MRS". Until he had retired, Alice's father had been Reverend Brooks of the Center City Baptist church, and her mother had been the dutiful reverend's wife, who always gladly bowed to her husband's wishes. She was sure that was the right thing for her daughter, too.

When Alice had gotten married, following in her mother's footsteps, she had also deferred to her husband in all things. Donnie had felt there had been no need for her to further her education, because he had a good job and could take care of the family's financial needs. Besides, he had said that she needed to be home for the children. But Alice had always had a pang of remorse about the avenues that she hadn't been able to explore and the experiences she had missed out on - not to say she didn't love her husband, her children, and her life.

"What class do you have in mind?" she heard herself asking.

"It's a survey class of comparative feminist literature. It concentrates on literature with cultural and political themes and other related topics." What Miss Bonnie didn't say was that it included LGBT studies, too. She felt that at least one of Jaden's parents should have an understanding of that movement, and perhaps it would increase awareness of the issues impacting their son. She knew there was not a chance that the parent would be Donnie, but hoped Alice could indirectly influence his opinions.

"I would love to do that!" Once again Alice couldn't believe her own ears. I think I'll do that instead of the women's group this year, she thought. Either one would be interesting, but to go to college again would be wonderful. "What do we have to do to enroll?"

"Why don't you come on over, and we'll enroll online."

Alice was smiling as she walked across the street, even as she was thinking that she wouldn't let Donnie know right away.

Chapter 5

Jenny was quick to find Mr. Anthony for a second time in that first week of school. She had a few things she wanted to ask him about, including the status of their favorite teacher from middle school, Mrs. Cohen. Mrs. Cohen had battled breast cancer their whole eighth grade year. She hadn't been able to finish the school year because of it.

"Hey, Mr. Anthony! You're kind of hard to catch up with sometimes."

"Hey yourself, Jenny. This is a much bigger campus than at the middle school. Even I don't know where I'll be stationed half the time. How is high school agreeing with you?" Jenny giggled.

"I don't know yet. We've haven't even been here a week. So far it's okay. I hope it stays that way. There sure are a lot more people here than in middle school." Mr. Anthony grinned at her.

"Are you just saying hello, or can I do something for you?"

"Actually, Mr. Anthony, I was wondering how Mrs. Cohen is doing. We worried about her all summer, and I guess you know what happened with Jaden. Part of it was because of worry about her."

Mr. Anthony frowned as he studied the sweet, young face that had changed from light and carefree, to heavy with concern.

Noticing his look, she quickly said, "Oh, he's a whole lot better now. He's been going to counseling all summer."

"Well, I'm certainly glad to hear that. As far as how Mrs. Cohen is doing, she's back at school, as busy as ever. She looks rested and seems to feel well."

"Oh, thank goodness! That makes me so happy! I can't wait to tell Jaden. And that brings up the other thing I wanted to ask you about. Does the high school have a TEAM Club?" Mr. Anthony had steered Jenny and her twin into joining the TEAM Club in middle school after their being bullied had ended in a fight. TEAM stands for Tolerance, Empathy, Acceptance, and Morality.

"I'm sorry to say that it does not, nor does it have any other club that would be the equivalent. As you know, that type of group has always been a special project of mine, and so far I've had no luck trying to get one started." Jenny's face fell. She had learned so much in the club, and Jaden had finally felt safe and understood. Mr. Anthony felt bad about her reaction, but he knew Mrs. Mackey, the principal, was only allowing curriculum-based clubs, at the direction of the school board.

As she left Mr. Anthony, Jenny had mixed emotions. She was thrilled about Mrs. Cohen, but very disappointed that no club existed for kids like Jaden and others who were bullied. When she saw her brother at lunch, she relayed all her information, and he, too, felt elation, as well as disappointment.

"All I have to say is that I hope the kids here are nicer than at middle school," Jaden said woefully. "So far, no one has said anything mean to me, but Ricardo said some kids were looking at him and whispering in one of his classes."

Jenny, her dander immediately up, said, "They better not let me see them picking on him!" Jenny was very protective of her brother and his friends.

"He hasn't pointed anyone out yet, so I don't know who they are," Jaden replied.

That afternoon at swim practice, Jaden pulled Ricardo aside and asked him if those same kids were still saying things. Pain filling his eyes, Ricardo merely nodded.

By the end of the first week of practice, Jaden and Devon had moved up into Trevor and Ricardo's lanes, with hopes of progressing farther the next week. The coaches had been complimentary to all four of them.

At Monday's practice, ten new swimmers who had been late getting their physicals showed up. Most of them were returners, so they went to lanes one and two. After a hard workout, Jaden was pleased to see that he could keep up with at least some of the recent returners who had missed three days of practice. It's pretty easy to get out of shape in swimming, he thought. The coaches called everybody over for some quick words.

Coach Swartout said, "Now that we've had a chance to see everyone swim, we'll be making cuts tomorrow. I'm sorry to say that there are only thirty spots on the team, fifteen boys and fifteen girls. If you're one of the cuts, please practice on your own, and come back again next year. We appreciate your effort."

As they walked to the change room, Trevor said to the others, "I'll bet I can tell you exactly who'll be cut. You know those girls that are always stopping to talk after every lap? They'll be gone in a heartbeat."

Devon replied, "I know, dude. Plus those whiney guys who keep getting leg cramps and having to get out of the pool to stretch." He mimicked a guy holding his toes, while he stretched his leg out. "It hurts, Coach, I can't swim," he said in a high-pitched voice. The others laughed, knowing it looked just like those guys. Jaden laughed, but felt a little bad about it, because he had been the victim of laughter many times. He rationalized to himself, though, that those kids weren't there to hear it. Mainly, he was happy that his friends all seemed to be getting along. Trevor was even being somewhat nice to Ricardo. At least he wasn't acting jealous or ignoring him.

Jaden wasn't getting to text with Trevor much at home, because Trevor had already started practicing for the fall play that he and his parents were in. Trevor was a fantastic actor, and he and Jaden had met a couple of years before in a Young People's Theater production. However, much of Trevor's acting was done with his parents in the adult community theater plays. The theater group had practice three nights a week, and Trevor was booking it to get there after swim practice. But at least he and Trevor had P.E. and swim practice together every day.

After practice the next day, Coach Staley asked seven swimmers to meet him on the pool deck before going in to change. Coach Swartout told all the rest to gather on the bleachers for a talk. The remaining swimmers knew what was going on over on the other side of the pool and kept surreptitiously glancing at the small group. They felt really bad for those guys, while at the same time feeling relieved that they had made the team.

Coach Swartout said, "We've got to order suits, so you need to bring in your money ASAP. Before you leave today, I'll give you a handout with suit prices, as well as optional gear prices, in case you want to order t-shirts or sweats."

"Oh, brother," Devon whispered. "Can't wait to get those suits," he said making a face.

"I need the guys to go in with Coach Staley to try on suits to check for sizes. Girls, come with me. I have suits for you to try on."

In the boys' change room, when Coach Staley held up a medium Speedo, all the boys howled with laughter.

"How are we gonna fit in that, Coach? It looks like it would be tight on a six-year-old," scoffed Devon. It was about five inches wide. The other new guys were nodding in agreement, while the returners were just laughing.

Coach Staley laughed, too, and said, "Yes, there is a trick to getting it on right. Let me school you on that."

The girls were having no problem with their Speedos. They were similar to any one-piece they had ever worn. In short order, the girls were all sized and ready to go.

"What's our suit gonna look like this year, Coach?" asked Chelsea, the girl who had explained double-dual meets to Jaden.

Coach Swartout answered, "It's going to have our galloping mustang across the front with goggles on its face. In the back there will be a single horseshoe."

"Woo-hoo! That sounds way cooler than the horse-head that was on the front last year," said Chelsea.

"When will they come in?" someone else asked. "I hope it's in time for the first meet. Last year we didn't get them until the third meet."

"This new company promises to have them here by end of next week. So be sure to bring your money tomorrow!"

"When's the first meet?" another swimmer asked.

"It's a week from next Wednesday. It'll be here before you know it!"

When all of the boys were finally sized, they walked out of the change room and over to where some of the girls were waiting.

Chelsea said, "What was all that laughing about in there? We heard you through the walls."

Some of the boys looked away, embarrassed, but Jaden said, "We were just having a hard time trying on our suits. They're so little!" That set off another round of laughter from the guys.

"I wish I could wear a boy's suit. At least it wouldn't ride up like mine does. I always have to tug on it."

"Oh, yeah," taunted David, a returner from last year. "I could just see you in a boy's suit. Actually, we probably couldn't tell the difference." Everyone started screaming at that. Chelsea laughed good-naturedly along with the others. She didn't mind one bit if they made fun of her small chest. There was nothing wrong with her body image, and she loved to tease, as well. Looking at her in a new light, Jaden decided he really liked this girl. I wish I could take teasing like that, he thought.

Chapter 6

Now that the team roster had been finalized, the coaches re-arranged the swim lanes, such that the first four lanes were the strongest swimmers. The only ones in the last two lanes were freshmen that showed a lot of promise, but still needed work on the strokes. Jaden was pleased to be in the third lane with Chelsea. He was planning to get to know her better. He thought it would be easy to do, because she was outgoing, and at times, outlandish. She really seemed to enjoy life, and she made him laugh a lot.

On Friday while they were catching their breath after a long string of sprints, Chelsea declared, "Man, I hope they don't completely wear us out today. I have a date tonight!"

David queried, "What are y'all going to do tonight?"

Chelsea answered, "I'm not sure yet. I told her I'd pick her up at eight, and she could choose. I was the one who decided the last couple of times." Jaden could hardly believe it when he heard Chelsea's date was a "she". Was it possible that this fun, popular girl could also be gay? Jaden, who had dealt with only ridicule and rejection as a gay guy, was amazed! Not only might she be gay, she didn't seem to care who knew it. In addition to this surprising turn of events, it was noteworthy that of the few gay people he knew, none were girls. He decided that when he had a moment in private, he was going to ask her outright how she managed.

"Well, ask Brooke if she wants to go to the movies with Kaitlyn and me. We could make it a foursome."

"Sounds good. Won't be near as tiring as the rock-climbing wall we did last weekend. It was lots of fun, though." As they began their next drill, Jaden swam with a lot on his mind.

After practice, Jaden asked Trevor, "Do you know some girl named Brooke who's a friend of Chelsea's?"

Trevor thought for a bit and replied, "No, I don't think so. Why?" Jaden was bursting to tell him what he had overheard.

"It's Chelsea's girlfriend. Chelsea has a girlfriend."

"How do you know that?" Trevor was eager to know.

"She told us all she had a date. Then I heard her talking to David, and she said she was going to let *her* decide what they would do tonight. David called her Brooke."

"I'm sure I could find out who she is if I knew her last name. Do you think she's a senior like Chelsea?"

"I don't know. Probably, although you're a sophomore and I'm not, so they may not be in the same grade." Trevor said he would text some friends over the weekend to see what he could find out, but as it turned out, he came up short. So when the boys went to practice Monday, they were still curious. Jaden was disappointed that he didn't find any time when he could get Chelsea alone to talk to her.

Some of the swimmers didn't have all their paperwork in, so after practice, Coach Swartout admonished the team to get it in. Everybody had their physical, which was the most important thing, but unless they turned in their insurance cards, some swimmers would not be competing in the first meet. Also, several freshmen, including Ricardo, had not turned in their birth certificates.

Jaden looked at Ricardo and said, "Why haven't you turned it in yet, mi amigo? Time is running out."

Ricardo turned his head, paused, then said, "My parents cannot find it yet. They are looking." Then he looked down. Jaden was oblivious to the sudden drama unfolding in front of him.

He just said, "Well, tell them to hurry and find it. I want you to be able to swim in the first meet." Coach Staley overheard this exchange and decided that he would go to the guidance office to see if a birth certificate may have followed Ricardo up from middle school.

The next day Coach Staley did just that. When he pulled up Ricardo's file, it only had half a year's grades in it, and those were from Lake Griffin Middle School. There was a document included in the folder that stated "Files requested from Brownsville school system." And there was nothing else. He thought that was odd.

———

The whole second week of school Brandon stared at Emily across the lunchroom, but she never turned to meet his gaze. If she would just let me explain that I didn't know I was taking steroids, he thought. I really believed the pills were supplements to make me stronger for baseball. That wouldn't excuse my behavior, but it would certainly explain it. I'd never have done it if I'd known how it would affect me. I lost my girlfriend, and I almost lost my little brother. Thank goodness I'm getting another chance with Jaden. I just wish I could with Emily, too. I hope she doesn't get together with that other guy, but if she does, I guess it's my own fault.

Across the lunchroom Emily knew that Brandon was looking at her. Her friends at the table were quick to point it out every day. It was hard not to compare him to Juan Carlos, the guy she was starting to like. They were both cute with dark hair, but Juan Carlos had dark eyes and mocha skin, where Brandon's eyes were blue and his skin, light. Juan Carlos played soccer and was a good athlete, but he wasn't witty and sarcastic in the funny way that Brandon was. Still, she was planning to go out with him Friday night. She didn't know if they would go to the game or do something else, but she had to get Brandon out of her mind.

The Hansens, as a family, had always gone to Brandon's games ever since he played Little League Baseball and Pop Warner Football, and all the way up through high school. Brandon's father and grandfather had been great athletes growing up, and he had continued their tradition. The family usually sat as a group that included Devon. The first football game of Brandon's senior year would be no exception. Crowding into the SUV, like they always had, was somewhat of a bittersweet moment for Donnie. He couldn't help but think that this was the beginning of the end. His pride in his older son's athletic abilities had never waivered, even during the tough times. And, now, he was beginning the last year his son would be at home where he could watch his every game, give him advice, and guide him into being the man that was simmering inside, waiting to boil over and spill into the world full-speed.

Not usually a sentimental man, it took effort for Donnie to push his emotions aside and enthusiastically say, "Let's get this show on the road!" When they got to the game and settled in their seats, everyone began watching the team warm up. Except Jaden. As usual, he was watching the cheerleaders. How he had longed to be a cheerleader in middle school! Of course, his dad would have none of it, but Jaden was finally at peace, because now that he was on the swim team, he wouldn't have had time to be a cheerleader, anyway.

As the pre-game formality began, Donnie's jaw dropped when he saw Brandon walk to the center of the field with the head coach. He was no stranger to the meaning and importance of that proceeding, and his chest swelled with pride as he saw his son shake the hands of the other team's captain and coach. The coin was tossed, and the momentous event was over, but it would live in Donnie's heart forever. Alice looked at her husband with tears in her eyes and squeezed his arm as the teams ran onto the field.

It was a good game, because Lake Griffin had scheduled an easy team so that the first game jitters wouldn't cost them a win. There were plenty of mistakes, but the Mustangs came out on top by a good margin. Emily and Juan Carlos went to the game and were in the stands, but Brandon was unaware. Emily was holding Juan Carlos' hand, but she watched Brandon's every move with an ache, and felt guilty.

Chapter 7

The team swimsuits had not arrived as promised on Friday, but UPS delivered a big box full of suits on Monday. Coach Staley passed them out at the beginning of practice, and everyone rushed into the change rooms to try them on. Most of the guys had bought jammers, but a couple of them had been brave enough to get the regular short ones. Jaden thought they were cute and wished he had had the nerve to try one.

"You look like a horse kicked you in the butt, Devon!" laughed Jaden.

"I know, dude. I like the horseshoes on the suits. You look the same way!" They all went out to practice in their new suits, and after a few laps, girls and guys alike remarked how sleek they felt, and how smoothly they moved through the water.

"I guess they're not as bad as I thought," volunteered Devon. "I'm sure I'll cut my time down now."

At the end of practice Coach Swartout pulled Ricardo aside and asked him about his birth certificate.

"I don't know, Miss. My father tell me I no have one," he spoke despondently.

"Where were you born, Ricardo? In Brownsville?"

"No, miss, I was born in Mexico, but my parents bring me to Brownsville every year to pick the vegetables. Last year the company ask my parents to move here to pick."

"Do your parents have a green card?"

"I don't know, Miss."

"Will you have your father call me, so we can try to work out this birth certificate issue?"

"I will ask him, Miss."

Ricardo was absent from Tuesday's swim practice. When Jaden hooked up with him on Wednesday, he was concerned.

"Ricardo, why weren't you at practice yesterday? Did you get sick at the end of the day?"

"No, mi amigo. I cannot swim anymore. My father tell me if the coach start to look around, we have to move. We don't want to go back to Mexico."

"What do you mean, Ricardo?" Jaden was bewildered.

"I have no birth certificate, and the coach want to talk to my father. My father, he say no. We don't want to be deported."

"That can't be right, Ricardo. Why would they deport you? I'll ask my mom to check into it. You have to swim!"

"Please, no, Jaden. No problem for us, please! My family need to work here." The look on Ricardo's face showed fright and panic.

"Okay, relax, Ricardo. I won't say anything. I promise. I just wish I knew how I could help." As Jaden walked on to class, he realized that Ricardo's problem was way worse than just not having a birth certificate. He felt bad for his friend.

At practice that afternoon, he told Coach Swartout that Ricardo couldn't be on the team, after all. He just told her that his father said he wasn't allowed anymore.

It wasn't the same without Ricardo at practice, but Jaden was working hard on his times, and at any little break, he watched for a chance to speak to Chelsea alone. She was easy to talk to, but it seemed everyone always had something to say to her at breaks. He had listened after the weekend to see if he could catch any comments between David and her about how it gone on the date Friday. He guessed it was old news, because it wasn't even mentioned.

Everyone suddenly realized the first meet was upon them, and Coach was going over things that were important, like paying attention so you didn't miss your event. Jaden, even though he had never played a team sport, had watched team sports since he was four years old. In a team sport, everyone takes the field together. In swimming, it was a new concept in that each competitor was responsible for his own part in being on the blocks at the appropriate time. You snooze, you lose. Additionally, Coach was reminding them of things that could make them faster, like turns. Devon had picked up so much speed by working on his turns! Jaden really couldn't compete with him anymore on the short races. But he had endurance and wanted to swim the 500-free and be on the 400-free relay. He was pretty sure he had a good chance to place in those events.

Chapter 8

Alice was relieved that the class she was going to take with Miss Bonnie was only meeting on Tuesdays from 10:00 until 12:00. That would leave plenty of time in the mornings with the kids, and she would easily be back to the house before they got home. She wondered if she could keep it from Donnie, or even if she should. She decided to wait until she had at least gone to the first class. That was going to be this coming Tuesday, the day before Jaden's first swim meet.

By the time Tuesday rolled around, Alice had been to Target three times – first, to get a notebook for the class, second to look at "school clothes" for herself, and third, to take back the first notebook, buy several binders and loose-leaf paper, and to actually purchase a couple of tops and jeans. It had been so long since she had been to school that she didn't really know what to get or what to expect. She thought, if I'm having this much trouble, what could Miss Bonnie possibly be going through? She's twice my age.

As it turned out, Miss Bonnie wasn't in the least concerned about how to dress or what supplies to take. She wore something out of her closet and took a spiral notebook. She felt she was too old to care what people thought about how she dressed. Finding seats together in the classroom, they looked around at their fellow classmates. Not surprisingly, everyone else looked like kids. A lot of students appeared to be bored, but two or three turned their way and smiled. Alice felt self-conscious, but smiled back. The instructor was a young woman who looked as if she were barely out of the classroom herself. As she got started on the introduction and syllabus, however, it became easy to tell she was passionate about her subject. She let her students know that she was a big believer in equality, as well as an activist on several battle-grounds. She explained that the class was a mini-course, meaning it met two hours a week for only half a semester.

The time passed quickly, and before they knew it, Alice and Miss Bonnie and the others were leaving class with their first assignment. There were to familiarize themselves with *The Book of the City of Ladies* by Christine de

Pizan, written in 1405, as well as *The Feminine Mystique* by Betty Freidan, written in 1963.

"Wow, I never realized that feminists went back as far as the fifteenth century," said an amazed Alice.

"Me, neither," commented Miss Bonnie. "It looks like we have our work cut out for us."

"I know! It's going to be a lot of reading, but it looks so interesting!"

"I know my reading is up to par, but I haven't written anything of substance in about fifty years. I hope I'm up to the task," said Miss Bonnie with a small smile.

"Oh, we can help each other. It'll be fun," replied Alice.

Chapter 9

It was dreary on Wednesday, the day of the first swim meet. Jaden awoke to the patter of falling rain and closed his eyes again to wish it away. When that didn't work, he slowly got up, dressed, and made his way to the breakfast table where the rest of his family seemed too cheerful for such a glum day.

"Mom, what are we gonna do if it's raining when it's time for the meet?" Jaden asked peevishly.

Alice, who had been in a great mood since her class the day before, said, "Don't worry about it, honey. It hardly ever rains all day, and if it does, you can still swim in the rain."

"Yeah, Jaden, are you afraid to get wet?" said Brandon, teasingly. But, not intending to be mean about it, he quickly said, "It's gonna stop, buddy. Don't you worry. And I'm coming to see you swim! We get out of practice at 4:30 on Wednesdays, so I'll have no trouble getting there."

"I'll be there, too, Jay," said Jenny. "I can't wait to see you race." Feeling somewhat appeased, Jaden smiled at his siblings.

Turning to his dad, Jaden asked, with hesitation, "Will you be able to come, Dad?" Without realizing it, he was holding his breath.

"Sure thing, son. I won't be able to get there until 5:30, though. Will that be too late?"

"No, that'll be great, Dad! I know you can't get out of work early." Any remnants of his gloominess had totally dissipated by now, and Jaden was eager to get to school and get the day started.

The rain didn't let up until 3:00, and after school the swimmers were huddled together under a large overhang of the building where the change rooms were located. They had been told that the meet would go on, rain or shine, unless there was lightning. So far, there hadn't been lightning, but there was no need to start warm-ups that early, since the meet didn't start until five. The other team wasn't due to get there until 3:30 anyway. The coaches were sitting at the score table making out the entry slips that each swimmer would give to the timer at the beginning of his or her event. The pulse of excitement for the first meet was palpable to the swimmers, even as they stood there just waiting. The kids from the year before were explaining the order of events and how each of them would pick up their entry slip and stand behind the blocks during the event before theirs. It all seemed so thrilling to Jaden and Devon. Even Trevor, who had tried to portray aloofness, seemed to be affected by the charged atmosphere.

At 3:25 a school bus pulled into the parking lot, and kids from the other team started streaming out. To the star-struck rookies on the Lake Griffin High team, the line seemed interminable, and the Newcastle swimmers seemed big and powerful. The older teammates from the Mustangs laughed at the wide eyes of the rookies and told them that this team put on their Speedos the same as they did, one leg at a time.

Both teams jumped in the water shortly thereafter and began their warm-ups. The timers and scorers arrived around 4:30. Unbelievably, the small bleachers were filling up with parents and friends. Jaden was delighted when he saw his mom and Jenny sit down, and a little later, Brandon. Seeing them made him swim that much harder in warm-up.

Finally, the long awaited time arrived. The starter talked to the timers, then blew the whistle for the meet to start. Jaden was happy, because he was scheduled to swim three of his favorite events. Not strong enough for any of the three A relay teams yet, he would be swimming on two of the B relay teams with Devon. Trevor was a sprinter and would be swimming in shorter events, as well as on the A relays. All three boys would be in the first event, which was the medley relay. Boys and girls events always alternated. All the returning swimmers got to swim four events each. Jaden looked forward to the time when he could, too.

Lake Griffin girls A medley relay won their event easily with Chelsea swimming powerfully in the anchor position. Jaden had known she was a good swimmer, but seeing her in competition form was really impressive. The boys A team barely won. They had been behind in the third leg, but Trevor grabbed the win by catching and barely passing Newcastle's last swimmer. The boys B team had a good race and only missed second place by half a second. Jaden did well, but his dive at the start was a belly-buster. He had been in the last lane, so when he landed, everyone laughed and ran for cover from the tidal wave. Because he had practiced at Miss Bonnie's, he had never had a starting block, so he had only begun learning to start off the block in the past ten days. Chelsea met him at the end as he finished and told him she would be working with him on his dive the next day, for sure.

After giving Trevor a one-arm hug, and doing a special handshake with Devon, Jaden rushed over to his family, so they could tell him how well he did. His next event wasn't until after the break, so he was allowed to sit with them as long as he paid attention to the meet. As he was basking in the glow of their praise, he looked over to see Chelsea sitting close to a good-looking girl. Wow, that must be the mystery girlfriend, he thought. As he inconspicuously tried to get Trevor's attention in order to point out the girl, he saw his dad walk in the gate. He felt a rush of excitement and ran over to meet him.

"Mom and Jenny and Brandon are sitting over here," he said as he proudly led his dad to the bleachers. After telling his dad all about his race and laughing ruefully as he recounted his dive, he went back to the poolside to cheer on the next race. He didn't want to miss Devon's individual medley where he had to swim all four competitive strokes for 50 yards each. The first leg of it was the butterfly, and Devon was strong in that. He finished almost half a lane ahead of the next closest swimmer. Next was the backstroke, and he was pretty good at that, too. His weakest was the breaststroke, the third leg. The swimmer in second place completely caught up to him by the end of that leg. The whole place was cheering loudly as the two boys started their final leg of freestyle. The Newcastle swimmer edged a little ahead at the turn, but with what seemed like superhuman effort, Devon seemed to speed up the last seven yards to finish a hair ahead of him. No one could really tell who touched first! The timers were the final decision on the race, and Devon's time read .015 second faster. Everyone began helping Devon out of the water and slapping his back. You could tell he was exhausted, because he went to the side and just sprawled out on the deck. The race was hard enough, but on top of that, Devon had sprinted hard in the relay just two races before. Thank goodness he didn't have any more events until the last race of the meet.

Next was the 50-free, Trevor's race. The girls' event was first, but it was so fast that Trevor was on the block almost before Jaden realized the girls were through. Trevor had a swimmer's body, long and lean, and was a natural at the sport. He did a long pike dive and didn't come up until he was two-thirds of the way down the pool. He went into the turn even with the

Newcastle swimmer who held a state ranking. Trevor's turn definitely needed some work, and the other swimmer finished the race about a yard ahead of him. Coach Staley pulled him out and told him that all he needed was improvement on his turn and a little more off his time, which should go down as the season progressed. If those things happened, he was state-bound for sure. Coach was amazed at Trevor's time, especially as a first-year swimmer.

"You have a big career ahead of you, Trevor, if you stick with it!" praised Coach Staley.

After the 50-free, there was a ten-minute break. Some of the swimmers jumped in the lanes to cool down, while others went to speak to their families.

"When do you swim next, Jaden?" asked Donnie.

"After the break, there'll be two races, then my race, the 500."

"You're going to swim 500 yards without stopping?" Donnie looked incredulous.

"Dad, we do that every day at practice. Several times." Donnie looked at his son with newfound respect. He, like many others, never realized that swimming could be a punishing sport and not for the weak of heart. He remembered that he had never even attempted to swim across the lake in Center City when he was growing up, and in retrospect, he realized that the lake wasn't even all that big.

When the break was over, the teams started in again. The races before Jaden's were over quickly, and he was on the starting block determined not to flop into the water again. Chelsea was at the end of his lane with the lap counters. It had made Jaden feel good when Chelsea had volunteered to count for him. Jaden hadn't even been aware that each 500 swimmer had a counter, but in practice he had learned that it would be difficult for a swimmer to keep track of laps in a race that long. He finished remarkably well, cutting a whole minute off his best practice time. He finished in second place, and his family was blown away. Who knew that little Jaden had it in him to be such a good swimmer? And such endurance! Jaden knew he would feel elated, too - as soon as he could catch his breath. Thank goodness his next event was the last race of the meet!

As Jaden leaned back on the bleachers, resting on his mom's knees, he noticed to his right, that Brandon was talking to the girl he thought was Chelsea's girlfriend, Brooke. He made a mental note to ask his brother about it that night.

Chapter 10

The rest of the swim meet finished with nothing out of the ordinary, and the Mustangs were ecstatic when they found that their first meet of the year had been a win. First-meet jitters were over, and all the swimmers vowed to work even harder to bring their times down.

When the Hansens arrived home, everyone was in high spirits. The twins were chattering about various swimmers and their races, and Brandon was proffering tidbits about the hot girls on both teams. Donnie was actually proud of Jaden, which was a new feeling for him, and also, a new experience for Jaden. He had praised Jaden for how well he had done in the 500, as well as his relay's winning the last race. Alice felt more light-hearted than she had in years.

"Hey, Brandon," sang out Jaden. "Who was that girl you were talking to in the bleachers?"

"Yeah, buddy! She was pretty smoking, wasn't she? Her name is Brooke, and she's a junior. She must be as smart as she is good-looking, because she told me she went from ninth grade last year to eleventh this year." Jaden frowned and had trouble processing these new facts. *Smoking?* I wonder if he knows that she's Chelsea's girlfriend? I wonder if he *hit* on her? Brandon continued, "She said she was at the meet watching her friend Chelsea swim. That chick is good!"

No more information was forthcoming from Brandon after that, and Jaden could hardly wait to let Trevor in on the gossip. He decided he would hold off until P.E. class the next day, though, because it was a lot to text, and he was keeping a low profile at home by not talking to Trevor on the phone.

The next day Trevor's response was, "Wouldn't it be funny if Brandon asked her out, and she told him she was gay?"

"I don't think that would be so funny, Trevor," Jaden said defensively. "It just seems like it would be weird. I hope he doesn't, because he's had a hard time with girls lately, and he doesn't need more rejection."

"Hey, can't you take a joke? I didn't really mean it." Lately, Trevor and Jaden had been sniping at each other when they were alone. Jaden thought that Trevor's head was getting too big with all the coaches telling him how great he was, and on top of that, he had a huge part in the adult play he was in. In addition, he had begun to hang out occasionally with a twenty-year-old guy in the play who, Trevor had told him, smoked pot. They had argued about that a few days ago and didn't speak to one another for a whole day, even though Trevor had sworn that he wasn't interested in the guy, nor had he smoked pot with him. Jaden had finally apologized, and they had made up, but occasionally tension would pop up again.

At swim practice, Chelsea was as good as her word. Before practice started, she took Jaden to one of the blocks and worked with him on his dive.

After a few attempts, she said, "Now, you're starting to get it. And, just be sure to keep your legs together and toes pointed when you enter the water." She told him she would work with him until he was confident. As they went back to join the others, Jaden walked slowly and watched Chelsea out of the corner of his eye. He suddenly felt shy.

Noticing, Chelsea said, "Jaden, do you have something on your mind?" Embarrassed, Jaden looked down. "Come on, out with it! What's up?"

Taking the plunge, Jaden asked, "Are you gay?" Chelsea laughed.

"Of course I am, but I prefer to be called a lesbian. You're gay, too, right?"

"Yes," he said hesitantly. "But you're so....no one makes fun of you... people know....", his voice trailed off.

"I think the word you're looking for is 'out'. I've been pretty lucky, because my parents are totally cool with it. We talked about it when I was twelve, near the end of sixth grade, because I had a big crush on an eighth grade girl, and they told me it was okay. Mom said some people are born that way. She told me that as I got older, I may or may not continue to have crushes on girls, but either way, she and my dad loved me." She grinned conspiratorially. "Now I'm older, and I still like girls."

"That's sort of what my friend Miss Bonnie told me!" Jaden said excitedly.

"Who's that?"

"She's my older best friend who lives across the street from me. Actually, she's really old, but she's still one of my best friends. If it hadn't been for her I don't know what I would have done back when I was figuring out that I was gay. I was a real mess."

Chelsea said, "I guess no one has made fun of me, because I have the same friends I've always had. They knew me before I had a girlfriend, and they know me now that I do. I'm the same person I always was."

"I know, you look and act like everybody else. I would never have guessed, except I overheard you talking about a date with a girl."

"I don't think of myself as different. It just happens that my relationship is with a girl."

"Are you two going to swim, or just talk away the practice?" yelled Coach Swartout. They hustled over to the group.

After practice, Jaden tried to tell Trevor the things that Chelsea had said, but it was as if Trevor couldn't be bothered.

He sort of brushed Jaden off, saying, "Sorry, but I really have to hurry today. I have to be at the theater earlier than usual. Talk to you tonight." With that he was gone.

Shrugging his shoulders somewhat disappointedly, Jaden set off for home, not sure whether to be upset with Trevor, or to concentrate on the new-found, promising idea that being gay could be seen as normal.

Chapter 11

Devon had settled in with a lunch group that he had picked somewhat randomly at the beginning of year. He knew two of the guys who were also freshmen, but the others were upperclassmen that he was just getting to know. Every day the talk was about the football season, and when the others found out that Devon was a personal friend of one of the star players, he quickly gained popularity.

"Yeah, Brandon and I have thrown the football around lots of times. His younger brother is my best friend."

One of the freshmen smirked and said, "You mean, gay Jay?" The others snickered. However, Devon had learned a lot about tolerance and acceptance in the past year. He believed his best friend had almost died due to his own misplaced prejudice.

He stood up to his full height of six feet, two inches and said with a glare, "You're not going to talk about my friend or anybody else that way! If you have a problem with that, let's settle it right now." The kid who had said it cowered in his seat.

"Chill, Devon! I didn't mean anything, man."

One of the others mumbled, "You got to admit, it's not like he ain't a fag."

Devon got right in his face and said, "Yeah, and it's not like you aren't an asshole, either! Jaden has a right to be whoever he is, and you don't need to make comments about it." The nearby tables had quieted down, listening and waiting to see if a fight would erupt. Several people started to gather around. Seeing the commotion, Mr. Anthony, who was on lunchroom duty, hurriedly strode over to the group.

"What's going on here, fellas? Devon, I didn't expect to see you here in the middle of this."

"I'm not starting anything, Mr. Anthony. I'm just stopping it. These guys want to run their mouth about things they don't know anything about."

"Everybody go back to your own table," he said waving away the on-lookers. "And you guys here need to calm down. Nobody needs to get into trouble."

"It's cool, Mr. A. I'm leaving this bunch of losers, anyway," said Devon. Nothing had really happened other than flared tempers and loud voices, so Mr. Anthony sent him on his way. One of the members of the swim team, sitting at another table, called him over.

"What was that all about, Dev?" he asked.

"Someone wanted to make fun of someone else, and I didn't want to hear it," was all he would say. The bell ended the conversation.

The next day at lunch, Nick, the swimmer from the day before, invited Devon to sit at his table. Nick mentioned that people made fun of them, too, saying that swimming was for wusses and fags.

"If they knew how hard our practices were, I bet they wouldn't say stuff," continued Nick. "And after yesterday, now that you're sitting here, no one will dare say anything!"

Devon had spent a lot of time over the summer thinking about Jaden and others whom people made fun of. He had always been big and tough for his age, as well as being an athlete. He had never experienced the humiliation of being ridiculed. Being bi-racial had never posed a problem for him, either. When he had learned that Jaden was gay, he had been caught off-guard and had responded poorly. But he was sensitive and kind and had come to realize that although people may seem different on the outside, on the inside they were the same and deserved respect. Devon answered Nick.

"I've played football and basketball, and swimming is just as hard as those sports. The only difference is that there's no contact. But, trust me, I'm willing to make contact with any jerk-face who tries to talk trash!" When Devon left the lunchroom that day, he decided that he needed to do something about bullies, other than fighting them. He texted Jenny to meet him in the courtyard right after school before swim practice.

"Hey, Devon, what's up?" Jenny smiled widely at Devon, who had always been a favorite of hers.

"Hi, Jen. You know that club you and Jay belonged to last year, TEAM? Do they have it here?" Jenny's face lost its cheery look.

"The high school doesn't have one. I asked Mr. Anthony. He said the school board thinks we shouldn't have any clubs other than academic ones."

"That's bull-crap!" spat Devon. "After I found out what Jaden went through last year, I've been noticing what all kids who are different go through. I think we need a TEAM Club more than any academic club. Do you know that they're even calling people on the swim team names?"

Jenny answered, "I didn't know that, but it doesn't surprise me. I don't know what makes some people think they're better than others. They should look in the mirror sometimes."

"I know, right? Can you think of anything we can do? I mean, I'm perfectly willing to take those guys down a notch or two, but I don't really want to get suspended."

"No, no, you don't need to do that, Devon," Jenny quickly responded. "Jaden and I already went down that road, and it's not the answer. You try to think of something, and I will, too. I wish I could ask Mom about it, but Jaden doesn't want to get anything started at home. He feels like things are going too good with Dad and doesn't want to bring stuff up." They parted so Devon could hustle off to swim practice. Walking home, Jenny thought, maybe I can talk to Miss Bonnie about it. Jaden used to talk to her about *everything*.

Jenny walked into her house and was surprised to find that her mother wasn't home. But, the car was there. Could her mom have gone for a walk? That didn't seem right. Kind of odd. While standing in front of the refrigerator with the door open looking for a snack, she heard the front door open.

"Mom, is that you?" Seeing her mom she said, "Where were you?" Alice looked flustered and surprised to see Jenny.

"I didn't know you were already home, honey."

"Where were you, Mom?" Jenny repeated.

"I was at Miss Bonnie's house. We're taking a class together at the community college."

"A class? Mom, that's great! Why didn't you tell us? What class is it? How long have you been going? Wait, you're taking a class with Miss Bonnie? Isn't she kind of old for school?"

"Jenny! How can you say such a thing? No one is too old to learn something new."

"It just seems weird, someone probably older than the teacher. But, you're right. I'm sorry; I shouldn't have said that. What's the class?"

"It's called Comparative Literature for Women. It meets once a week, and we've been once. Lots of reading!"

"Sounds boring. Why is it supposed to be for women?"

"The focus is on feminist literature. So far, we've read what women have written about women's rights starting in the fifteenth century. Can you believe someone wrote about women's rights way back then?"

"Still sounds like a yawner, but if you like it, that's what matters."

"Honey, I haven't told Dad yet." Jenny's eyebrows lifted. "I guess I'll tell him tonight, but whenever I tell everyone else, just act like you didn't know either. Okay?"

"Sure, Mom, I can keep a secret." Jenny thought, boy, *can* I keep a secret!

After doing a few chores and her homework, Jenny walked across the street to see Miss Bonnie.

"Jenny, what a surprise!" Miss Bonnie ushered her in, wondering if she knew her mother had recently been ushered out.

"Mom told me about the class the two of you are taking. That's way cool! Mom is gonna tell Dad tonight, I think." She paused thinking, then, started again, "Miss Bonnie, Devon and I are worried about the bullying that goes on at school."

"Oh, dear. Have they started in on Jaden again?"

"No, I'm not talking about him specifically. Oh, I'm sure he's included, but it seems that people are picking on the swim team now. The high school doesn't have a place that feels safe for kids to go, like the TEAM Club last year."

"Why, that's ridiculous, honey. Why not?"

"The *school board* thinks the only clubs we should have should be for academics," Jenny said sarcastically. "Don't they know that kids can't learn school stuff if they're looking over their shoulder to see who's going to pick on them next?"

"Let me check into a few things, Jenny, and I'll get back to you."

"Thanks so much, Miss Bonnie. Jaden was right. You always know what to do!"

Chapter 12

Alice wasn't sure how she would broach the subject of her class with Donnie, so she waited until everyone had gone to bed and the house was quiet. That was about the only time they ever had to talk privately, anyway. As they lay in bed with the TV on, she decided to go for it.

"Honey, I don't know why I didn't tell you ahead of time, but I've signed up for a class at the community college." Alice's nerves were on edge. She guessed it stemmed from the past when she never did anything without Donnie's express approval and encouragement. Her anxiety heightened when he didn't respond at first. He rolled over and examined her tense face.

Then he took her in his arms and said, "Alice, you know I support whatever's best for you. I'm a little surprised that you didn't want to talk about it with me before enrolling, though. I realize we've been through some stressful times lately, and taking a class will probably be a good release for you, but I just wish you had discussed it with me first." His tone made Alice feel somewhat like she was a child being reprimanded, and the insecurities she had felt before joining the women's group the year before, resurfaced. But suddenly, insight she had been gaining from her class readings bolstered her resolve. Women had been fighting oppression for centuries.

She took a deep breath and said, "I made the decision on the spur of the moment and didn't want to wait another minute to sign up. Miss Bonnie and I signed up together. It won't take any time away from the kids. I do apologize for not discussing the cost with you." Alice really loved her husband, but for the past year had been enjoying a growing feeling of empowerment, a feeling that she was as capable as Donnie of making decisions. Donnie's face had darkened for a brief moment when he heard Miss Bonnie was taking the class, too, but he didn't comment on that. He just told her that he hoped she would enjoy it.

Chapter 13

The next day at swim practice Jaden could hardly wait for Chelsea to help him again, so he could ask her more questions.

"So, Brooke is your girlfriend?"

"Yes, isn't she cute?"

"She's hot. How long have you been together?"

"I met her last October. I was at the park by the lake throwing a Frisbee for my dog. She walked up to pet Zoomer, and we just started talking."

"Did you know she was gay – I mean, a lesbian?"

"I didn't know for sure, but I just felt it, sort of 'gay-dar'. I thought she looked kind of familiar, and we discovered we both went to Lake Griffin. We started hanging out after that."

"When did you first kiss?" Jaden asked, and then looked down, cheeks reddening. Chelsea laughed out loud.

"It didn't take long, I'll tell you that! She's gorgeous! And so much fun."

"Can I meet her at the next swim meet?"

"Absolutely! By the way, are you dating anyone?"

"Yes," Jaden said shyly. "He's on the team, Trevor Kinney."

"Oh, Trevor! He's a pretty good swimmer for his first year. If he works at it, he'll be great." Jaden's eyes flashed with pride. Then, as they noticed the others gathering around the coaches, they quickly joined them.

When Jaden got home that day, he was eager to report his information to Jenny, with whom he shared everything. He had already told her all he knew about Chelsea, and Jenny had been thrilled that he had someone else to talk to, besides Trevor and her. Not that he couldn't talk to Devon, but Jaden just didn't talk to Devon about stuff like that. Now he told her all about Brooke and how Chelsea and Brooke had met.

"I hope some day you can feel as free and good about things as Chelsea does, Jaden," said Jenny, eyebrows knitted.

"I hope so, too," he said pensively. Then his excitement returned. "But in the meantime, Chelsea is going to introduce me to Brooke at the swim meet Thursday, and I want you to meet her, too. Can you get there early?"

The end of the week promised to be busy for the Hansen family. On Thursday, Alice was going to meet with Miss Bonnie to do homework, and then the family was going to the pool for Jaden's meet. Friday night, Brandon had another football game that they would all attend. Saturday evening, Brandon was going to hang out with some of his gamer friends. Alice and Donnie continued to be pleasantly surprised at how nice Brandon was being to his siblings and how well he was getting along with his friends this year.

Even Trevor was excited about the meet on Thursday. Now that the coaches had singled him out as a great prospect, he was ready to see if he could cut his times down. It was another home meet, but this time it was to start at 4:30 instead of 5:00. Because of the change in time, Donnie was upset that he would miss half of it. Jaden was disappointed, too, but he was so psyched about competing again, meeting Brooke, and getting to know Chelsea better, that he hardly let it bother him.

Before warm-up started, Jaden was on the bleachers talking with Trevor about how they both might decrease their times and do better.

"What are you looking at?" Trevor spoke sharply as he saw Jaden's face light up and focus on the gate to the pool.

"That's Chelsea's girlfriend, Brooke, coming in. Chelsea's gonna introduce us. Geez, Trevor, you don't have to jump down my throat!"

"What, are you all about girls now?" Trevor sneered.

"Don't be like that, Trevor. You should meet her, too. I just think it's cool that we could know other gay people. Maybe even do stuff with them." Trevor sighed.

"Okay, I guess I could meet her. But, I still don't see what you're getting so excited about." Jaden knew that Trevor had never had the difficult times with his parents, or with people making fun of him, that he had. He knew Trevor had never officially told his parents that he was gay, but it didn't seem to matter either way to them. They seemed to accept Trevor and let him do pretty much whatever he wanted. The kids at school just thought he was a metrosexual, because he always dressed great, and he always took a girl to the dances. Plus, he drove a Mustang! Jaden figured he could excuse Trevor for not understanding how great it would be for him to expand his social life. He had never had that problem.

"Come on, Trevor, Chelsea's waving us over!" Jaden slowed his step to match Trevor's so he wouldn't seem so eager – so needy.

"Hey, Jaden, this is Brooke."

"This is Trevor." Jaden continued, saying, "Brooke, I'm so glad to meet you. You sat with my brother at the last meet."

"That was your brother?" she asked. "He seemed really nice."

"He thought you were nice, too, and really hot." Jaden laughed self-consciously. He felt funny telling a gay girl that his brother thought she was hot.

Chelsea said, "I've wanted you all to meet ever since Jaden and I first talked. Trevor, it's nice to actually meet you, even though we're on the same team and have practiced together for a few weeks. Practices are so intense that we don't get to talk a lot or get to know people."

"It's great to meet both of you. Maybe we can all hang out some time. Hey, I've got an idea. Jaden, his twin sister, Jenny, and I are going to a movie at the mall Saturday night. Maybe you'd want to meet us there? Jenny's totally cool with everything."

"Trevor, that's a great idea!" said Jaden. He beamed at Trevor, shocked at his invitation. "Do you think you could?" he beseeched Chelsea.

"That sounds fun," Chelsea replied. "Want to, Brooke?" Brooke, who had never met a stranger, smiled and nodded. She always enjoyed getting to know new people and was forever expanding her circle of friends.

"Just say when and where, and we'll be there," she said. It was time for warm-ups to start, and the swimmers split up to hop into the pool.

When the meet was over, everyone had dropped a little off their time, and Jaden, Devon, and Trevor all had a first place finish to their credit. Jaden had won the 500-free, Devon, the IM, and Trevor, the 50-free. Full of motivation, the three friends vowed to practice that much harder.

At Friday's swim practice Jaden and Trevor made plans with Chelsea to meet at the mall food court at 6:00. They would have a bite to eat and then decide on a movie. Jaden rushed home to tell Jenny the plan. They talked about the upcoming event right up until they left for Brandon's game.

Saturday morning Jaden was up early asking his mom if he had chores that needed to be done.

Surprised, Alice said, "What's gotten into you, honey? I've never known you to get up early just to do chores!"

He said, "I don't know, Mom. I'm just anxious for the day to go by, so we can go to the movies tonight. What did Dad say when you told him Trevor was in the group?"

"He was just glad that you were going to get together with a group of friends and have some fun. He didn't say anything about Trevor. You know he's been worried about you, sweetie." Jaden breathed a sigh of relief. He knew he had been given permission to go, but had been worried his dad would nix it at the last minute if he knew Trevor was going.

That afternoon at 5:45, Trevor boldly drove into the driveway. Before he could get out and go to the door, however, Jaden and Jenny had poured out of the house heading for the Mustang. They certainly didn't want to push their luck with their dad.

Everyone met on time at the food court. After discussing the various options, they decided to go out of the mall to Five Guys Burgers next door. Pulling two tables together, Jaden was flanked on either side by Trevor and Jenny and sitting right across from Chelsea and Brooke. He could hardly wait to talk to Brooke again.

"I think it's so cool that everybody knows about you guys, and no one seems to care! What do your parents think, Brooke?" asked Jaden.

"They don't think anything, because they don't know about Chelsea and me," answered Brooke.

"They don't?" Jaden was surprised. "I thought both of your sets of parents knew. Do you think they would be okay with it?"

"I seriously doubt it, and I don't want to find out. My dad is ex-military, and I'm pretty sure he would freak even though they both really like Chelsea. They think we're just friends."

Chelsea added, "Yeah, it's not a big deal for us, because they always let us do stuff together and spend the night at each other's house. Of course, at my house, we can hold hands while watching TV and kiss each other in front of my parents. I mean, we wouldn't have a make-out session or anything like that, but I wouldn't do that with a boy if I were straight, either." Everyone laughed.

Trevor said, "I've never talked about it with my parents, but I'm pretty sure they know. They're in theater big-time, and lots of people in theater are openly gay, and they don't care."

"Why don't you talk about it with them, Trevor?" asked Chelsea.

After shrugging his shoulders and squirming a bit, he answered, "I probably will before I graduate, but I'm just not ready yet. Jaden's parents would go ballistic if they found out, so no need to push things." Jaden looked at him affectionately and squeezed his arm.

Jenny said, "Well, I just have one thing to say about this whole subject. Jaden's life has sucked the past few years, and I've always thought it was so unfair that I could talk to my parents about anything, and he couldn't." Nods of assent went around the tables.

When the food arrived, all talk turned to choosing a movie.

Chapter 14

In Alice and Miss Bonnie's next class, the young teacher enthusiastically laid out a consolidated timeline of that part of the feminist movement that progressed from 1405 to 1963. She was eager to provide information that even long ago, women had felt they could be active participants in society and should have the same education and rights as men, but their ambitions and petitions had been squashed, or even worse, ignored. As inspiring as the instructor was, however, many of the young students in the class had trouble identifying with that feeling of oppression. It was hard for them to believe that the rights they presently enjoyed took decades, even centuries, to become the status quo. A few of the black students, though, were nodding their heads as the instructor spoke.

After a good discussion, the instructor closed by saying, "I want to spend the next few classes exploring the trials of black women and of lesbians. You need to read Andrea Dworkin's *Lesbian Pride* and Zora Neale Hurst's *Their Eyes Were Watching God*. See you next week!"

Alice had cut her eyes over to Miss Bonnie when *Lesbian Pride* was mentioned, because Miss Bonnie had admitted she was a lesbian to Donnie and her at the beginning of the summer. Alice had been surprised, and Donnie had been displeased. He had told Alice, in private, that he was upset that their son had been getting guidance for years from a lesbian! Alice had experienced mixed emotions, but had defended Miss Bonnie. She had said she was certain that Miss Bonnie would never have done anything to hurt Jaden and that he had assuredly needed an adult to talk to, because they absolutely hadn't been there for him. Miss Bonnie had told them that she wished she had come out to them earlier, because she believed that if she had spoken up, she might have helped Donnie and Alice to accept and support their son for the person he is. As a result, his suicide attempt might well have been avoided.

Alice asked, "Did you know that the study of lesbians would be part of this class?"

Miss Bonnie, with a small smile, replied, "I was certainly hoping so. Anything that might possibly help you better understand Jaden's feelings could only be a good thing."

"I know you must be right, but I don't want Donnie to find out. By the way, I did tell him about the class the other night."

"How did he take the news?"

"I suppose he was okay with it. But, as usual, he had to tell me how I should have talked it over with him." Then, with a little more spunk, she said, "But I'm beginning to realize that I don't have to ask his permission to do something I want to do!"

It was hard to believe the first month of school was already over, and Halloween was approaching. The leaves had just started to show hints of color, and on some nights and early mornings, there was a little nip in the air. It never seemed to last through the day, but the promise of a new season was slowly revealing itself.

At school Brandon still glanced longingly at Emily across the lunchroom, but he had come to the conclusion that she and that Hispanic guy were rock solid now. She never looked his way, and if he saw the two of them in the halls, they were always holding hands. On those occasions, her mouth would smile at Brandon, but her eyes never seemed to fully make contact.

Several girls had expressed interest in Brandon, and his friend, Dan, had even tried to hook him up with a friend of the girl he was dating. They had gone out a couple of times, and Brandon had really tried to like her. He knew he needed to move on, but he just couldn't seem to get interested. Thankfully, football occupied a lot of his time, and with games on Fridays, one of the two prime date nights, there were only Saturday nights to contend with. Football had spiked his popularity and provided a plethora of parties to which he was invited. He attended them all, always looking for something different or someone new to catch his interest.

One Friday night, after a particularly close game in which Lake Griffin had barely eked out a win, one of the football players announced that his parents were going out of town the next morning, and he was inviting all the players, all the cheerleaders, and whoever else wanted to show up, to his house the next night for a blowout.

"It'll be the biggest party this town has ever seen!" he bragged. "Just don't tell your parents where you're going, because I don't want my parents to know how many people are coming. I know they don't care if I have a party, but they seem to think the bigger the crowd, the more likely there'll be alcohol." Then he grinned with a sly look. "We wouldn't want that now, would we?" he said and winked.

There had been the occasional wine coolers and beer at parties before, but Brandon had never participated. He was a strong believer that an athlete shouldn't mess up his body with drugs or alcohol. His unknowing encounter with steroids the year before had reinforced that idea. He would go to the party, but as far as alcohol was concerned, he would be an observer.

Saturday night Brandon got ready to go, and before he realized what he was saying, he told his parents he was going to Dan's house to watch a movie. He had always told them when he was going to parties before, and right after he said the lie, he felt guilty and wondered why he hadn't told them the truth. I guess I was just reacting to Zach's request not to tell our parents where we're going, he thought. Yeah, that was it. It must be.

When Brandon arrived at 9:00, there were cars parked up and down the road. Geez, there *must* be a lot of people here, he surmised. As he walked in and looked around, he saw empty beer bottles, wine coolers, and three or four half-gallon bottles of vodka and rum. The living room was packed. Music was blaring in surround-sound and some kids were dancing on the pool deck. Two guys and two girls were in the pool without their shirts on. They each had the inevitable beer bottle in their hand.

A tipsy Zach stumbled out of the house and yelled, "Don't you guys know you're not supposed to have glass in the pool?"

"My bad, man," answered one of the guys. "I'll switch out for cans." He actually climbed out of the pool to comply. It only took him a minute to walk over to the big cooler, grab four cans of Budweiser, and reenter the pool.

"S'up, Zach?" said Brandon. "How long has this thing been going on?" he asked.

"Hell, buddy, some of these guys showed up at three this afternoon to swim, and we started drinking then. You better catch up!" He pointed to a cooler.

"Later," Brandon put him off. "I'll just walk around and see who's here." He saw Dan and his girlfriend in the media room and joined them on a sofa. "How long have you guys been here? I'm guessing not as long as some people, judging by the fact that you're still coherent."

Dan laughed and said, "Not by a long shot! We got here about an hour ago and have had only one drink each."

"You're drinking?" asked Brandon.

"Come on, Brandon! Everybody drinks a little, some more than others," he said with another laugh. "Don't be a prude! Just have one beer. Or maybe a rum and coke?"

"Nah, I'll leave the drinking to the rest of you. The body's a temple, you know. Gotta stay in shape!"

"Are you sure? I brought a bottle of rum I got out of my dad's liquor cabinet, and it's pretty good. One wouldn't hurt you."

"No, thanks, I'm gonna wander around a little. See you guys later."

"Okay, buddy, see you." He whispered something in Audreonna's ear, and she laughed as Brandon strolled off.

Brandon drifted from room to crowded room. He couldn't believe how many people were there and how many were in various stages of intoxication. Even the bathtub was full of beer and ice. He was about to head back to Dan when he saw, much to his disbelief, Emily chugging a beer, and then laughing hysterically. When they had dated, they had discussed drinking and discovered that neither of them had ever had a drink. She had been proud of him, and he of her, for ignoring peer pressure and staying away from drinking. It must be that Juan Carlos, he thought. Seeing Emily really put a damper on Brandon's evening, and his interest in the party immediately waned. Before he could leave the room to head for the front door, Emily looked up and saw him. He saw her gasp, then turn her head to say something to her date. Brandon's eyes followed Juan Carlos as he walked to the cooler and pulled out two more beers. Juan Carlos was having fun and was oblivious to the emotions playing out in front of him.

As Brandon was leaving the room, Eric stepped out of a throng of people to stop him. The year before when Eric and his girlfriend, Kristin, had been having problems, she had broken up with him and had come on to Brandon. She had never meant to stay broken up, nor had she really wanted Brandon. Kristin had just been making a point to Eric, but she had used Brandon in a way that he would never forget. It was the first time he had really had a serious heartbreak, and later in the year, when he was under the influence of steroids, he had given Eric a hard time for months. Eric had an even temper and had never risen to the bait of fighting Brandon, but he had gotten plenty tired of Brandon's attitude. Watching Brandon looking at Emily, Eric thought he would at least get in a jab at Brandon.

"So, Brandon, what's it feel like to see your girlfriend having fun with another dude?" Brandon's face flushed, and he felt his breathing quicken.

"What's it to you, jerk-face?" he answered.

"Oh, I was just wondering how a super-jock like you might handle things when the shoe is on the other foot. Your girl and that dude have been sucking down the brews and getting mighty cozy." It was all Brandon could do to not flatten Eric. He took a deep breath and just turned and walked out of the room. He knew Eric wouldn't have a prayer against him in a fight, but the valuable lesson he had learned last year was not to fight, because he would be suspended, and lose a sports season.

When Brandon returned to the room where Dan and his girlfriend were, he was fuming. His face was blotchy, and his hands were clenched into fists. Dan noticed immediately.

"Hey, bro, what's going on?"

"I don't even know where to start. First, I saw Emily and *that dude* chugging beer and hanging on each other. Then Eric tried to start something with me. I'm so pissed I can't see straight."

"Have a drink, bro. It'll calm you down and make you feel better."

Much to Dan's surprise, Brandon answered, "Make me one!" Dan got out his bottle of rum and made Brandon a stiff one. Brandon gulped it down.

"Make me another one!" he demanded. Smiling, Dan complied.

After the third drink, Dan said, "You better slow down a little, dude. You're not used to drinking, and they'll hit you quick. What time do you have to be home?"

Brandon looked at his watch and said, "It's only 10:00. I don't have to be home until midnight. I have plenty of time." He had quickly lost a lot of his ability to reason, and he was now no longer able to think responsibly. With a fourth drink in his hand, he ambled back to the room where Emily was. He didn't know what he hoped to accomplish, but when he saw her and Juan Carlos making out, his bravado dissipated. He turned back with tears in his eyes.

Watching the whole episode, starting in the room with Dan, then following him back to this room, was Sheila, one of the girls who had the hots for him since the beginning of the year. As he turned back with tears in his eyes, she was there to envelop him in her arms.

"It's okay, baby. I know how you feel. You just let me hold you until you feel better," she said. She caught him right at the moment of his greatest weakness, and she let her lead him into a bedroom. As she was holding him and soothing him, it seemed only natural that they would lie back on the bed and start kissing. He later remembered her hands caressing him, her speaking softly and then, himself sinking into nothingness.

Awareness returned a while later when he was in the bathroom throwing up. He didn't know how he had gotten there, but Dan was holding his head. He had never felt so horrible. Wave after wave of nausea overtook him.

"Okay, bro, that's the fifth time. Are you about through?" Brandon couldn't manage to say anything. He just kept his head hung over the porcelain throne.

"Come on, Brandon. You've got to get up, so we can get you home. It's 11:45!" He moaned, tried to rise, and collapsed on the floor again. Dan said, "I'm gonna go get somebody to help me lift you, so we can get you in the car. I'll be right back." While Dan was gone, Brandon tried his best to clear his head. His stomach felt a little bit better, but he really didn't know if he could move. He wondered how he got to the bathroom. Dan came back shortly with one of Brandon's teammates in tow. He said, "All right, now, Brandon, the two of us are going to get you up, walk you to the car, and then Audreonna and I are going to take you home. Come on, bro, up!" They managed to get Brandon out to the car with no more vomiting episodes, but he still wasn't doing that great.

Dan said, "I'm gonna drive your car, and Audreonna will follow along behind in my car. Where are your keys?" Brandon fumbled through his pockets and came up with the key.

He was now alert enough to say, "Oh, man, I really hope my dad's not up. He'll kill me." As Dan was driving, Brandon asked him, "How did I get to the bathroom? How did you find me?"

Dan chuckled and said, "You got lucky tonight, bro. That Sheila chick you went into the bedroom with came and got me. She said that a few minutes after you got in there, you passed out, but after a while, you woke up and started heaving. She didn't want you puking all over the bed, so she came and got me, and we got you to the bathroom. Since it was getting late, she left to keep from getting in trouble with her parents." Bits and pieces of the evening started coming back to Brandon. He felt worse than ever, but now along with his physical discomfort, he couldn't believe he had gotten drunk, done who-knows-what with a girl he barely knew, and then passed out.

"What have I done?" he groaned. "How could I have done that?" And, on top of all that, he had an ache in his heart when he thought of Emily. "Now I've really messed things up."

The lights at the Hansen house were all out when Dan drove up. He parked the car, wished Brandon luck, and left with Audreonna. Brandon slowly walked to the door, hoping he could get in without anyone waking up. Now I know how Jaden must have felt when he was sneaking out the window, he thought. He let out a big sigh.

Brandon did manage to slip in undetected, and he had enough foresight to shower with his clothes on. They had puke on them in several places. He figured he would tell his mom he got thrown in Dan's pool in his clothes.

Chapter 15

Miss Bonnie had done some research on the Internet for Jenny. She had found that the most prominent tolerance-promoting club in high schools across the nation was the Gay-Straight Alliance, or GSA. From the literature, she noted that this club was all-inclusive in that it invited all students who perceived themselves to be "different" to join, not just LGBT kids. After reading many reviews, she decided that the GSA most closely resembled the TEAM Club at the middle school, except that it went a step beyond by identifying those with sexual identity issues.

Miss Bonnie was eager to share this information with Jenny, but she didn't want to do so without Alice's knowing, because Donnie had made it clear that he hadn't been happy with the guidance and information she had given Jaden in the past without their knowledge or permission. She was convinced, though, that poor Jaden would have been even more confused and tormented than he had been, had she not stepped forward. She also knew that Alice's mind was slowly being opened in their class. In addition, Alice, by reading Andrea Dworkin, was beginning to get an idea about what it was like to be homosexual in an un-accepting society.

Alice completely surprised Miss Bonnie one day after class. As they were leaving, Alice paused to ask the instructor for recommendations for books based on teenage boys struggling to come out of the closet.

She replied, "I would suggest *Maurice* by E.M. Forster and *The Front Runner* by Patricia Nell Warren. These two would give you an idea how things changed from the early 1900s to the 1970s. They both explore how difficult and touching it can be for kids discovering their sexuality. In addition, you should read *Straight Parents, Gay Children: Keeping Families Together* by Robert Bernstein. It's a survival guide for all parents who want to help their children deal with bullying."

At Miss Bonnie's curious look as they walked away, Alice said, "Women and minorities have been suffering at the hands of others for centuries. In becoming more aware of their trials, I felt that I should try to learn a little more about the pain of those who are like my Jaden. I know he has suffered." Miss Bonnie spontaneously reached over and gave Alice a big hug.

"My dear, you have come a long way. Jaden has so much to gain by everything you learn." Miss Bonnie decided this would be an excellent time to bring up the research she had done for Jenny. After explaining Jenny's dilemma to Alice and telling her that Jenny had come to her for help, Miss Bonnie told Alice that she thought Jenny should go to a school board meeting and plead her case for a GSA in the high school. And, even though she would be glad to go with her, Miss Bonnie said her mother should be the one to accompany her. "I haven't said anything at all to her yet. I wanted to get your permission and, hopefully encouragement, first." As Alice was digesting this startling disclosure, random thoughts and emotions were racing through her brain. She thought, I couldn't go to a school board meeting without Donnie. Oh, wait, what *about* Donnie? He would have a fit if he found out about this. But, I can't leave Jenny without support either. And, I really can't let Jaden dangle without a net again! Did I just waste my time going to the women's group and feeling like I had grown? I guess this is sort of a litmus test to see if I really have changed any at all.

Finally getting her thoughts under control again, she said, "From now on, I'm going to help my children in any way I can and will just have to figure out a way to make Donnie understand."

"Atta girl," said Miss Bonnie and hugged her again.

The next day, seeing Jenny walking home after school, Miss Bonnie went outside to meet her.

"Hey, Jenny! I've done a little research. Have you ever heard of a club called GSA?"

"No, ma'am, I don't think so. What is it?"

"It stands for Gay-Straight Alliance, and there are clubs in schools all over the country."

"Schools have clubs like that? Wow, that sounds really cool, but do you think our school board will allow something like that if they won't even allow TEAM?"

"Years ago, students with disabilities went to different schools from other kids. Then lawmakers came up with a law about 'inclusion'. The original goal of inclusive education was to have students of various levels of disabilities be an integral part of the learning environment of the regular classroom. They rightly believed that school is where kids learn to be members of society. Later, a law called the Equal Access Act came along that prohibits schools from denying students the right to start a new club as long as there are already other clubs at the school. Those lawmakers also believed that in school is where kids become a part of a multi-cultural, diverse society. TEAM was really a great club to have at the middle school, but I found out that it was totally a product of Lake Griffin Middle School and the teacher who created it. GSA, on the other hand, is a national organization that is protected by that same federal law I was talking about. If there are other clubs in your school, then the school can't deny students who want a GSA."

"Does the school know about those laws?" Jenny asked.

"They certainly should, but in case they don't, I think you should educate them."

"Me? They're not going to listen to a ninth grader! I'm sure of it!"

"Jenny, to make changes in this world, we sometimes have to do it one person at a time. Even you, a freshman, can create change in your school that will enable Jaden to be treated equally and with respect, as well as all others like him who feel like they don't fit in."

Jenny thought about it, and replied, "I can't believe I'm saying this, but I'm gonna do it. Tell me how."

"The first thing you should do is go talk to your mom. She wants to support you and Jaden in any way she can."

"Mom? Did you talk to her already? Whoa...that would be so cool. I've always wanted to talk to Mom about stuff like this, but I was afraid of what she might say. I know Dad would be against it, and she always agrees with him."

"Go talk to her, Jenny."

Chapter 16

As the October nights had been getting cooler, the pool water had started cooling down, too. The team knew they had to suck it up, though, because they had the rest of the month before the season was over. Getting in at the beginning of practice was the worst part, but after swimming a few laps, the water magically seemed warmer than the outside air making no one want to get out of the pool to practice on the starting blocks.

One meet started on a cool, overcast day, so everyone brought extra towels and jackets to wrap up in when they weren't in the water. Trevor was only scheduled to swim the medley relay, the 50, and the 200-free relay. After he finished that last relay, he went into the change room, took a hot shower, and put his clothes on. As it turned out, one of the guys in the last relay got sick, and Lake Griffin needed to win the relay to win the meet. Coach Swartout looked for Trevor to replace the sick swimmer in the event.

"Trevor! What are you doing in your school clothes? I need you in this race."

"It was so cold, Coach. I took a hot shower and got dressed. I don't ever swim that race anyway."

"Well, I need you to swim it today! Go get your suit back on!"

"I can't, Coach. I'm too cold." Jaden, who was listening, couldn't believe his ears! Trevor was going to let the team down, because he was too *cold?"*

Jaden spoke up, "Trevor, come on! You have to swim! The team needs you."

Trevor glared at Jaden and responded, "Let David do it. He's only had three races today, too."

Coach Swartout said through gritted teeth, "I don't have time for this, Trevor! Alex, you're in for Patrick. Do the best you can." Then looking at Trevor once more, she said, "I will talk to you later. See me at the end of the meet!"

Alex did the best he could, but it wasn't enough, and Lake Griffin lost the relay and the meet. The team was subdued as they listened to the coaches go over their performance. After the team meeting, when Jaden went over to talk to his family, he saw Trevor looking at the ground as Coach Swartout read him the riot act.

Noticing, Jenny asked, "What's that all about, Jaden?"

Jaden said, "I don't really know, Jen. Coach asked Trevor to swim in the last race, and he wouldn't. Doesn't he realize he's part of a team? I don't know what's up with him lately. Sometimes, he acts like the old Trevor, and then sometimes I feel like I barely know him. I bet it has something to do with Brian, that twenty-year-old guy that he's been hanging with at the theater."

"I'm so sorry he's acting that way with you, Jay. He seems all right when we're all together on Saturday nights. I'm really glad you've become good friends with Chelsea and Brooke. I like them a lot."

Momentarily forgetting how Trevor was acting, Jaden said, "I know! I can't wait 'til Saturday when we go to the concert at the lake. That's gonna be a blast!" Then remembering Trevor, he said, "I sure hope he's back to normal by then."

The next day, Friday, Jaden wanted to know why Trevor had acted as he had at the meet.

In P.E. class, he asked, "Why wouldn't you swim in that relay yesterday, Trevor?"

"Don't you get on my back, too!" Trevor scowled. "Coach Swartout already ripped me a new one yesterday!"

"I'm not on your back. I just don't understand why you wouldn't swim. The team needed you."

Trevor mumbled something under his breath, and then said, "It's not that big a deal, Jaden. I was too cold to swim, so I wouldn't have helped the team anyway. I would have been as slow as Alex. Just let it go!" Jaden slowly shook his head, not knowing what to say. He decided that the only thing he *could* do was let it go.

———

During the week following Zach's party, Brandon felt somewhat awkward, wondering who knew he had gotten drunk, and who knew he had disappeared into a bedroom with Sheila. He didn't really want to face Sheila either, because his recollection of the evening was sketchy. He was pretty sure they had done things, but he wasn't totally sure how far they had gone.

On the other hand, Sheila was not one bit reluctant to encounter him again. In fact, when she saw him for the first time at school, she smiled broadly and rushed over to him.

"I had such a good time the other night, Brandon," she gushed. As she stared into his eyes, she continued seductively, "Who would have thought that you and me would be the first ones to go in a bedroom?" Then she winked at him. Brandon was embarrassed and didn't know what to say, so he just smiled and nodded. Sheila asked, "Are you going to the big Halloween party coming up? We should go together."

"Uh, I don't know. Who's having it?"

"Justin Branch, you know he lives over by the lake."

"I don't know him…"

"That doesn't matter," Sheila said. "He doesn't send out invitations; everyone will be going," she said and smiled coyly. "It's only two weeks away."

Brandon replied, "Yeah, well, maybe I'll go." He thought, what do I have to lose? Emily doesn't want me. I might as well date someone who does. Before turning to walk away, Sheila pressed a piece of paper with her number on it into his hand.

Chapter 17

The headliner for the concert at the lake was At Large and the warm-up band was Bear Roses who played a lot of Grateful Dead songs. Jaden and Trevor loved the Grateful Dead and were really looking forward to hearing Bear Roses. After swim practice on Friday, Trevor had told Jaden and Jenny he was leaving work early and would pick them up at 5:00, so they could get a good spot in the park to put their blanket. Chelsea and Brooke made plans to get there at the same time.

Around 4:30 Jaden received a text from Trevor that was very upsetting. He rushed into Jenny's room where she was putting the final touches on her outfit.

"Trevor's screwing up again, Jen," Jaden stated.

"Why? What do you mean?"

"He just texted me that we should get a ride with Chelsea or have Brandon drop us off. He said he'd be there, but he'd be late. He didn't answer when I texted back asking why."

"Try not to be so paranoid, Jaden. Maybe he couldn't get off work as early as he thought."

Frowning, Jaden replied, "You don't know how he's been acting, Jenny. You haven't been around him like I have. If that was the case, why wouldn't he just tell me he couldn't get off, instead of being so mysterious?"

"I don't know, Jaden, we'll just have to wait and see," Jenny spoke practically.

Reluctantly he answered, "Okay, I guess I'll see what Brandon's doing. Maybe he can take us."

At 5:10 Brandon dropped his younger siblings off at the lake with a, "Text me later if you need to be picked up. I'll be out and about somewhere."

A grateful Jaden and Jenny thanked their brother and started looking for Chelsea and Brooke. They quickly spotted them under a shade tree protecting a patch of grass large enough for two blankets.

"Where's Trevor?" Chelsea asked when they caught up to her.

Jaden scowled, and Jenny said, "He'll be here in a while. He texted that he's gonna be late."

"Oh, that's too bad. Anyway, we got a great spot here. We have a perfect view of the band shell, and shade to keep us cool 'til it gets dark."

"Yeah, this is a great spot!" said Jaden, feeling better every minute. He loved hanging out with Chelsea and Brooke. "I guess Trevor will get here when he gets here."

A barrage of sounds reverberated off the walls of the band shell as musicians strummed, tuned, and tested their various instruments.

"Look at all the people coming in," exclaimed Jenny. "This is gonna be an awesome concert!"

"I know, and look at all the tie-dye, Jen," enthused Jaden. "I told you we should have worn ours."

"I would have worn tie-dye," said Brooke, "but I didn't know what kind of band Bear Roses was."

"Me, neither, but I know I'm gonna like them!" Chelsea chimed in. The crowd all looked to be between sixteen and thirty years old, and the din was getting louder as the park filled up. At 6:10 the music started with no Trevor. At 6:40, Jaden's phone vibrated.

The text said, "where r u?"

"Undr bg shade tree." A flash of bright blue, pink, and green tie-dye caught Jaden's eye a minute later, as Trevor wound his way through the crowd to meet them.

"Look, Trevor has on tie-dye," lamented Jaden. Then he gave him a half-hearted smile. "Why were you late? Wait a minute, what's wrong with your eyes? Why are you squinting?" Chelsea laughed.

"He's just stoned, Jaden, can't you tell?"

"I'm not stoned, I just had a couple of hits."

As Trevor tried to slide in between Jaden and Jenny on the ground, Jenny fumed, "I can't even believe you did that, Trevor!"

"Did what, Jenny? What are you, my mother?" She turned her back on him and slid over to another spot beside Brooke.

"I guess I can see why you're late," said Jaden flatly. "What happened to 'I'll never smoke pot with him, we're just friends'?"

"I told you I'd never done it, but I also told you I wanted to see what it was like, Jaden."

"No, you didn't! You *never* said you wanted to try it!" Luckily the band was playing, because their voices were rising.

"It's not that big a deal, Jaden. A little pot will never hurt anyone. You might lighten up if you tried it!"

"Yeah, right. Trevor, I can't begin to get my head around this, and I don't want to talk about it anymore right now. Let's stop fighting and just listen to the music. No sense in ruining it all for everybody."

Chelsea spoke up, "Chill, Jaden. I've smoked weed before, but I don't now. I think swimming is more important than getting high." The whole conversation was making both the twins uncomfortable, but Jaden decided to try to salvage his former exhilarated mood. He had waited for weeks for this concert, but try as he might, he couldn't help but feel hurt and angry.

The concert really was good, though, and before it was over, they all were on their feet dancing. Tension eased as they rocked and swayed with the crowd. Jenny was as boisterous as anyone, yelling and clapping to get the band to come back out and do one more song. When it was obvious that the very last song had been played, they gathered up their blankets and headed for the parking lot with the other happy attendees.

"Jaden, I'm gonna ride with Chelsea and Brooke, so you and Trevor can ride together."

"Okay, see you later at home." When Trevor and Jaden got to the Mustang, Jaden's hurt and anger resurfaced, and he wanted some answers.

"Okay, Trev, so tell me what's going on. You owe me an explanation. Sometimes I feel like I don't even know you anymore."

"I'm really sorry, Jay. I didn't mean to be late. Brian drove by when I was leaving work and stopped. He wanted to go get something to drink. I figured it would only take a half hour at most, so I said okay. On the way he pulled out half a joint. I only took a couple of hits, like I said." Trevor pulled Jaden close. "Don't make a big deal out of it. I wish I hadn't done it. We're still together and fine. Brian doesn't mean anything to me."

Jaden didn't resist. When Trevor was being sweet and was apologetic, too, it always melted any anger he felt. He really did love Trevor and didn't want to stay upset with him. By the time Trevor dropped him off, they had kissed and made up.

Chapter 18

Jenny picked an afternoon to talk to her mom when she knew everyone else would be occupied.

"Mom, I've wanted to talk to you about Jaden for a long time."

Alice drew a quick breath. I knew this was coming, but I'm still not sure of what I'm going to say, she thought.

Jenny continued, "You know I've always come to you when I had a problem, and you've always helped me or made me feel better. The thing is, I've wanted to talk to you about Jaden, but I didn't think you'd understand. I'm not sure what you actually know, but Jaden is gay." Jenny studied her mom's face. Expecting shock, she saw tenderness, instead.

"Honey, I know about Jaden. After his suicide attempt, Miss Bonnie had a long talk with your dad and me."

"Dad knows, too? What does he think?" Not waiting for a response, she said, "Jaden has wanted to talk about some things lately, but he says Dad has been so nice these past few weeks, that he doesn't want to upset anything."

Alice felt her eyes moisten and thought, my poor little Jaden, how could I have let this happen? But she said, "Dad has had a hard time with it, but he's trying to find peace about it."

"I've always felt so bad for Jaden, because he only had Miss Bonnie and me to talk to. Thank goodness he had her!" Alice's head bowed, and Jenny was afraid her mom was going to cry. Sensing the emotion running through her mom, Jenny reached over to hug her. It was a liberating moment for both mother and daughter. No longer did either have to hide what she knew. Not wanting the moment to end, the hug endured, seemingly suspended in time.

Finally separating, but clasping each other's hands, Jenny exhaled deeply in relief. Now, being able to share her thoughts with her mother, for the first time, she felt a ray of hope for Jaden.

"Mom, Devon and I are trying to get a club started at school to help kids who are bullied, and Miss Bonnie thinks I should go to a school board meeting to talk about it. Can you believe that? Like I could do anything to help?"

"I know, sweetheart. Miss Bonnie talked to me, too. She told me it was called GSA. I want you to know that I'll support you in this; I'll go to the board meeting with you. You never know what difference one voice could make. I don't know what Dad will think, but I'll deal with it. I love you and Jaden very much."

That night after dinner, Jenny wandered into Jaden's room as he was doing his homework.

"You having any trouble with today's math?" she asked.

"No, I think I got it. This part's not so bad."

"I talked to Mom about you today, Jaden."

"Talked to Mom? What about?"

"I told her you were gay."

"Oh, my God, Jenny! How could you! I've always trusted you over everybody! You promised to keep whatever we talk about private. I can't believe you did that!" He clinched and unclenched his fists as he stared at Jenny with a stricken face.

"Jaden, you know you can trust me! And I trust Mom. I would never tell a secret that would hurt you. Anyway, I found out that Miss Bonnie had told Mom and Dad about you when you were in the hospital."

"Oh, that's great, Jenny, absolutely great. Now you're telling me that they knew all along and that Miss Bonnie told them? Oh, my God! Just get out of my room! Leave me alone!"

"Jaden, no! It's not like that. Please listen to me!"

"Leave, Jenny! I don't want to talk about it right now." He lay down on his bed and turned his face to the wall. Feeling terrible, but not knowing anything more to say, Jenny left him alone.

Neither twin got a good night's sleep. Feeling betrayed and abandoned, Jaden tossed and turned until the wee hours of the morning. Jenny, who had felt she was only trying to help her brother, was offended and hurt by his reaction. But as the night wore on, those emotions faded, and despondency set in as she began to believe she had failed him once again.

Jenny skipped breakfast the next morning saying she wasn't hungry. Jaden sat with his head down, picking at his toast. He wouldn't make eye contact with his mother. The usually talkative walk to school was uncomfortably quiet. Jenny tried once to explain that it wasn't a bad thing, but

Jaden wouldn't talk. The siblings separated as soon as they reached the school grounds, and Jaden went to find Devon. It was as if he needed to confirm that at least one important person in his life was steadfast.

"Hey, buddy, what's with the sad face?" Devon immediately noticed.

"I don't know, Dev. It seems like I can't trust anybody anymore."

"You can trust me, buddy. Who's giving you grief? Do I need to have a word with them?" Jaden really wanted to confide in Devon, but he was a little hesitant, because he had never openly talked about the "gay thing" with him. When Devon had found out about him the year before, his initial rejection of Jaden had contributed to Jaden's suicide attempt. Even though Devon had come to grips with his friend's sexuality, Jaden still wasn't comfortable talking about feelings with Devon. As if he sensed what was going on inside his buddy's head, Devon said, "Is somebody giving you shit about being gay? You can tell me, Jaden. Now I really do understand how people feel when they're getting picked on. That shouldn't be happening!"

Jaden was overcome with emotion. To know, to finally believe for certain, that his best friend really did accept him for who he was, was unfathomable. Suddenly, his burden felt lighter.

He said, "Last night I felt that Jenny and Miss Bonnie had betrayed me. Jenny told me that she talked to my mom about me being gay, and when I freaked out about that, she told me that Miss Bonnie had told my mom and dad about me a long time ago. Then I really freaked out. I wouldn't even listen when Jenny tried to explain. But, I really do know that neither she nor Miss Bonnie would do anything to hurt me. I just wasn't thinking straight."

"I get it. You were just taken by surprise. But you were way off base, dude! You know that Jenny and I have been trying to figure out a way to get a GSA club started here. Your sister is your biggest ally, and I'm sure Miss Bonnie is, too."

"Yeah, I know. I feel bad now. I shouldn't have acted like I did last night."

"Don't tell me, dude. Go tell Jenny." With that encouragement, Jaden did just that.

The apology went well. No one understood Jaden as well as his twin.

"Jay, will you go to the school board meeting with mom and me? It would really help if they could hear from a gay student firsthand." Jaden hesitated.

"I kind of want to, but I just can't. If someone there knew who I was and then kids at school found out about me for sure…I just don't think I can face that right now." Jenny hugged her brother.

"It's okay, Jay, you don't have to go. Mom and I can do this."

Chapter 19

Despite Ricardo having left the swim team, he and Jaden still tried to meet in the hall to walk to their classes. Because of his language difficulty, he had been put in a special class for students whose first language wasn't English. In that class he had made friends with several Spanish-speaking kids. One of them was a senior, Emily's new boyfriend, Juan Carlos. Ricardo admired him because he was a good athlete and popular in school, and he didn't seem to mind that Ricardo was only a freshman. He had spoken to Ricardo about Emily when they had first started dating.

"I'm dating the ex-girlfriend of your friend brother. She is cute and sexy, eh?" Ricardo quickly agreed. He liked the fact that a senior confided in him.

"I show her what a real man is like," he laughed. When Ricardo later told Jaden what Juan Carlos had said to him, Jaden just shrugged.

"I don't think Brandon would care one way or the other," he said.

———

Swim season was rapidly coming to a close. The district tournament was scheduled for the Friday before Halloween. The swimmers would get to miss a full day of school and would have to be transported over to Jack's Creek, in the south end of the county, where there was an Olympic sized pool with ten lanes. The entire team was excitedly talking, and Coach Swartout was having trouble getting their attention in order to pass out the permission slips and absence-from-class forms.

"You have to get a parent to sign the permission slip, and all your teachers have to sign the other form. These must be turned in by Wednesday, or you won't get to go to the meet. We'll be swimming against seven other teams, and some of you will qualify to go to the regional tournament if you do as well as you have been. Three girls and three boys from each team can enter in every event, so you can probably count on doing the event of your choice. I need to know by tomorrow what you'd like to swim."

When the team was dismissed, Trevor said, "I know I definitely want to do the same events I've been doing. I've dropped my 50-free down to 23.01."

"I bet you'll probably qualify to go to the regionals," said Jaden. "I hope I can qualify in the 200-free. What about you, Devon?"

"I for sure want to do the IM. Other than that, though, I don't really care what they put me in." Coach Swartout, walking by, heard his comment.

"That's the attitude, Devon!" Then she looked hard at Trevor, but didn't say anything.

"What was that all about?" bitched Trevor. "She's been on my back ever since that day it was so cold."

"Just let it go, Trev. You have a really good chance in districts. Don't go in being mad at the coaches," said Jaden.

"Yeah, Trevor, let it go," said Devon. "You know you were wrong not to swim that day." Trevor shot him a nasty look, but Devon ignored it.

They all got their forms and permission slips in by Wednesday, and Friday morning at 6:00 A.M., they were standing sleepy-eyed at the bus loop, awaiting their transportation. They were laden with coolers, towels, blankets, and Ipods. It was about a forty-minute drive to Jack's Creek, and warm-up started at 7:00. Every event had several heats scheduled, and the meet would last the better part of the day. When they arrived at the pool, Jaden couldn't believe who was waiting at the gate.

"Chelsea, did you know Brooke was going to be here?"

"Yeah, her mom let her miss school to come. I just wish she could have ridden on the bus with us. I would have sneaked her on if there had been a way, but her mom said she'd bring her."

"That's so cool. I wish Jenny could have come today, too."

Without delay, the swimmers jumped into their assigned lanes and began warming up. When Coach Swartout signaled that warm-up was over, they huddled around the coaches, feeling the cool of the October morning air, even wrapped in their towels. The pool was heated and comfortable, but it was hard to get out. Coach Swartout told them that the fastest three swimmers in each event would go to regionals, but since there were three heats in most events, even if you were in the top three of your heat, it wouldn't guarantee a placement. After listening to their coach, the swimmers in the first couple of events headed for the starting blocks, while the others piled up together under blankets.

Lake Griffin Mustangs made a good showing in almost all their heats before the break that followed the 50-free. Both girls and boys medley relays came in first, Jaden came in second in the 200-free, and Devon easily powered through the IM. Trevor came in first in the 50 by a long shot, but as the other heats were swimming, he was concerned about the times of those winners. When all the heats were finished, he was relieved that only one time was better than his. Much to everyone's delight, Devon's IM time remained the best! Jaden was crestfallen to realize his first place turned out to be fifth place overall, but he knew he had one more big event that he had worked on all season – the 500-free. Still, he was thrilled about how his friends had done.

During the break Jaden headed for the bathroom. Suddenly, he was overjoyed at the sight of his mom, sister, brother, and Miss Bonnie coming in the gate.

"Mom! Miss Bonnie! I didn't know you were coming! This is so great!"

"We wanted to surprise you and let you know that we're here for you in everything you do! I just wish we could have gotten an earlier start." Jaden hugged his mom, Jenny, and Miss Bonnie, and high-fived Brandon, then, began to excitedly describe the races they had missed.

The break was soon over, and the new group found seats in the bleachers. Jenny spotted Brooke and waved her over to sit with them. The next event that they were particularly interested in was the 100-free, which was two events away. They knew Chelsea would be in that one, and Trevor would be in the boys' event that followed.

Brooke had purposely taken a seat between Jenny and Brandon, so she could talk to both of them.

"Brandon, are you dating that girl, Sheila? I heard you were." She raised one eyebrow at him. Brandon flushed and stared straight ahead. "Well, are you?" He looked at her sideways and tried to give her the "not now" look. She smiled, obviously enjoying putting him on the hot seat. In a low voice, she said, "Relax! Your mom's not paying any attention at all. She's talking to the lady that came with her."

Brandon breathed a sigh of relief and replied in a muted voice, "I guess you can say we're dating. We wound up at a party together, and supposedly, we're going to Justin's Halloween party together tomorrow night."

"Oh, cool! Chelsea and I are going to that one, too. It's her birthday, you know."

"No way! She was born on Halloween?"

"Yep, so her birthday has always been a really fun day for her, what with costumes and trick-or-treating growing up. We decided that instead of having a separate celebration this year, we would just go to the big Halloween party at Justin's. Chelsea and he are neighbors."

"I guess I'll go for sure, then."

Jenny, not sure why she felt a little irritated, said, "Heads up, guys. It's Chelsea's race." Maybe she was feeling left out. The small group joined the others in the stands yelling encouragement to their favorites. Chelsea had a bad start, but swam powerfully through the short race to come in first. Trevor's turns had vastly improved, and he had no problem taking a first, too.

When the time came for the 500-free, Jaden was so psyched and ready that his toes were twitching on the block. Out of the corner of his eye, his attention was drawn to the swimmer to his left who was pulling nervously on his suit. That one moment of lost focus did him in. When the starter bellowed the command, "Take your mark", he was so ready to dive that his weight shifted slightly forward, and he couldn't stop himself from leaving the block just as the horn blared to start the race. Did he leave too soon? It was so close that the race continued to the end. As Jaden was climbing out of the pool, one of the officials pulled him aside and said he had disqualified for leaving the block early.

Disqualified? Are you kidding, he thought? And then he saw his name on the board with a blank where his time should have been. He was mortified. He had DQ'd in the race that he was hoping would qualify him for regionals. He was fighting back tears as he left the pool area to go sit by himself, away from everybody.

Coach Staley was scanning the crowd, looking for Jaden. Chelsea, who had been his lap counter, realized what must have happened and found him in a corner, his face a mask of disappointment and shame. She put her arm around him and spoke in a soothing voice.

"Jaden, everybody DQ's some time in their career. It actually happens a lot, especially on relays. You're a first year swimmer, and it didn't happen to you all season. You were due, especially in the stress and excitement of the biggest meet. Don't feel bad, and especially don't feel ashamed. It's not the end of the world."

"But I wanted to go to regionals with you and Trevor and Devon so bad. This was my only chance. And I know Coach Swartout is probably pissed, too." Coach Staley, who had spotted the two, walked up in time to hear Jaden.

He said, "Jaden, you've done an amazing job all season. No one is mad or disappointed in you. You're your own worst critic. Jumping the gun is a fact of life in swimming, and you'll learn from it. Now, get your mind focused, because you have a relay yet to swim."

Jaden walked back over to where the team had staked out a spot at the beginning of the day. He was feeling better, and when Devon and Trevor both told him he swam really well regardless, he felt almost back to normal. Devon said he had timed Jaden's race, and he had cut off another forty-five seconds from his best time! At least that was something.

The swim meet finally wound up around 5:00 with both the boys and girls 400-free relay, and Chelsea, Devon, and Trevor set to go to regionals in their individuals the next week. Unfortunately, for everybody else, swimming was over for the season.

Chapter 20

When Brandon got home from the swim meet, he decided to give Sheila a call. She seemed nice enough, and she certainly seemed to like him, so why not go out a few times and get to know her. She was pretty, and it was always more fun to go places with a date than to go alone.

"Hey, Sheila, it's Brandon. You still thinking about going to Justin's Halloween party with me?"

"Brandon! Yes, I'd love to go with you. You going in costume?"

"Costume? I didn't know about that. I'm not sure. Are you?"

"I'd been planning to go as Lady Cleopatra. You could go as Marc Antony. Everyone will be dressed up!"

"I guess I could do that, if you'd help me get it together."

"Oh, it'll be easy. All we need are some sheets that we can cut up, and a couple of other little things. Why don't we meet at the mall tomorrow around 3:00, and we can accessorize! It'll be fun!" Although still uncertain about wearing a costume, Brandon agreed.

Sheila gave Brandon costume details the next day at the mall, and when Brandon found out he could wear sandals and shorts covered by some sheeting, he decided it might not be so bad, after all. To look Roman, he would have some leather straps crisscrossing up his legs and a wide leather belt. Sheila would have a low-cut, long, flowing gown (made of sheets, too). All in all, they thought they would look good together, and Brandon was privately relieved that the costumes wouldn't be excessive. After he told her he would pick her up at 7:00, they went their separate ways. The party was due to start at 7:30, and Brandon wanted to be a little early, so there wouldn't be any surprises like when he walked in on Emily and Juan Carlos at the last party.

Brandon's plan worked well, because when he and Sheila arrived at the party, fewer than ten people were there. All were in costume, however, so he was glad Sheila had talked him into wearing one. A couple of people were incognito, because their costumes had full-face masks. There could be advantages to that, Brandon thought. I could look at people without their knowing, as well as people not knowing who I am. He had made up his mind, though, that no matter what, he wasn't going to get drunk tonight.

Close to 8:00, people started arriving in droves. Brandon was relieved when Dan and Audreonna got there, but when he began to introduce Sheila to them, his face flamed red when Dan pointed out that they had met previously under inauspicious circumstances.

Brandon tried to cover it up by saying, "Oh, yeah, right. Hey, did you bring anything to drink tonight?"

Dan pulled a small flask out from under his costume and said, "Let's get cracking!" Brandon had resolved to have only one drink, hoping it would mitigate his anxiety should he run into Emily.

With drinks in hand, the four began walking around and mingling with people they knew. After a while they ran into a cute set of salt and pepper shakers, who turned out to be Chelsea and Brooke. They had drinks in plastic cups, and Brandon was curious whether they had alcohol in them. Not wanting to call attention to himself, though, he abstained from saying anything.

"Isn't the house outrageous?" said Chelsea. They always go overboard for Halloween. Did you see the witches and ghosts at the door when you came in? Out back the whole yard is a maze of spider webs with humongous spiders in them!"

"Yeah, this place is awesome," added Brooke. "I've never been here before but Chelsea has. And the food! Did you see they have tables inside and outside, with real food, not just chips and stuff?"

"I know," said Dan. "I've had my eye on those chicken wings and the pulled-pork sandwiches." Suddenly feeling hungry, the group turned toward the food tables. They loaded their plates and found seats on the pool deck. The music was loud outside, and people had started dancing.

"Come on, Brandon, let's dance." Sheila tugged on Brandon. Feeling somewhat emboldened by his drink, Brandon followed her out to the others. Chelsea and Brooke were behind them soon after. It occurred to Brandon that he was actually having fun – something that had eluded him all this school year. He decided Sheila wasn't so bad to hang out with. She had neither done nor suggested anything that had made him feel uncomfortable. He let his guard down a little.

As it got later, the noise increased, and the hard-core partiers were disappointing no one. As usual, a few were pushing others into the pool, more were staggering, and loud voices could be heard above the din. Suddenly, Brandon perked up his ears. Although all the voices were mostly indistinguishable, he was almost certain he recognized Emily's voice. He was sure he heard her yell, "Juan Carlos, stop! I said no!" He was both concerned and conflicted right away. He didn't want anyone to hassle Emily, but he felt awkward wanting to respond to what he assumed to be an ex-girlfriend's argument with her boyfriend, while he was on a date with someone else. Still, he excused himself to go to the bathroom and walked in the direction of the voices. Looking around he didn't see Emily or Juan Carlos, and the loud voices seemed to have stopped. Feeling a little better, he made his way back to his friends.

Their group had grown a little since the evening had started. Justin, the host of the party, had led David and Kaitlyn to them, as well as Kris and Kelsie, all members of the swim team. They had arrived with balloons and small presents for the birthday girl. Justin gave Chelsea a peck on the check and offered up a toast with his wine cooler. They all cheered, but everyone except Dan and Audreonna abstained when Justin asked if anyone needed a drink refill. No one, not even Dan, had encouraged Brandon to have another drink that night, and all he had sampled was the one. He was somewhat relieved and grateful to be with people who weren't going to push him. The ten of them had a great time dancing, teasing each other, and laughing at people when their costumes tripped them up or made it impossible for them to do anything with ease.

For those with curfews, the party started breaking up around 11:30. That included the group Brandon was in, so they were saying their goodbyes. When Brandon and Sheila were heading for the door, Brandon was startled to see Emily glaring at a tipsy Juan Carlos in the living room. Feeling like a voyeur, he quickly turned away and ushered Sheila out the door. She didn't mention a thing, and he was sure she hadn't noticed the unhappy couple.

Brandon dropped Sheila off and sincerely told her that he had a good time. He kissed her briefly and tried to keep thoughts of Emily out of his head as he drove home.

Chapter 21

Alice had decided to enlist Miss Bonnie's support when she called to put the GSA item on the school board meeting agenda.

"I'm pretty sure I know who to call, but it would make me feel better to just have you in the room."

Miss Bonnie laughed and said, "Everyone feels better when they're not alone. There are plenty of things I probably wouldn't have done without a friend standing by." The call went smoothly, and the item was placed on the agenda of the meeting the Monday of Thanksgiving week.

Alice said, "Thank goodness it's not next week! This gives me a little time to decide how to tell Donnie."

"What *are* you going to tell him?"

"I don't honestly know. I'm really worried about how he'll probably react, but I feel like I have to do this."

———

The week before Thanksgiving, was also Brandon's final high school football game. In addition, it would be senior night when, before the game, all the twelfth grade players would be escorted by their parents to the middle of the field, and all would be introduced. Ever since he had found out about the event, Donnie had thought of little else. He vividly remembered his own senior night, years ago, where he and his dad together had basked in the accolades of the announcer who had recounted unrivaled feats from his own season, as well as his dad's, the generation's before. Donnie had been the only senior that year whose dad had starred on the same field when he was in high school.

He knew it wouldn't be the same for Brandon and him, because they didn't live in the same town that Donnie had grown up in. But nevertheless, he was looking forward to walking out with his son, a well-known and popular player, who was also the captain of the team.

Jaden, Jenny, and Devon were psyched to go to Brandon's last football game. In seasons past they always had been eager to go, but now that they were in high school, there was a lot more to it. Cheerleaders had been selling spirit ribbons all week, as well as plastering the walls with banners, and they had made little goody bags for each player with his number on it. The twins had bought ribbons, and Brandon had given Jaden his goody bag, which Jaden had carried around at school for two days. He was so proud of his brother! There was even an hour-long pep rally the day of the game.

It had been disappointing at the regional swim meet earlier that week, because not one of the Lake Griffin High swimmers had advanced to state. But they had made a good showing, and most of them would be returning the next year. Jaden was doubly disappointed, first, because he hadn't been able to go and watch, and second, because no one had advanced. But that letdown feeling only lasted a day, because everyone had become so caught up in the excitement of the last football game. Trevor was the only one that seemed indifferent to the activities.

The day of the game when Jaden asked Trevor to come to the game for the umpteenth time, he had replied, "No, Jaden, for once and for all, I'm not going to the game. You know I don't like football."

"But it's Brandon's last game! Everyone's going. I don't like football either, but I like to see Brandon play."

"You just watch the cheerleaders anyway. You told me that yourself."

"That was a long time ago. You know I like to watch Brandon now. He's great!"

"Then, you go watch him and have fun. I think I'm gonna call Brian and see what he's up to."

"So you can get stoned again?" accused Jaden with eyes flashing.

"No, not 'so I can get stoned again'," mimicked Trevor. "I just don't want to go to the stupid football game, and I don't want to stay home by myself. Don't be so suspicious." Jaden's stomach turned to bile as he swallowed the acidic words he wanted to say. He shrugged his shoulders, sighed, and turned to go to class, fighting back tears.

The Hansens and Devon got to the stadium early enough to get decent seats. Before they left the house, Brandon had given his dad his "away" jersey to wear for the introductions, and Donnie's heart had not stopped soaring.

Seeing other fathers donned with jerseys at the stadium intensified his anticipation. Finally, the moment came when Brandon, standing between his parents, lined up with the other seniors. As they walked toward the middle of the field, Donnie was bursting with pride. The solemn ceremony was over too quickly, but Donnie and Alice had it imprinted indelibly in their hearts. This was a moment they would cherish over and over, replaying it in their memories.

The game was close, and the players were hitting hard. Suddenly, in a hapless moment near the end of the second half, it was over for Brandon. He got hit from the side with a blow that knocked him to the ground, causing his helmet to make a forcible thunk! He lay there, out for a few seconds, but when the coaches and trainer got to him, his eyes were open, and he insisted he was fine. Regardless, he was taken out of the game with a possible concussion. After an examination by the team doctor on the sidelines, he was told he was done for the night. Since there were only a couple of minutes left in the game, they told Brandon he could stay and watch the rest from the sidelines.

Alice was beside herself with concern, but Donnie persuaded her to keep her seat and let the team take care of Brandon.

"See, Alice, he's up and sitting on the bench. It must not be too bad, or they would have taken him off in the ambulance." Shaken nevertheless, Donnie felt the game was over for him, too, and he watched the rest in a fog. After the final play, he and Alice rushed to the field to talk to their son and the doctor. Because a mild concussion was a possibility, they were given instructions to take Brandon to the ER to be checked out further, just in case.

On the way, Donnie and Brandon talked about the game and the accident. Because there were no abnormalities in the neurological test he performed, the ER physician felt imaging was unnecessary. Brandon was released and father and son consoled each other with the fact that baseball was still to come, and that was the best sport, anyway.

Now that the big game was history, Alice knew she had to say something to Donnie about Monday night's meeting. Saturday morning her face reflected her anxiety.

"Honey, I'm going to the school board meeting Monday night, and I need to talk to you about it."

"What? Why are you going?"

"Actually, I'm going with Jenny. She's going to ask that a club be started at Lake Griffin High."

"Jenny? What club?"

"It's called GSA, and I think it's only right that I be there to support her. It's a club similar to the one she and Jaden belonged to in middle school. It's designed to help kids of all sorts fit in and get to know each other."

Starting to feel skeptical, Donnie asked with a sardonic tone, "What does 'GSA' stand for?" Dread filled Alice's chest and rendered her almost breathless. She tried to speak calmly.

"It stands for Gay-Straight Alliance."

"Oh, no you don't! No one in my family is going to any school board meeting for that purpose!" Donnie's voice grew louder. "I forbid it!" Alice flinched. Waiting to see if Donnie was going to continue his outburst, she took the time to gather her thoughts. After a pause, she continued.

"Donnie, our children need us." Alice was trying to speak in a reasonable tone. "I know it's difficult for you to handle the fact that Jaden is gay, but I thought you had made a little headway in that respect over the past few months. Jaden didn't *choose* to be gay. Why would anyone *choose* a life where people, including his parents, don't understand him, think something's wrong with him, and even ridicule him? But, the fact that he is gay doesn't change him as a person nor diminish him in any way. Your daughter understands that and wants there to be a club on campus where he can feel safe to be himself and others can get to know him as a person, not as a misfit or a 'fag'."

"Where did you get to be so high and mighty? So knowledgeable?" he said sarcastically.

"Donnie, please. This is our son, and we love him. Actually, I've learned a bit more about what its like to be gay from the class I'm taking, but that in itself has not changed how I feel about Jaden one bit. I realize you had an incident early in your life that has negatively influenced your feelings, but the only way you're going to ever sort through that is to go to counseling, like you said you would." Donnie glared at his wife, almost spoke again, then abruptly left the room. Alice shook her head and thought that she hadn't wanted this to happen, but had been afraid it would.

Donnie decided to take a walk to try to let his temper subside. His face was contorted in anger, and his breathing was rapid. He knew if he didn't subjugate his rage, he would either explode or say something he would regret. How dare Alice, without even consulting him, make plans to go to a public meeting to expose and humiliate the whole family? How dare she try to tell him what to do or how to feel? He knew he had said he would go to counseling, but really, what was the point? What had happened to him had been when he was a kid and was long past. No amount of talking would change the fact that Father Tom had touched him. Nothing else had really happened, and he had gone on with his life.

As he walked and walked, his breathing became normal again. His thoughts turned to Jaden. I only said I would go to counseling because Jaden tried to commit suicide, and back then, I blamed myself because of how I had treated him. But, that's all changed now. We get along great, and Jaden's happy. And, I can't see any reason to start some club that will announce to the whole school that he's gay. That's the last thing he should do. Plus, I don't see why Alice and Jenny want to get everyone at the school board agitated just because some kids don't like the way the school is run. Things just need to calm down. What I need to do is go home and apologize to Alice for losing my temper, and then try to talk some sense into her.

By the time he got back home, he was ready to try to be reasonable with Alice, but no one was home. Alice had left a note saying she had gone to the grocery store, and the kids had gone to see friends.

When Alice got home from the store, Donnie was waiting. He helped her unload, and they put away the groceries in awkward silence. When they finished, he asked Alice if they could talk again. Not knowing where it was heading, she agreed reluctantly.

"Look, I'm sorry for blowing up at you like I did," Donnie started. "I know that we don't have the type of relationship where you have to ask me if it's okay to do something. The thing is, I can't see how this club could be beneficial for Jaden. The only people who would join would probably be more gay kids, and I don't want Jaden to be involved with a bunch of queer kids talking about sex." Alice was flabbergasted.

"Do you think being gay is only about sex?" she asked incredulously. "Do you think that Jenny only talks about sex when she is in a room full of heterosexual kids?"

Donnie blustered, "That's not the same thing. Normal kids have a lot of shared interests to talk about." Alice's eyes turned to steel.

"I don't want you to ever again say that Jaden is not normal," she said unequivocally. "He's bright, fun, caring, and I'm sure he wants to have a lasting relationship with someone some day, just like any other fourteen-year-old wants. He can't help it that he wants that relationship to be with another boy, because that's who he can emotionally bond with. And back to the club. It would be open to all students. It would give kids from all cultures, disabilities, and sexual orientations a chance to get to know one another, instead of being biased against each other." Donnie didn't really know what to say. He felt his temper rising again.

"Well, if you're dead set on doing this, I just wish it could be done without the whole town knowing about it at a school board meeting," he finally said.

"Honey, as long as things are hidden and not brought to the surface, no one will ever realize that gay kids are typical kids, just like all other kids." Donnie realized he was fighting a losing battle. He didn't feel good about it, but he knew there was nothing he could do about it.

Chapter 22

Friday night, instead of going to the last football game, Trevor had hung out with Brian. Brian had said he would pick Trevor up, but in a way, Trevor thought he should be the one to drive, because he knew Brian would be smoking weed. But, in another way, he was sort of glad Brian would be driving. He hated to admit it, but with Brian driving, it would feel like a date, and he liked the feeling.

As they pulled away from Trevor's house, sure enough, Brian grabbed a roach from the ashtray and lit it up. After inhaling long and deep, he passed it to Trevor.

"I'll just have one hit," stated Trevor, "but I'll make it a good one."

"No need for more than one, dude. This is some good shit." Minutes later Trevor knew exactly what Brian meant. Brian had his system turned up, and Trevor's brain was delightfully fixated on the music. Brian didn't really want to drive around, so he had gone to the lake and parked, so they could chill to the tunes. They settled back and were quiet for a while, just listening.

After a bit, Trevor casually asked, "Hey, Brian, you going out with anyone?"

"Nah, I don't have time with college, work, and the theater. You?"

"Yeah, I have been, but we haven't been getting along too well for a while."

"Too bad, dude."

"Well, I think I'm up for a change," said Trevor, glancing at Brian. Brian was oblivious to Trevor's implication. But when Trevor put his arm around Brian's shoulder and leaned in to kiss him, he was suddenly fully aware.

"Dude! Stop! I'm not that way! Not that there's anything wrong with it, but I'm definitely on the other team. I thought you knew that. I figured you were gay, but I just wanted to, you know, hang out with you. You're cool." The buzz that Trevor had been enjoying vanished like a puff of smoke, so to speak.

Flushed with embarrassment, he blurted out, "Oh, God, I'm sorry! I thought..." he groped for words, "Never mind, just take me home!"

Unsure of how to handle the situation, Brian just said, "All right, sure."

Jenny went to school Monday filled with an air of excitement, but mixed with a heavy dose of apprehension. Speaking at the meeting that night would be a monumental step for her, but although she was scared, she was also convinced that it was the right thing to do. Plus, she felt really good about the fact that Devon had whole-heartedly agreed to go, too.

When she saw him she said, "Are you getting psyched about tonight, Dev?"

"I am, but I don't have to say anything, do I?"

"No, and I wish I didn't. I'm really nervous about having to talk. I sure don't like getting up in front of people." The two friends grimaced, then grinned at each other. "We just have to remember that we're doing this for a good cause."

The school board meeting was due to start at 6:00, and by 5:15, uncharacteristically, there was not a seat left in the room. The local newspaper had featured an article about the meeting's agenda, and it was headlined "Will School Board Adopt GSA?" Apparently, that had stirred up quite a bit of attention. When Alice, Jenny, and Devon arrived at 5:30, there was a long line of people waiting to sign up for comments.

"Jenny, you need to get in that line over there and fill out a form, so you'll be called on to speak," said Alice, who had researched the procedure. Jenny looked at Devon, took a deep breath, and bravely walked to the end of the line. Devon scrambled after her and took her hand.

"I'm in this with you, Jenny." She looked at him with surprise and relief.

"Thanks, Devon, I'm so glad you're here with me." They smiled warmly at each other.

The school board quickly dispensed with the mundane agenda items, and soon the moderator said, "We will now hear comments addressing the issue of clubs without academic focus being allowed in our schools." The first five speakers addressed the need for students to learn to serve in their community by belonging to clubs such as Interact and Key Club, sponsored by the Rotary Club and Kiwanis. However, things heated up when the next ten people spoke to the need of the GSA, citing examples of how bullying would be decreased, school safety would increase, and even more to the point, gay kids would feel the school cared about them as people. Alice, Jenny, and Devon were pleasantly shocked at the number of people who spoke in support of the GSA.

Immediately after the GSA advocates spoke, though, a long line of people gave impassioned speeches about homosexuality being a sin, and how they didn't want their children to be associated with kids who were "that way". As Alice listened, she couldn't believe what they were saying. It became very up-close-and-personal when Jaden was one of the kids they were talking about. And then, she became horrified when she realized her own husband believed the same way as those narrow-minded people.

Next to speak were some parents and siblings of current and former gay students. It was heartwrenching to hear how some of those students had begged not to have to go to school because of how they were treated there. And how others would come home with black eyes or bruises, but wouldn't let their parents take action for fear of worse consequences. Suddenly, Jenny Hansen's name was called. Listening to all that was being said, her fear had turned to outrage.

"My name is Jenny Hansen, and I'm in the ninth grade at Lake Griffin High School. My brother is one of those kids who has been bullied and ridiculed. In middle school we had a club called TEAM started by our great teacher, Mrs. Cohen. TEAM stands for Tolerance, Empathy, Acceptance, and Morality, which it seems that a lot of you are lacking. Mrs. Cohen made us all feel welcome in the club, regardless of what issues we might have personally been facing. I believe that the Gay-Straight Alliance would do the same thing. It's not just for gay kids. Straight kids who get to know gay kids as people, instead of queers, wouldn't be mean to them. They would begin to realize that we're all alike." Jenny was on a roll, but the timer called out that her time was up. She left the podium to scattered applause.

A few more anti-GSA people made their comments, and the marathon meeting was finally over. The chairman announced that the board would have to take some time to consider what everyone had said tonight. They would vote on the issue at the next month's meeting. Walking out of the room, several people congratulated Jenny on her speech.

Her mother said, "I'm so proud of you, sweetheart. What you did was not an easy thing, and a lot of people took notice of what you said."

"You were great, Jenny," exulted Devon. "No one could have said it better. I know Jaden's gonna be really proud, too." Jenny beamed at the praise.

"I just hope it does some good," she said.

Jenny had been excited to talk to Jaden when she got home from the meeting, and she had given him a full rundown. Jaden had been brimming with enthusiasm.

"Jenny, you are so awesome! And brave! I can't believe you said all that in front of all those people. I didn't know Devon was going with you. Did he say anything? Was he nervous? I can't wait to see him." Jaden went on and on. While Jenny answered all his questions, Jaden didn't even notice the little smile that played across her face as she thought about Devon's taking her hand in his. She thought, he was probably just trying to calm my nerves and support me. It probably didn't mean anything more. I've never thought of Devon that way, anyway. But, the more she thought about it, the more she liked the idea that maybe it did mean more.

Chapter 23

Donnie hadn't had much to say when they got home, but the next morning at breakfast, when he opened the paper, there was Jenny's picture on the front page. He was mortified.

"Holy shit! Alice, did you see this? Jenny's on the front page, and it's captioned 'Sister Champions for Brother'. There's a whole article about that meeting last night."

"Let me see that." As she read the article, her reaction was the polar opposite of her husband's, as her sense of pride for her daughter swelled up again. "Donnie, it took a lot of courage for her to get up in front of all those adults and speak what was in her heart. You should be just as proud of her as I am."

"I'm always proud of her, but this is outrageous! How could you let the newspaper take a picture of her and put it on the front page! I'm humiliated. What am I supposed to say at work? And just like that, bam! You act like you condone it! Have you lost your mind?"

"Just like what, Donnie? Just like standing up in support for our kids and others who are bullied and ridiculed? I think you're the one who's lost his mind. It's past time for you to get over it! Things are going on in our family, and you can join in or get left behind. You need to make a choice." Alice had never in her life spoken so forcefully to anyone, much less her husband. Like a chameleon, her color was changing. She had found her voice. Her own mother wouldn't recognize her now.

Donnie wasn't too sure he recognized his wife, either. Nor was he sure he wanted to. This woman standing before him was nothing like the woman he had married. Or, was she? He knew he still loved her, but could their marriage survive such a profound controversy? He snatched the paper back from her and began to read the article. The more he read, the more upset he became. By the time he had finished, he was too incensed to speak. He threw the paper down on the table and left for work. He couldn't imagine how he was going to face his co-workers. How could Alice have allowed this fiasco to happen?

When Jenny came into the kitchen for breakfast that morning, her mother had presented her with the picture in the paper, and she had read the article three times. When Jaden saw the paper, however, the implications of what Jenny had done suddenly hit him. His breathing became constricted, and his heart began to race. This year he had been kind of flying under the radar at school. Now everyone would be reminded of just what he was, a fag, a queer. He couldn't believe he hadn't seen this coming.

As they walked to school, Jenny was puzzled about his silence.

"Is something wrong, Jaden?"

"Kind of. It's not that I don't appreciate what you and Devon did, but now everyone's gonna start in on me again. Being part of the swim team helped distract from who I really am. But swim season is over, and that article in the paper outs me. I dread walking down the hall today. I'm really starting to freak out."

"Oh, Jaden, I never thought of it that way. But it might be okay, anyway. Look at Chelsea. Everyone knows about her, and no one bothers her. It's like the more gay people that people know personally, the more accepting they'll be. Remember how the swim team accepted you – not because you were gay or straight, but because you were a good swimmer. Someday people will accept people for who they are, and not judge them because of something stupid, like their color or their sexual identity." They walked on in silence while Jaden was contemplating what his sister had said. Still, he worried.

When the twins found Devon in the hall, Jaden wanted to know what Devon thought about the whole situation. Jenny let Jaden carry the conversation, which was almost totally a repeat of the one she and Jaden had on the way to school, while she studied Devon to see if she could pick up on any difference in his feelings about her. When Jaden and Devon quit talking, Devon turned his attention to her.

He smiled widely and said, "I think you and I need to get together right away and plan our strategy for the next meeting. I think we should get other kids to show up with us next time." Then he hugged her and said,

"There's the bell. Time to get going." This time she was sure the hug meant something.

That afternoon after school it seemed as if Devon might have been waiting for Jenny. He was right behind her as she left her locker.

She said, "Devon, last night you said you were in this with me. What did you mean by that?"

He took her hand again and replied, "I meant you and I will go the distance to try to get the club here, but I also meant a little more." He looked into her eyes and continued, "I want you and me to be more than friends." Jenny laughed in delight.

"Devon, I would love that!"

Jaden hadn't had contact with Trevor for days except in P.E., and the contact there had been standoffish. Jaden knew they hadn't left each other on the best of terms that past Friday before the football game, but he had been extra nice on Monday, trying to mend fences. Trevor had been very distant and didn't want to talk. Jaden had gotten used to his moods in the past few months, so he decided to bide his time until Trevor lightened up. Therefore, he was totally taken off guard when Brooke waved him over in the hall at school with a concerned look.

"Hey, Brooke, what's up?" She spoke tentatively.

"I don't know if I should be the one to tell you, but you're my friend, and you need to know."

"Need to know what?"

"One of Chelsea's friends was at the lake Friday night, and she saw Trevor in a car with some guy."

The color drained from Jaden's face, but he managed to say, "Oh, that was probably Brian. Trevor said he was gonna call him and hang out, but I didn't think it would be at the lake or in Brian's car..."Jaden's voice trailed off.

"Jaden, it was more than that." She paused. "Kaitlyn told Chelsea they were making out." Jaden was stunned. He felt like he had been kicked in the gut.

"Was she sure?"

"Pretty sure. Trevor was in the passenger seat, and she saw him lean over and kiss the guy." Brooke put her hand on Jaden's arm. "He hasn't been that nice to you lately anyway, Jaden. Maybe this is for the best." Jaden couldn't think. All he knew was that he didn't want to cry in the hall at school for everyone to see. Things were bad enough already. He pulled away from Brooke and headed for the boy's bathroom. He stayed inside a stall until he regained enough composure to go to class. Even though he was late, the teacher was kind and seemed to accept his excuse of being sick in the bathroom.

Jaden wasn't sure how he was going to handle this. Should he confront Trevor when he saw him in P.E. class? Or should he wait until he had his emotions under better control? The last thing he wanted to do was cause a scene at school. He decided to wait, and he was glad he did, because Trevor seemed like he was in a horrible mood. Neither of them spoke to the other.

Jaden and Jenny walked home from school that day, each lost in his own thoughts. Jenny was thinking about the kiss on the cheek that Devon had given her at the end of the school day. Jaden was wondering what else could go wrong in his life.

"Mom! Mom! Guess what! Devon and I are going out!"

"Jenny! That's big news! Devon is such a nice boy. He's always been such a great friend to Jaden, and now the two of you are a couple. How sweet."

"Mom, we're not a *couple*, and it's not *sweet*." Jenny cringed. "We're just starting a relationship, and it's awesome. The two of us are going to make some changes in our school. He's so smart and has such a good head on his shoulders. He's already thinking of the next school board meeting."

"Jaden, how do you feel about your best friend being your sister's boyfriend?"

"What? Oh, yeah, cool. Cool for them." Then he turned away to go to his room. Jenny quickly caught up with him.

"Did someone at school say something about the article?"

"No. No, it's not that. Jen, I found out that Trevor made out with that guy from the theater."

"No way! How do you know?" A tear slid down his cheek.

"Brooke told me. Some friend of Chelsea's saw them."

"That jerk! Did you get in his face about it?"

"Not yet. I didn't want to start anything at school. Jenny, I don't even know if I want to be with him anymore, or even if he wants to be with me. He's changed so much. But I really love him. I don't know what to do."

"I think you should take a break. If it's meant to be, you'll get back together. But you don't want to hang on to somebody who cheats on you. I don't even think you should say anything to him. You deserve so much better. If he cares, let him come back after you."

Jaden took her advice, even though it was painful, and steered clear of Trevor. When Trevor made no attempt to approach him, Jaden brokenheartedly felt the relationship was over.

Chapter 24

The day before Thanksgiving there was no school. Jenny asked her mom if Devon could come over for Thanksgiving dinner.

Hearing that, Jaden asked, "Can Ricardo come over, too, Mom? I don't think his family does anything special for Thanksgiving. I think his parents work."

"His parents work on Thanksgiving? That's terrible. Of course he can come, and Devon can, too."

"We'll help with the dinner, won't we, Jaden?"

"Heck, yeah! I want to make something special!" Jenny was pleased to hear enthusiasm in her brother's voice. He had been so down the last few days.

Alice said, "By the way, Dad won't be here for Thanksgiving." Her face clouded over.

"What? Why not?" asked Jenny.

"He hasn't seen Grandma and Grandpa Hansen for a long time, and he wants to spend a couple of days with them."

"Why don't they come here?" Jaden wondered aloud.

"They just can't get away right now, so Dad is going to see them. He'll be going straight from work today and staying until Saturday or Sunday." She didn't want her children to think they had any part in Donnie's decision. Brandon walked in to hear the last part of the conversation. "Do you have anyone you'd like to invite for Thanksgiving, honey?" asked Alice.

"I'll check with Sheila to see if they have a family deal."

"Good idea! We'd all like to meet her. Tell everybody that we'll eat at 2:00. You kids need to find out who can come, and then we'll plan the menu, and I'll go to the grocery store." They all reported back in the affirmative, so Alice and the twins sat down to plan the food.

The next morning the Hansen kids were in the kitchen, getting in each other's way, but having a good time preparing for the arrival of their friends. Alice had put the turkey on early, so all that was left was the side dishes.

Jaden was making a scrumptious sweet potato casserole with pecans. Even Brandon was involved, although he was just dishing out cranberries, pickles, olives, and stuffed celery. As soon as Jaden put his casserole in the oven, he went in to set the table exactly as Miss Bonnie had taught him years ago.

When the guests arrived, introductions were made as heavenly smells led them to a veritable feast on the table. Ricardo's eyes widened. He had never seen so much food on one table! Although Alice was not happy about her husband's absence, she was tickled that each of her children had a special friend to share the day with, and she hid her heavy heart well.

The food was delicious, and the conversation was animated. The small group acted as if they had known each other for ages. When the meal was finished, everyone helped clear the table, while Alice began the task of taking the rest of the turkey off the bones. By the time she was through, all the dishes had been washed, dried, and put away. Brandon and Sheila decided to try to walk off some of that wonderful dinner. Jenny and Devon plopped down on the couch to watch football, while Jaden took Ricardo in to show him his room.

"Your room is so big, mi amigo. I share mine with two little brothers."

"I used to share a room with Jenny, but now she's next door."

The boys settled in to talk, as good friends do, and inevitably the conversation turned to school.

"Is anyone messing with you in class, Ricardo?"

"Not really. It's the halls that are worse. But, some people know Juan Carlos is my friend, so they don't say much. He is big and strong."

"I guess that's a good thing. Is he still dating Emily?"

"No, she broke up with him a couple of weeks ago. He don't care. He said he got what he wanted."

"Yeah, it seems to be going around. Trevor and I pretty much broke up last week."

"What happened?"

"Oh, you know how he was acting and treating me. I think we just needed a break. Maybe we'll get back together eventually. Who knows?" Although it made him feel better to think that they might, in a way, it was a relief not to wonder what kind of mood Trevor was going to be in every time they saw each other.

The kids all decided to take in a movie that night. Jaden told Ricardo it would be his treat. Ricardo's eyes were shining in gratitude. A movie was a luxury never enjoyed in his family. While they were gone, Donnie called home to check in.

"How was your dinner?" he asked in a stilted voice.

"It was lovely. Friends of the kids came over, and we all had a good time."

"That fag friend of Jaden's wasn't one of them, was he?"

"Donnie, I will not talk to you if you use that term. I thought you went to your parents to think some things through. Now here you are being just as negative as ever," Alice rebuked him.

"I *have* been thinking, Alice," he said coldly. "It's just that every way I turn, I face more and more undermining of my way of life. You know, men being men, and good wives who honor their husbands."

"Honor?" she said. *"Honor?"* Her voice became loud and was dripping with sarcasm. "Perhaps you need to stay over there in Center City for a while and think some more." She hung up.

Alice was glad she had told the kids that their dad might not be back until Saturday or Sunday, because Donnie didn't drag in until Sunday evening. He seemed cheerful and glad to see everyone on the surface, but she was going to reserve her judgment.

When they went back to school after the Thanksgiving break, Jaden found it was easy to take Jenny's advice, because avoiding Trevor did not turn out to be a problem. He hardly ever saw him at school except in P.E. anyway. He started timing his entrance into the locker room, so that Trevor would already be dressed and out to class. Likewise, he dawdled at the end of class to let Trevor finish first then, too. Trevor didn't seem to mind; in fact, he appeared preoccupied. What Jaden didn't know was that Trevor felt like a fool for coming on to Brian. Plus, he *had* noticed that Jaden was obviously ignoring him and felt even more like a fool, because he figured Jaden must have found out somehow. He increasingly became aware that he had really screwed this one up, but didn't know what to do about it.

Chapter 25

Basketball practice had started in the middle of November, and Devon had made the J.V. team with no problem. He really hustled on the court, and the high school coach was as pleased with him as the middle school coach had been. Jaden had always been his fan, and now Jenny was as excited as he was. She couldn't wait to see her new boyfriend play on the team! The first game was early in December, and time couldn't pass fast enough.

Donnie and Alice hadn't had a serious talk since he had returned home at Thanksgiving, but he was obviously trying to make an effort to be less confrontational with Alice and more sympathetic toward Jaden.

At breakfast the day of the first basketball game, he said, "Jaden, I want to go to Devon's game with you and Jenny tonight. Maybe we can go as family like we used to go to the football games." Jaden was always thrilled when his dad made a point to personally mention him in activities.

"That would be great, Dad, right, Jenny?" Jenny, who had always been her dad's princess, agreed whole-heartedly.

Alice was on board, and Brandon said, "What the heck, might as well."

During pre-game warm-up that night, Devon's eyes searched the stands for Jenny, and when he saw the whole family, his face lit up. Through the years he had become close to all of them. The Hansens were like family to him. His mother couldn't make it to all the games because they started at 5:00, and most of the time, she was still at work. His dad had split years ago.

The game was exciting and fast-paced. Devon roamed around under the goal, and because he could jump so high, he frequently snatched the ball away from the waiting fingertips of the opposing team. On defense, many a fast break was initiated by his rebounding ability. Right at the halftime buzzer his mom walked in, and he gave her a little wave as the team retreated to the locker room.

Jaden saw her too, and yelled, "Over here, Mrs. Mulder! Come sit with us!" She turned toward the voice and smiled.

"I'll be right up, Jaden. I'm a little hungry, so I'm going to the concession stand to get some popcorn and a Coke. Any of you want anything?" Everyone smiled and shook their heads, so she headed for the concession stand.

"Who was that, Jaden?" asked Donnie. "How do you know her?"

"That's Devon's mom. She's awesome."

"But, she's a… she's black," stammered Donnie.

"Donnie!" Alice spoke sharply.

Unperturbed, Jaden said, "Yeah, she's black, and his dad was white. I guess he gets all his jumping ability from her." Then he grinned.

Donnie whispered to Alice, "I always thought Devon was Hispanic, because of his skin color and all."

Alice whispered back, "Does it really matter, Donnie? He's a wonderful friend to Jaden, and we all love him."

"Well, it sure matters now. He's Jenny's boyfriend."

"Don't even go there, Donnie. I swear that would be the last straw." Donnie managed a smile and a handshake when Mrs. Mulder joined them in the stands. Jenny sidled up to her, and the two of them began talking about Devon's athletic prowess. Even Donnie had to admit that Devon was one hell of an athlete. The game ended with the Lake Griffin Mustangs on top, and Devon had made six points, along with eighteen rebounds.

After the game, since it was Friday night and still early, Brandon asked, "Dad, would you drop me off at the mall? I made plans with Sheila to hook up and find something to do." His dad agreed, and they headed to the mall. In the back seat Jaden spoke to his brother in a low voice so that his parents couldn't hear.

"Did you know Emily and Juan Carlos broke up?" Brandon stared at Jaden.

"How do you know that?"

"Ricardo told me. He said Emily broke up with him, but Juan Carlos said he didn't care, because he had gotten what he wanted from her." Brandon was stunned. I wonder if that Halloween party had anything to do with it, he thought. I wonder what happened that night. Now, she's free again. But, I'm not. He smiled at his brother, but his eyes were sad.

"Thanks for the info, Jaden."

The little group that hung out together most Saturday nights had lost one member, Trevor, but had gained another, Devon. Sometimes they had specific plans, and sometimes, they just hung out. This night they were just wandering around the mall trying to plan a zip-line adventure.

"I want to go next Saturday!" Chelsea was emphatic.

"But I don't have enough money saved, yet," pleaded Jaden. "I don't think Jenny does, either."

Chelsea replied, "You never used to have money problems. What's up?" Brooke made a face at Chelsea and tried to catch her eye to make her stop this line of questioning. She knew that Trevor had a job and had often footed the bill for Jaden and him. Devon halted the conversation by casting the deciding vote.

"No way I can go. When I have something coming up that costs that much money, I have to do odd jobs around my neighborhood to get the cash. I can do it, but not that quick." Chelsea pouted a little, but gave in.

"Besides," Devon continued, "Jenny and I have something coming up in just ten days that we want you guys to help with." Peevishness forgotten, Chelsea was interested.

"What is it?"

"Remember a few weeks ago when Jenny and I went to the school board meeting, and Jenny told them we need a GSA club?" Nods all around. "We have to go plead our case again Monday after next, and we figured the more people who show up on our side, the better."

Jaden said, "I didn't go last time, because I was chicken. But I'm going this time. I can't let everyone else fight my battles." Jenny beamed at him.

"Count me in," said Brooke.

"Me, too," said Chelsea. "I'm sure I can get some more people to go, too. I know my parents would go." Brooke looked distressed when she heard that.

"I know my parents wouldn't go, and I don't even want them to know that I'm going. I'll just say Chelsea and I are hanging out."

"I'm gonna ask some guys from the swim team who eat at my lunch table. They've talked about getting picked on a lot," said Devon thoughtfully. "I'm gonna ask my mom, too. Who else can we get?" Thinking caps on, the group came up with about ten more names.

Sunday when she had her mom alone, Jenny recounted the previous evening's conversation.

Alice said, "Well, I'll certainly ask Miss Bonnie to go. Maybe she'll know some other people, too."

"That's a great idea, Mom! I don't know why Jaden and I didn't think of her."

On Monday, Alice walked over to Miss Bonnie's house with a cup of coffee in her hand. The two had become good friends during their class and frequently had morning coffee together. She brought Miss Bonnie up to speed on the plans for the next school board meeting. Miss Bonnie spoke enthusiastically about Alice's growth and Jenny's burgeoning confidence.

"Plus, I always thought that Devon had a good head on his shoulders, and now our little Jaden is starting to find his voice," she proclaimed. "I know some people at the MCC who will be glad to come."

"What's the MCC?" asked Alice.

"It's the Metropolitan Community Church. It's a place for all people to worship whether they are gay, lesbian, transgender, or straight." Alice thought, I wonder what my father would have to say about that. As a minister he had often spoken of other churches, but not that one.

Aloud, she said, "I've never heard of it. That sounds like a wonderful place."

The next day Miss Bonnie informed Alice that the pastor of the MCC would attend the meeting, as well as eight members of the congregation. Several more were maybes. The pastor had suggested that everyone wear red and sit together. She was also going to notify a friend who was a columnist for the paper.

"Wow, Miss Bonnie, when you get going on something, you really make things happen."

"This isn't my first rodeo, dear," she said with twinkle in her eye. "I've been in the background for many a protest. It's only been since Jaden's near tragedy that I've had enough nerve to come out publicly."

"I can't tell you how much its meant to me that you took him under your wing. I guess I can say the same for myself, too. Without your courage, none of us would be where we are now. You've affected me and both my twins immeasurably, and I'll be forever grateful."

Chapter 26

Alice had relayed all of Miss Bonnie's information to Jenny, Jaden, and Devon. They, in turn, had told all their friends what she had said.

"We want to be sure to get there early enough to get seats," said Jenny. "And be sure to wear red," she emphasized.

The week passed quickly as plans were being made. Thanks to Miss Bonnie's friend, there was a nice article in Thursday's paper. Then, Friday, there was a little update article about the meeting that stated the venue for Monday's school board meeting had been changed to the high school auditorium, because large crowds were expected. When Alice read it, she was a bit unnerved, but the kids whooped it up.

"Those old school board members will know we mean business!" cheered Jenny.

Jaden said, "I know! I'm scared, but I'm really getting excited!" In the privacy of his and Alice's bedroom, Donnie pleaded one more time.

"Is there anything I can say that will stop you from going through with this, Alice? Continuing to follow this path will surely lead to disaster for our family."

"Donnie, what you persist in believing is that Jaden can just change himself to fit in with your vision of a happy family. Because he couldn't, he tried to commit suicide. It's up to us to make the changes needed to help our son feel he has worth, that he is loved and accepted. And I, for one, have taken that vow. So has Jenny." Donnie just shook his head and walked away.

Monday night arrived, and Miss Bonnie, Alice, Jaden, Jenny, and Devon were shocked to see that two of the local TV channels had camera crews outside the school. There was a large assortment of people wearing red, from kids to senior citizens. But, there were also a large number of solemn-looking people carrying Bibles. The little group pushed through the crowd, astonished at all the people. Once inside, they hurried to find seats, as the auditorium was filling up fast. The majority of people on the left side had on red, with a few more red shirts sprinkled throughout. Once their seats on the left were established, the twins and Devon went to look for Chelsea and Brooke.

"There they are, in the front," blurted Jaden. "Let's sit with them. Let's tell Mom and Miss Bonnie that we're gonna sit down there." Alice reminded Jenny to sign up to speak.

Jenny, Chelsea, and a few more of their friends got in line to fill out a form. Miss Bonnie fell in behind them. The line seemed to stretch out forever, and before long, Miss Bonnie was chatting with the couple standing behind her.

"I'm so glad you could come," she said. "We haven't gotten together like this for a while, but the time is ripe for us to become active again." The couple smiled, and the three of them talked softly as the line slowly moved forward.

At last, the moderator announced that the meeting would begin in a few minutes, and that anyone who wasn't in line now wouldn't be allowed to sign up. She also announced that anyone who didn't have a seat would need to go out into the lobby and watch the proceedings on close-circuit TV. When the meeting finally started, the only people standing were the TV crews.

When the first person to speak introduced himself as a Southern Baptist minister, Alice rolled her eyes. Having had a father who was a Baptist minister, she didn't look forward to what he had to say. He didn't disappoint her, either. His topic dwelled on how gay children would burn in hell if the adults in charge didn't take action to save them. He said all God-fearing people must keep these clubs out of schools everywhere, as they were nothing but the devil's workshop. He was prepared to go on and on, but thankfully, the buzzer stopped him.

The next two speakers weren't quite as graphic, but they stressed that they didn't want their children to be exposed to a club that advocated homosexuality.

Someone in a red shirt was next. She gravely spoke to the fact that clubs like GSA were sorely needed, because back in Indiana, her neighbor's son had killed himself as a result of bullying at school.

The mother of a gay son spoke next. She sadly told the story of how her son had tried to pretend he wasn't gay, so he could fit in at school. As soon as he graduated, he moved across the country, in order to be who he was without ridicule. He had told her when he left that he never wanted to return, and he hadn't.

The next lady who spoke said, "I'm a minister at a church here in town. It is one of the many MCC churches across the nation. At our church we don't believe that God makes mistakes. We believe that he made each of us exactly how he wanted us to be and loves us for whom we are. Many of you don't understand gay people, and you fear what you don't understand. There is nothing to fear. We aren't trying to recruit you. You can't change how you were born any more than we can. We love our partners and are committed to each other just as you are to your spouse. We seek to excel at our jobs and make a difference in the world, just as you do. The reason the GSA is so important in our schools is that in a safe club like the GSA, young people can intermix with and accept others without attaching a label to them." When she finished speaking, the whole left side of the auditorium gave a standing ovation.

Next to speak was a twenty-something young man.

"In high school I used to date the most incredible girl that I've ever met. She was smart, witty, beautiful; she had the whole package. We dated from freshman year to the start of senior year. We were both Christians and decided together not to experiment with sex until we were adults. We had so much fun and loved to do everything together. Then one night her mom called to tell me Diane was in intensive care at the hospital. She had tried to take her own life. I was crazed. I got up there as quick as I could. I held her gently and asked why. She told me that in the last few months she had discovered she was a lesbian. She said she didn't feel that she could ever break it to me or to her mom, so she decided she would be better off dead. Dead! Can you believe that? If she had had a place at school to go that would have helped her feel less isolated and not alone in her feelings, maybe she could have dealt with things in a different manner." Once again half the audience stood and clapped.

An older man stiffly walked to the podium.

He said, "I have talked about this issue with my preacher, and he told me we shouldn't judge other people. We invite gay people to our church. We would never turn away any sinner. We pray for them. But until they ask for forgiveness and divine grace to be normal, we cannot have outside fellowship with them. Thank you."

Chelsea was next.

"I'm a lesbian, and I don't care who knows it. I have lots of gay friends and even more straight friends. My parents think I'm normal. But, on the other hand, I have gay friends who are scared to death to let people know. One guy's dad told him if he were gay like the kid down the street, he would disown him and kick him out of the house. Others have been picked on ever since elementary school, even before they realized they were gay. I believe the reason I don't have any trouble is because my parents always supported me and my friends knew me as a person before they knew me as a 'gay' person. That's what the GSA could do. Let people get to know each other without barriers and prejudices."

When she returned to her seat, Brooke said, "Way to kick butt, Chelsea!" The others grinned, nudged her, or high-fived her. When Jenny went up, she had added a few things to her first speech and taken a little out. Her final point was that kids learn prejudice and bigotry from their parents, and the only way to stop that cycle was to be exposed to diversity on a safe, level playing field, such as the GSA. This time, she wasn't stopped by the buzzer.

Some of the people who spoke seemed to think the club might be okay, but they believed the parents should have to sign a permission slip for their child to join.

"Just great," bemoaned Brooke. "How many kids are going to ask their parents if they can join a group like that, when they don't want their parents to have a clue that they might be gay?"

"Yeah, and how many parents would even sign a permission slip for their kid to hang out with gay kids?" offered Devon. "I wish they'd just let us kids get together, and figure it out. Like Jenny said, most of the problems come from parents teaching their kids their own prejudices."

When Miss Bonnie stood at the microphone, she stated that she was speaking both for herself, as well as for friends not present. She told the crowd that the world was a much different place when she and many of them grew up.

"Back then gay people were afraid to come out, not just because of ridicule and scorn, but because we could have lost our jobs. We could have been arrested. We couldn't adopt children or even be a foster parent. Many of us tried to blend in and keep our lives a secret from the public eye. But now there are laws that protect some of us from workplace discrimination. We can adopt. Just about everyone knows a gay person, has a gay friend, or has a gay family member. Kids in school are much more open and accepting than their parents were because we are everywhere. But, unfortunately some kids still come to school bearing the burden of their parents' prejudice and hatred. Because of these narrow-minded parents, our schools need GSA clubs, and children need to be free to join, without parental permission."

Everyone stood and clapped, and the row where the kids sat was cheering loudly. The last person to speak was a man in a suit and tie. He told the board that they should consider carefully when it came time to vote, because a "No" vote would set an ACLU lawsuit in motion on behalf of a person who wished to remain anonymous unless the suit became necessary. When he sat down, the moderator told the audience to take a ten-minute break, followed by the board members vote.

When the meeting reconvened, the chairman asked for questions or comments from the board before proposing a vote. The first and second members said they had no questions. When it came to the third, apparently what the ACLU guy said had struck home with her.

She said," I don't think we should take a vote now with a possible lawsuit looming. I think we should delay the vote until we have had time to pursue it with the school-board attorney. I move that we not vote and conclude this meeting." After a few minutes of back and forth, all the board members concurred, and the meeting was over.

On the way home Jenny commented, "What a copout! I can't believe we still don't have an answer."

Miss Bonnie replied, "We'll just to wait and see, but at least we haven't lost. Even though the vote won't come until a later date, I think once they huddle up with the attorney, they'll come to the conclusion that they should okay the club." The kids in the car cheered, but Miss Bonnie cautioned them, "Let's wait to see how this plays out. Those church people are a powerful force."

Chapter 27

Sitting on the couch with the TV on, a terse Donnie watched Alice, Jenny, and Jaden return from the meeting.

"I guess you know the TV crews were at your meeting, and teasers about the upcoming news broadcast have been showing on the hour."

"Really, Dad? Did it show me up there?" questioned Jenny.

"Actually, it did, princess," he replied with a tight smile.

Alice quickly said, "You two need to scoot and do your homework. It's late and will be bedtime soon. I'll call you when the news story comes on." She wanted to divert Donnie in case he had been going to say anything of front of them.

"I'm not happy about this, Alice, but you needn't worry that I'll say something to the kids. I know they think they're doing the right thing, but they just don't realize the ramifications that can occur when the public gets into someone's private business."

"Nobody's getting into anyone's private business, Donnie. The kids want, and need, an inclusive club at school that models tolerance and acceptance, rather than prejudice and hate."

"If the public's not getting into it, then why is it plastered all over the TV set?"

"I guess because narrow-minded people like you are trying to deny kids access to a place at school where they all feel safe from bullies and bigots. Bigots are always big news." Clearly angry, Donnie threw down his newspaper, flipped off the TV, and left the room.

Just returning from working on a research project at the library, Brandon asked, "What's up with Dad? How did your meeting go?"

"I guess you can safely say that Dad's not too happy that we went to the meeting."

"What does he care if the school gets a new club?"

"Brandon, you're right! But Dad feels like we're airing the family's dirty laundry all over town."

"He's really ashamed of Jaden, isn't he?" That did it for Alice. The composure that she had maintained all evening yielded to tears. She turned her head away, unwilling for her oldest child to witness her sorrow and frustration. "Mom?" When no answer was forthcoming, he walked to her and hugged her from behind. After a moment, she faced him again.

"Honey, your dad has always wished both of his sons had been athletes, like you are." She was carefully choosing her words. "He has slowly and painfully realized that Jaden will never be as he had hoped, but he has always loved your brother and, in his mind, has come to accept that he is different. His issue is that Jaden's difference should be kept in the family. He feels that everyone in town will ridicule him, and us, when they find out Jaden's gay."

"Mom, I've discovered there're lots of gay kids in school. There was even this big guy, Deek, who came out for the football team this year. He moved here from Connecticut, and the first day in the locker room, he said, 'Listen up, you guys, I'm gay. If any of you panty-waists are afraid to be in the locker room with me, then get out now. But, none of you have to worry, you're not my type!' Then he got a load of the shocked looks surrounding him and laughed. Nobody messed with him, because he was so big and looked like he could handle himself. For the first few days, the guys would whisper 'Deek the freak' behind his back and make fun of him, but when we started hitting on the field, no one had much to say anymore. When we started playing the games, he hit the other teams so hard that they had to double-team him to stop him. By the end of the season no one cared if he was gay. He was just another player, and a valuable one, at that." He went on.

"I used to think Jaden was wussy because he was gay. I thought the two went hand in hand. But, he's not a wuss. He was just trying to learn sports that weren't right for him, because of Dad. He's great at swimming! Sometimes, it's hard not to join in with the other guys when they're teasing or making fun of someone, but then, I remember Jay. Everybody's good at something and has a place somewhere."

"Oh, sweetie, you've grown up so much!" Alice teared up again, but this time with pride.

Brandon blushed, and then said, "I guess I just told you all that in hopes that you might make Dad realize that our family won't be singled out.

There are lots of gay kids around. And that, when people get to know people, they don't keep on making fun of them."

"Brandon, you're wiser than half the people in this town." Alice flipped back on the TV and called the twins to watch the news segment. They all felt the report was fairly presented and were pleased with the coverage. Alice was so proud of all her children for taking a stand on the issue and sorely regretted that her husband didn't feel the same. She went to bed that night planning to clue him in on what fine citizens their children had grown to be.

Alice wasn't the only parent in town who had been watching the evening news. The Gormans, Brooke's parents, were quite interested in the news story.

"Wayne, I can't believe what we just saw. What are we going to do about this?"

"I'm not sure, Justine. Was Brooke there? She better not have been!"

"I don't know. I didn't see her. She was supposed to be studying with Chelsea. Chelsea certainly didn't look like she was studying, though. I really don't know what to make of it." When Brooke got home, she went straight to her room, and her parents decided not to bring the matter up to her until the next night at dinner.

The next night when everyone was seated and passing bowls of food around the table, Justine Gorman casually said, "Did you have a test today, Brooke?"

Looking perplexed Brooke replied, "No, why?"

"I know you and Chelsea were studying last night, so I assumed you had a test today." Blood rushed to Brooke's ears, then, flushed her face, and she looked down.

"I did…we did…it was a project, not a test," she finally was able to say.

"Brooke, did you know that Chelsea was on TV last night? On the news?" Unable to think of a response, Brooke sat quietly, staring at her plate. "Honey, we know you're lying to us, but right now we have an even bigger problem to address than that."

Her dad spoke sternly, "Don't just sit there biting your lip. Don't you have anything to say?" Not knowing how much they knew or what they were thinking, Brooke continued to be mute. As the silence wore on, her appetite fled and she began to feel sick to her stomach.

Finally, her mom said, "Were you at the school board meeting last night, Brooke?" She nodded. "Did you speak to the group like Chelsea did?"

Before she could answer, her dad asked sarcastically, "Are you a homosexual, too, Brooke?" Oh, boy, I'm really in for it, now, Brooke thought. She looked at their grim faces and knew, without a doubt, that she couldn't tell them the truth.

"No, Dad, no, I'm not!"

"Well, you had to know that Chelsea is one," he persisted.

"Sure, Dad, everyone knows that. Even her parents. But, no one cares. We're just all friends."

"Why did you go to that meeting?"

"I just went to support her and some other friends who get picked on in school. All they want to do is start a club."

"Are those other friends homosexuals, too?" He said the word homosexual like he had a nasty taste in his mouth.

"Some of them are, but some of them just dress funny, or are nerds, or have some kind of disability. People make fun of them. It's hard to walk around school when nobody's got your back."

"Honey, I don't want you hanging around those homosexuals," chimed in Justine.

"Mom, how long have you known Chelsea? Have you ever thought she was a freak or that something was wrong with her? No, you've always said what a nice girl she is and what a good friend I have. Why is it suddenly different?" Her mom sniffed derisively.

"Well, that was before we knew…what if she tries to change you? You know, *recruit* you?" Brooke let out an exasperated breath.

"Gay people are born gay. No one suddenly decides to be gay. People aren't *recruited*. Geez, Mom! I'm not hungry anymore. May I be excused?"

"You may be excused, but don't come looking for something to eat later, just because you don't want to keep talking now," said her dad, Wayne. Brooke went to her room, wondering what the next round of conversation would be like. She knew it wouldn't end there. Not wanting to text Chelsea with her news, Brooke waited until she saw her the next day at school.

"What's wrong, Brooke?"

"My parents decided to have a little talk with me last night. About you."

"Me?"

"They saw you on TV at the board meeting. They asked me if I'm gay, too! Actually, they asked me if I was a homosexual, too. My dad made it sound so gross."

"What did you say?"

"What could I say? I said, no, we're just friends."

"Did you consider that it might have been a good time to come clean and tell the truth?" Chelsea seemed a little hurt. "You know, let them know how we feel about each other?"

"I couldn't do that, Chelsea! They would have forbidden me to see you. I know they would have. I'm scared even now, because I know the subject will come up again."

"You're fifteen years old! What are they going to do, lock you in your room?"

"I don't know. Remember, my dad was military, and they look at things differently."

"I guess you're right," said a subdued Chelsea. "I just wish your parents were like mine."

"You and me, both."

Chapter 28

As much as he tried, Brandon still couldn't keep his thoughts away from Emily for very long. After Jaden had told him she and Juan Carlos had broken up, he had started to unobtrusively watch her from across the lunchroom again. Emily seemed so melancholy, and he hated to see her like that, but what could he do? He and Sheila had been having a blast together, but there were no deep feelings there. At least, not on his part. But, he couldn't very well try to cheer Emily up. He was sure Sheila would have a hard time with that. Besides, Emily had made it clear she wanted nothing to do with him.

Emily was spending too much of her time having regrets. At the lunch table, she confided to her friends.

"It seems like ever since Brandon and I broke up, things have been going downhill. I had to break up with him because he was being such a jerk, but I never stopped caring for him. And talk about a jerk! I had thought Juan Carlos was cool and fun. It wasn't long, though, before I found out he only had one thing on his mind, and if he didn't get it, he'd pout and act like a baby. We did do some fun things, but when he got drunk at that last party and wouldn't stop with me, that was the last straw. If someone hadn't heard me yell, no telling what he would have done. I should have broken up with him before then. It doesn't much matter, though. I'm right back where I started – alone and missing Brandon."

Chapter 29

Christmas holidays were only a week away, and Jaden was feeling a little down as Devon, Jenny, Chelsea, Brooke, and Brandon were all talking about what gift to get for their loved ones. His heart was filled with the bittersweet memory of his excitement last Christmas when he was trying to find the perfect present for Trevor. He had been missing Trevor a lot the past few days, but Jenny had told him to give it some more time. Trevor had been the one at fault, and Trevor should be the one to apologize and try to get back together. He guessed she was right, but he couldn't help wondering if Trevor were missing him, too.

Right before the holidays, the Gormans sat Brooke down again to talk. Her dad began.

"Brooke, your mother and I have decided you can continue to be friends with Chelsea, but you won't be allowed to stay the night at her house, nor her here. We don't want you alone with her at all."

"It's not that we don't trust *you*," her mother continued. "We just feel like it would be too easy to give in to temptation if the opportunity was placed right in front of you. You two have been friends for a long time, and you could become confused if she pressured you. You're too young to understand how homosexuals are."

"That's not fair, Mom! We haven't done anything wrong, and we're being punished anyway!"

"You're not being punished, Brooke," said her father. "You can spend time with her as long as it's with other people. That's more than fair."

"Honey, it's only a matter of time until she starts to pressure you, and we don't want to see you do something that you will regret later and perhaps, the rest of your life."

"I don't believe you two! I'm being held prisoner in my own house at night, and I can only hang out with her in a group? I'm not allowed to do what other kids do all the time. My life might as well be over."

"That's enough, Brooke! You're exaggerating and over-reacting, and I'm not going to let you be a drama queen. If you continue acting this way, we won't let you see her at all." Under her breath, Brooke muttered words to the effect that her dad was a Nazi and should never have retired from the military.

When she texted Chelsea that night, Brooke was still angry about her new rules. But Chelsea replied that they would figure something out and not to worry.

"Dude!" Devon had called Jaden. "Want to go with Jenny and me to help my mom with a dinner and to give out Christmas presents to under-privileged people Saturday?"

"Where do you do that?"

"Most of the employees where she works do it every year at the community center. The company she works for sponsors it, I guess. This year she asked if we wanted to help, you know, to sort of give back in thanks for all we have."

"Awesome! Count me in. What time?"

"We'll pick you and Jenny up around 10:30 Saturday morning. It goes from 11:30 to 2:30. Everybody eats around noon, and then we get to play Santa."

"Sounds good to me. I guess Jenny already knows the details?"

"Yep! See you then."

When Saturday arrived, Jaden and Jenny were both dressed in red and green. Devon came to the door looking festive, too. His shirt had bells on it that actually jingled as he walked. When Jenny commented on them, he made a face, but then grinned. Everyone was in a good mood. Christmas was in a few days, they were hanging out together, and Mrs. Mulder had promised ice cream after the event.

When they got to the community center, Mrs. Mulder said brightly, "Come on, kids, we need to help get the serving line set up. Devon, you and Jenny start putting the silverware on all the tables, and Jaden, you and I can help those two guys over there get the warming trays ready. We need to fill them with water and light the fuel underneath, so they'll heat up before the trays of food are put over them."

The two guys, to whom Mrs. Mulder had referred, were looking at the trays with puzzled expressions.

Devon's mom said, "Hi, guys! Don't worry, we're here to help you. I'm Mrs. Mulder, and this is Jaden Hansen."

One of the two replied, "I'm Nolen, and this is my brother, Ward. Nolen and Ward Crenshaw. We could use the help, because we're not exactly sure what to do. Our mom just sent us over here and said to do something with the trays."

"Well, Nolen and Ward, you sure look an awful lot alike."

Ward chuckled, "Everybody says that. We're twins."

"Hey, me too!" exclaimed Jaden.

"Is your brother here, too?" Now it was Jaden's turn to laugh.

"Yes, she's right over there."

"Whoa, she's cute! A lot cuter than you," said Ward. He snickered.

"Wait a minute, Ward," disputed Nolen. "Jaden's pretty cute, too." He laughed.

"All right, guys. We're not getting anything done. Let's talk less and work more. Here's how we'll do it," said Mrs. Mulder, as she started them on their task.

When that was done, they started putting ice in glasses for the drinks. They could smell turkey from the kitchen and could see several people scurrying around in there getting things ready. The group was expecting up to a hundred people and had been cooking since the wee hours of the morning. There hadn't been a lot of time for the boys to talk, but Jaden was planning to find time before the dinner was over. These guys were really cute, and Nolen's comment was very much on Jaden's mind. He wondered if there was any chance...

When it was time to line up to serve, Jaden introduced the new guys to Devon and Jenny, making it clear that they were a couple. He didn't want Ward to try to horn in on his best friend. Ward just laughed at Jaden.

"Not to worry, my friend. I have a girlfriend, but that doesn't keep me from looking at hotties." Jenny blushed, and Jaden turned red. And then, the doors opened, and the crowd jostled in.

There were big families, as well as single parents with only one or two kids. Jaden had left the serving line to get another pan of rolls when he saw Ricardo and his parents come in, along with all of Ricardo's brothers and sisters. Their dark eyes were shining at the prospect of a good Christmas dinner and presents, too. Jaden waved Ricardo over while his parents got in line. The little ones couldn't take their eyes off of the big Christmas tree with its profusion of pretty presents.

Not meeting Jaden's eyes, Ricardo said, "It's for the little ones that we come. I'm too big for presents. My papa says times are tough." Jaden felt bad because his friend seemed embarrassed.

"Devon's mom told us that the presents were for all ages. She said they would go to waste if they weren't taken today." The first part was true, but he made up the latter. "Go get something to eat, and I'll personally bring you a big kid present." Ricardo smiled his thanks at Jaden's attempt to make him feel at ease. Jaden got the pan of rolls and went back to his place in the serving line. He whispered to Devon that Ricardo was there with his family.

"Great! I'll ask Mom to pick out something special."

Once everyone had gone through the line and was eating, the helpers began to take the dirty pans back to the kitchen. By the time the serving area had been cleaned up, most of the people had finished their meal and taken their empty plates and utensils to the cleaning station. Holiday music had been playing, and many of the parents seemed to have dropped the stress of a hard life at the door and were laughing and chatting with strangers. The children kept eyeing the tree and pulling on their parents' arms as if to ask when the presents would start.

Mrs. Mulder gathered her little group around her for instructions. She told them each of the little kids would get three presents, one from each of three areas that she pointed out. The older kids would get one present, but it was a more expensive one than the little kids' toys.

"Devon, you, Jenny, and Ward pass out the little kids' presents, and Jaden and Nolen will hand out the big kids' presents. After I make the announcement, you may begin." She cheerfully called for everyone's attention. Suddenly, through the door appeared Santa! He was carrying a big bag over his shoulder, and he walked to the center of the room.

"Merry Christmas, everyone! I know it's a little early, but I have a lot of stops to make this year, and I wanted to make sure I got to this one. There are some wonderful people here, and I want to make sure that their wishes come true. My elves will start giving presents to the little ones, but I have something special for the big folks." He nodded at Devon, Jenny, Jaden, Ward, and Nolen to get started. Then, with a 'Ho, Ho, Ho!' he walked around and presented each parent, or each set of parents with a card containing a fifty dollar gift card to Toler's Super Store, which carried everything from groceries to electronics to clothes. Mr. Toler himself played Santa each year and generously donated the gift cards to help people in need. He had never forgotten his own childhood when he had been lucky to get a Christmas stocking with an orange in it, and perhaps a few nuts. His dad had died when he and his brothers and sisters had all been under the age of ten. His mother had struggled her whole life to provide for her family. He was a wealthy man now, and he believed in sharing what he had.

Meanwhile, the little kids were ripping open packages and squealing with delight at the toy or game or box of candy they received.

"Oh, Devon, look how happy they are," said Jenny with a delighted smile. "I'm so glad you asked us to help today. Did you see that little boy's face when he opened up that dump truck? You'd have thought he'd gotten a million dollars!"

"I know! And did you see that little girl who had been sitting behind her mother the whole time? She never said anything or smiled or anything. She wouldn't even open her box, but when her mother opened it for her and she saw that doll…she grabbed it and started hugging it and whispering to it. Her mom told me she hadn't talked since her dad left a week ago."

"Oh, my gosh, I think I'm gonna start crying. That's so sweet."

Jaden had made a beeline over to Ricardo with his gift.

"Open it, Ricardo! Let's see what it is!" Ricardo fumbled with the paper on the little box and finally got it open.

"Amigo! It is MP3 player! I've always wanted one! I can't believe it!"

Jaden said, "I'll help you load it with lots of good music. It'll be so great! But I better get going for now to pass out some more presents."

By the time 2:30 rolled around, a roomful of strangers had become friends. There was something uplifting in the fact that they all had the same struggles and heartaches, but that they also shared similar love for their children and hope for a better life. The gifts from Toler's Super Store reinforced the belief that there were a lot of good people in the world, and they left the event with warm feelings in their hearts.

Ward and Nolen were invited to join Mrs. Mulder and her group of Santa's elves for ice cream at the Dairy Creme. They told their mom, who thought it was a great idea. As soon as they got their cones and shakes, they left the two mothers to chat at a small table and commandeered a big table of their own.

"What school do you guys go to?" asked Jaden.

"We live here in Williamsburg, but go to school at East High, the fine arts magnet school in Shelby County. Ward is a great artist, and I'm into photography and graphic design, and stuff like that," said Nolen.

"Nolen's not sure what he wants to do," scoffed Ward. "He changes every year, but he really is good with photography. I guess all of you go to Lake Griffin High?"

"Yes, we're freshmen there. What grade are you in?"

"We're sophomores, and if Nolen isn't careful, he'll be a sophomore again next year."

"Oh, come on, Ward! My grades aren't that bad. Just because I don't make straight A's like you do doesn't mean I'm going to fail."

"If you would study even just a little, instead of playing with that camera all the time..."

"It's not like you don't always have your drawing pad," retorted Nolen.

Devon started laughing, and before long, everyone joined him.

"You sure can tell you two are brothers," he said good-naturedly.

"We know Ward has a girlfriend, but how about you, Nolen?" Ward jumped in before Nolen had a chance to say anything.

"He doesn't swing that way, do you, Nolen?"

"Ward, my God, give me a break," countered Nolen tersely, his face turning bright red.

"Hold it, hold it! Let's don't get started again," said Devon with a grin. Jaden's eyes had widened when he heard what Ward said. He wondered if he had enough nerve to speak up. He looked at Jenny.

As if she could read his thoughts, Jenny said, "It's okay, Jaden plays on Nolen's team, too. He's had a lot of trouble with it, but hopefully, we're getting things straightened out, no pun intended." Everyone laughed, the awkwardness dissipating.

Jaden grabbed that opportunity to say, "Did you ever have trouble with your parents or at school, Nolen?"

"Nah, my parents don't care, and we go to a school where there's lot of gay kids. It seems like a fine arts magnet school draws them in."

"I sure wish it was like that at my school," Jaden said wistfully. Jenny smiled up at Devon.

"But, we're in the process of trying to make things better, aren't we?"

"Yes, we are!" was his forceful answer. Devon got the high sign from his mother and said, "Guess we need to wrap it up. Mom's saying time to go." The new friends exchanged telephone numbers and promised to stay in touch.

Chapter 30

Chelsea and Brooke spent practically every day during the holidays with each other, sometimes with friends, sometime alone, but they were still aggravated that they couldn't spend the night. It wasn't like they would do anything wrong. They didn't smoke or drink or do drugs. They just wanted to be together. True, they had drunk a drink or two at the occasional party, but they didn't get wasted or anything. Everyone did it.

The first evening that they got together with Devon, Jenny, and Jaden, Chelsea was griping about how unfair it was.

"I know, right?" said Jaden. "When my dad wouldn't let me hang out with Trevor, I used to sneak out my window at night, and Trevor would pick me up in his Mustang."

"You snuck out at night?" Chelsea was incredulous. "I've always thought you were a 'good' boy, you know, always following the rules."

"Well, I've got to say I was scared to death every time. I almost couldn't have fun because my heart was pounding so hard. I never felt safe until I was back under my covers in bed." Chelsea looked at Brooke.

"Do you think you could sneak out at night?"

"Wait!" Jaden interjected. "You need to hear the whole story. I finally got caught. My dad was waiting for me in my room. It was so horrible, I can't even tell you how horrible it was."

"What did he do?"

"He yelled at me and told me if I ever did it again, I would never leave the house again."

"That doesn't sound so bad."

"That's not the whole story. It was bad, trust me. But I don't want to talk about it."

Chelsea looked at Brooke again.

"Could you?"

"No! I couldn't sneak out. I would never have the nerve."

"Then maybe I could sneak in." Devon and Jenny had been silent throughout the conversation.

Deciding to speak, Jenny said, "It was worse than you could imagine. I was scared when Jaden would sneak out, and then it turned out really bad. I don't think it's a good idea at all." Seeing Jaden squirm, everyone decided it would probably be best to just drop the subject, and the talk turned to the up-coming basketball tournament that Devon would be playing in.

Donnie and Alice had called a truce for the Christmas holidays. They were going to leave certain topics off-limits. It hadn't been a great Thanksgiving with Donnie gone, and neither parent wanted to spoil Christmas for the kids. It had gone well, but it was no secret that things were somewhat tense.

At the end of the holidays, the kids were ready to get back to school. They were getting a little bored now that Trevor wasn't around to drive them places. Jaden, Jenny, and Devon had to rely on parents or Brandon to get them around, and it wasn't always an option. Jaden had learned that his new friends, Nolen and Ward, would turn sixteen in February, though, and their parents had promised the use of their car occasionally. He and Nolen had talked and texted a lot during the holidays and gotten to know each other better. Nolen had promised when they got together again, he would show Jaden some really cool pictures of wildlife he had taken at the lake and in the woods. Jaden had told him all about the camping trip he had been on and how beautiful the mountains and wildflowers had been.

"Did you get any pictures there?" Nolen had asked.

"Only on my phone, but they look pretty good." Nolen smiled to himself when he thought of how Jaden would like his pictures. He had received much acclaim for his photography, and a magazine had accepted a couple of his pictures for a wildlife spread they were doing. "Maybe we can get together this weekend."

Brandon and Sheila hadn't spent a lot of time together over the break, because she had gotten a seasonal job at the mall. Brandon had originally thought that not seeing her on a daily basis would be a drag, but he was surprised to find that he hadn't really missed her much. He had hung out some with Dan and Audreonna and a couple of the other computer geeks, but he had spent a lot of time at the gym getting ready for his senior year of baseball. Now that it was time to focus on that, he considered breaking up with her. He knew parties were pretty much out of the question during baseball season, and they didn't do much together except go to parties, anyway. The more he thought about it, the more he decided it was probably the right move. He was sure that thinking about Emily had nothing to do with his choice.

"What are you doing here? I didn't know you were coming over," was Sheila's surprised greeting when Brandon rang her doorbell. When he didn't return her smile, she became apprehensive. "What's happened? Has something happened? Is your family all right?" Her immediate concern for his family made Brandon feel like an ass.

"No, everyone's okay, nothing's happened. I just felt like we need to talk." Her expression turned from concern to dread. She had known all along that this day would probably come. It had to be Emily. He had never gotten over Emily, and she had never felt that he cared about her as much as he had cared about Emily.

"You're back with Emily," she blurted out.

"No! No, I'm not back with Emily. I haven't even talked to her."

"I heard that she and Juan Carlos had broken up, but I never said anything, because I thought, somehow, that maybe if you didn't know, you might stay with me longer."

"Sheila," he took her hand. "You know we've always had a great time together. It's just that baseball season is around the corner, and I won't have time to go to parties, or even have a girlfriend anymore. There isn't anybody else, honest."

"Are you telling me that none of the other baseball players have girlfriends during the season? Come on, Brandon." She jerked her hand away.

"I'm not telling you that. I'm just saying that I need to really concentrate this year, because I'm trying to get a baseball scholarship. That's the most important thing to me right now. It's not about you. We can still be friends."

"You need to leave, Brandon," she said as the tears started. When he hesitated, she said more forcefully, "Just get the hell out of here!" She turned away and slammed the front door.

Chapter 31

At school that first week back, Jaden, Jenny, Devon, Chelsea, and Brooke got together to set up a date for the zip-line adventure. They all had gotten at least a little money as Christmas gifts and could afford the splurge now.

"Over break we met these cool twin brothers that go to East High. Can we ask them to go, too?" asked Jaden.

"Sure, the more the merrier," replied Chelsea. "A small group is always fun, but a big group is even better!"

"One of them is gay," added Jaden.

"Way cool," answered Brooke. "Can't wait to meet them."

"I'm ready this time," said Devon with a chuckle. "My Christmas money was a lifesaver."

"Let's go this Saturday. I can drive all of us if those other guys can meet us there," said Chelsea.

"I'll call them tonight," exclaimed Jaden. He really hoped they could go. He wanted to see Nolen again.

Brandon, who later heard the twins planning, said he'd like to go, too.

"I've never been on a zip-line, but I've always wanted to," he said.

"They have lots of other stuff there, too," contributed Jenny. "I looked it up online, and they have a total adventure course. It's gonna be so fun! I can't wait!"

"Me, neither. I'm so glad the Crenshaw guys can go with us. They'll be fun, too!"

"Who are they?" asked Brandon.

"Some twins we met when we were helping Devon's mom at the Christmas party at the community center. They're sophomores at East High."

"If Mom lets me take the car, the three of us can pick them up and meet the others over there. Devon can ride with us, too. We sort of go near East High to get to the park." Jaden beamed at his brother. He still couldn't get over the change in Brandon from last year to this year. He had always wanted to please his brother, but had never succeeded. Now Brandon acted like he wanted to please him. Bizarro world, he thought, but it was all good.

When Saturday came, the two drivers decided to follow each other. Brandon's car was in the lead, because he seemed to know where he was going. As it turned out, he wound up having to use the GPS on his phone to get to the zip park. It was near East High all right, but it was out past a neighborhood full of twists and turns that finally opened into unpopulated acreage.

"I'm so glad you were in the lead, Brandon," exclaimed Chelsea. "I have no idea how we got to where we are, and you better not lose me on the way out!" Everyone laughed. "There's the gate, let's get going!"

Introductions took place as the group made their way to the big gate, behind which was a wooded area with numerous tall trees. As they got closer they could see platforms in the trees, and the conversation's energy level rose with excitement. They paid their fees at the entrance and were directed to the area where they would get their harnesses.

"You put yours on first, Devon," said Jenny as she let go of his hand. "These look weird. Oh, I guess that guy coming over is going to show us how." One by one they were shown how to step into their harness and strap it up. There were two carabiners on each harness, and the instructor told them one of them would have to be attached to a wire at all times. Every time they had to change wires, they were to snap the second carabiner on to the new wire before unhooking the first one from the old wire. Next they got heavy gloves to use to slow themselves down on the zip-line. There was a practice area, low to the ground, where everyone took a turn working with the carabiners and gloves until each got comfortable with the process. It was perfectly safe, because the first carabiner would never be undone until the second was attached to the wire. Worst case, they would fall and dangle by a carabiner attached to their harness.

"Follow me," said Devon as he grabbed Jenny's arm and headed to the first course. Everyone watched as he climbed a twisting, wooden stairway up the tree to the first zip-line. He hooked himself to the wire and pushed off the platform. He flew across the path and over toward the second tree. The line went from high to low, and he stopped himself with his gloves when his feet touched the ground. "That was awesome!" he shouted. Jenny was clambering up the stairs, followed by Brandon.

"I'm after Brandon," said Chelsea. "This is going to be great!" The first zip was the easiest and the group started to become comfortable using their gloves to stop. When everyone had finished the first three zips, they were all confident about stopping. They had noticed that actually getting on the zip-line from each platform often proved demanding. It wasn't just a case of climbing steps and walking out to a platform. Often they had to reach halfway around a tree to hook their carabiner before figuring out how to get their body to the same place.

The next challenge wasn't a zip. They saw two parallel wires about twelve feet up, and one more above those about fifteen feet high. They had to hook their carabiner on the top wire and walk on the bottom ones for about thirty feet to another tree. Jaden decided to go first on this one. When he finally balanced himself with a foot on each wire, his legs were wobbling so much that the wires started bouncing up and down. He was screaming, and the others were practically on the ground laughing. When he got to the far side, he started laughing, too.

"I think I have to go to the bathroom, now," he said, and everyone laughed that much harder.

Nolen said, "I'll go with you. I think I better go *before* I get up there."

"Don't be a baby! I'll go next," exclaimed Ward.

"We'll see who's a baby. Bet you'll have to go, too, when you get off." Nolen and Jaden headed off to the bathroom, hurrying so they would get back before all of the others had walked the wires.

"It wasn't that it was so scary," maintained Jaden. "It's just that when I was on both wires, I totally lost control of my legs. The wires were so bouncy that my legs felt like spaghetti. I can't wait to watch the others." As expected, each of them wobbled precariously, and everyone laughed hilariously.

The next challenge also had a wire up top for the carabiner, but this time there was a series of twelve-inch by twelve-inch platforms about two feet apart that led to the other side. Because the stepping boards were strung on wire, they, too, were very wobbly.

"I'll go first on this one," boasted Brandon. "It's looks easy." He scrambled up there, and he did make it look easy. He was across it in thirty seconds. Brooke went next, and it only took a second for her to realize that Brandon's height and athletic ability had gone a long way toward making it look easy. When she tried to step out for the second platform, it was too far away. As she stood there pondering the situation, the platform she was standing on started to sway.

Chelsea's advice was, "Swing your platform forward, and when it gets close to the next one, leap over to it." Her platform had to swing back and forth a couple of times before she had the nerve to jump for the next, but it worked. She continued across, and her friends mostly did the same procedure or something similar. Devon, however, was as competent as Brandon.

After thrill on top of thrill during the afternoon, the finale was the longest zip-line in the whole park that started extremely high in a tree and traversed 1000 feet across a lake. It was super fast and super fun.

At the end of a perfect afternoon, everyone was jubilant about the park.

"I can't think of anything I've done in a long time that was so much fun," said Chelsea.

"I know," said Brooke. "Who heard about this in the first place? It totally rocks!"

"I sure am glad you asked us to come, too," declared Ward. "It was great, and it was fun getting to know all of you." Nolen agreed wholeheartedly.

"You guys will have to start hanging out with us on Saturday nights. We almost always get together to do something fun," said Devon.

Ward said, "We'd like to do that for sure." After high fives all around, they split for the parking lot.

When the Hansen car got loaded up, Jenny immediately snuggled into Devon's shoulder and was asleep before they got back to the main road. Jaden was still wired, and he, Brandon, and the Crenshaw boys talked about the different challenges all the way home.

The next day after church, Nolen called Jaden.

"That was so much fun yesterday!" he raved. "I didn't even know that place was there, and it's so close to our school."

"None of us had ever been there, but we heard about it a while back."

"I want to go again. I told my parents about it, and they were interested in going. Maybe if we go, you could go with us."

"Nice!"

"Hey, listen, any chance we could get together this afternoon? I want to show you some of my pictures."

"Hang on, let me ask my mom." After a minute he returned to the conversation. "Mom says I can't go over there, but you can come over here. Can you get here?"

"No problem. I can ride my bike. I ride all over town. What time?"

"Come over around 2:30. We'll be finished with lunch by then." When Nolen arrived, Jaden was outside waiting.

"Man! That's a cool bike! It's got shocks and everything!" Nolen grinned.

"I know. I love my bike, and I love to ride off-road. There's a mountain bike area not too far from our house that Ward and I go ride in all the time. We don't play any sports, but we stay pretty active. Want to try my bike out?"

"Right now?" Nolen jumped off the bike and leaned it toward Jaden.

"This is awesome! It's a little tall for me, but Mom says I'm going through a growth spurt, and I've already grown a couple of inches. I'll be glad when Jenny isn't taller than me anymore." He rode down the street and back, laughing and waving at Miss Bonnie who was in her flower garden.

"Amazing!" he said when he got back to Nolen. "When you hit the bumps in the road, it seems like the wheels absorb them instead of your arms and your butt," he added laughing. "I want a bike like this." Nolen's face beamed his pleasure. "Come on in the house, I want to show you my room." They went inside, and after pointing out his Grateful Dead poster to Nolen and showing him a few other things, Jaden suggested they sit on the bed to look at Nolen's pictures. Expecting Nolen to pull a thick album out of his backpack, he was surprised to see him pull a tiny flash-drive out of his pocket.

"I assume you have a computer we can use? I keep a lot of my pictures stored on my computer at home, but I loaded these to show you."

"Yeah, let's go into the family room. We have our computer in there." Jaden pulled up an extra chair to look, but wasn't prepared for what he saw when Nolen opened his files.

"Oh, geez! How did you get these pictures? It looks like you were two feet away. And, they're so clear!" The first picture was of a female cardinal with her beak inside her baby's beak, feeding it. Another picture showed the nest was up high in a tree, but the next shot looked as if Nolen were up there with it. Jaden could practically count the tufts of feathers on the little bird.

"For that bird-nest picture I used a 400mm prime lens. I had to have a very high shutter speed, too." The next picture was of a pine tree with a big droplet of water on one of the needles. It was a magnified close-up of the droplet, and Jaden could see a small deer on the ground reflected in it. "That might be the best picture I've ever seen!" praised Jaden. Another picture loaded, and Jaden was dumbfounded for a moment.

When his words came back, he asked, "How in the world did you get a still shot of that hummingbird's wings?" Nolen laughed outright.

"It's just stop-action photography. Did you know that hummingbirds can flap their wings eighty times a second? That's a *second*! I had to use a 400mm lens with a shutter speed of 1/1000 of a second." Jaden was stunned with Nolen's fantastic photography. But, not only did he think his photography outstanding, his former regard for Nolen soared to unbridled admiration. The next two pictures were the same shot of foliage along a creek bed, but one of them looked like the sun was shining, and the other was duller. "The first one was done with some photo enhancement software. The camera isn't able to pick up all the light in all parts of the picture, so the software makes it look like it did."

Looking at the all the fabulous pictures made the time fly by, and before they knew it, Nolen said he had to get going.

"Aw, man, I wish you didn't have to go yet. This has been so fun!"

"I've had fun, too. I hope we can do it again soon." He looked around to make sure they were alone, and then he leaned over and kissed Jaden on the cheek. "See you soon." Jaden sat unmoving for a while, with his hand on his cheek where he had been kissed. Funny, Trevor hadn't entered his mind all afternoon.

Chapter 32

One afternoon at the end of January, Jenny was startled in English class when a runner from the office came to get her. She thought, what have I done? I know I haven't gotten in trouble with any teacher, but nothing good ever comes from being summoned to the principal's office. As she followed the aide into the main office, she saw Devon sitting in a chair.

"What are you doing here, Devon? Are you in trouble? Are we in trouble?"

"I don't know, Jen. They just came and got me out of class." The principal's door opened, and Mrs. Mackey waved them both into her office. Sitting inside was Mr. Anthony with a big grin on his face. It must not be that bad, if he's smiling like that, thought Jenny.

"Please sit down," invited Mrs. Mackey. "The superintendent and district school board have met with me about your proposal to have a GSA club on campus. They have decided to allow it provisionally here at Lake Griffin High School for the rest of this year."

"What does that mean, 'provisionally'?" asked Jenny.

"It means that they will study the issue further this summer in a school board workshop and decide then whether the whole district, including this school, can proceed with the non-academic clubs. Also, it was decided that students must get at least one parent's signed permission to join."

"That's not fair!" Devon's eyes were fiery. "A lot of kids won't join, because they're afraid to, or can't, get their parent's signature. It sounds like they just don't want to face a lawsuit." He remembered what that guy from the ACLU had said.

"That's right, and until just a few weeks ago, my brother and I wouldn't have been able to join, because my father would never have permitted it," said Jenny forcefully. Mr. Anthony spoke up.

"Guys, we have to take this one step at a time. I'm pleased that it has gone this far. Mrs. Mackey is going to let me sponsor the club. You, Devon, and I will work together to make sure it's a success."

Mrs. Mackey said, "You don't realize the progress that you've made. The school board had previously been adamant about having no clubs that weren't curriculum based. This opens the door to getting service clubs and social clubs back in the school. You students need to be commended for your courage and determination."

"Thank you, Mrs. Mackey," said Jenny, surprised at the praise, but still worried about access to the club for a lot of kids.

Mr. Anthony continued, "The three of us will meet this week to plan publicity and to decide when we'll make an announcement for the first meeting. I know you're both disappointed about the parental permission requirement, but this is a good start."

As they were returning to class, Devon said, "It's better than nothing, Jen. We can have the first meeting and get ideas from others about how to make sure that every kid who wants to can join."

"I hope so. I just don't like the idea that parents have to sign for a kid to join a school club."

By the end of the week, Mr. Anthony, Devon, and Jenny had met and planned an introductory meeting that would not require permission slips. They decided to put an announcement in the school news for a week, as well as posters in every hallway. The posters would emphasize that everyone, not just LGBT kids, would be welcome. A couple of posters in the freshman wing would specify that the club would be similar in some ways to the middle school TEAM Club. As an added incentive, it was stated that refreshments would be served at the first meeting. The date was to be February 9. Mr. Anthony had told Devon and Jenny that he would get the meeting started, but then it would be student led.

"I wonder how many people will actually show up," mused Jenny. "The freshmen who were in TEAM definitely, but I wonder if the name of the club will discourage other people."

"If they're decent people, that shouldn't stop them," said Devon.

"You know how you were at first, Devon. You stopped being friends with Jaden when you found out about him." Devon looked crestfallen.

"I know, and that was so wrong. Jaden was my friend, and the fact that he was gay shouldn't have bothered me. I was a real jerk back then. I wish I could take it back." Jenny noticed his anguished look and softened.

"Don't beat yourself up, Devon. The two of you got over that problem, and it's in the past."

"I know, I was just...oh, well, that's why we're trying to start the club."

Trying to change Devon's train of thought, Jenny said, "Why don't you plan to come over to my house the Sunday before the meeting and help me make cookies. Mr. Anthony said he would provide drinks."

"That sounds good. I know Jaden will help us, too."

That afternoon Jenny was excited to tell her mom about her meeting with the principal.

"Mom, Mrs. Mackey seemed really nice. I've never talked to her before, but she wasn't stern or anything. She even said something nice about Devon and me."

"What did she say, honey?"

"She said we were to be commended for making as much progress as we did with the school board. Devon said they were just afraid of a lawsuit, though."

"Lawsuit or not, Jenny, nothing would have ever been done if you guys hadn't brought it up."

"And parents have to sign a permission form before kids can join the club."

"You know I'll sign for you and Jaden."

"Yes, but what about the kids who are afraid to talk to their parents about it?" Alice sighed.

"I don't know, honey. I guess it will have to go in front of the school board again, at some point."

"That's what Mrs. Mackey said. The board is going to study the issue again this summer."

"Honey, you can't save the world all at once. Let's take this one step at a time." Brandon came in from baseball practice at that moment.

"Save the world from what?"

"We're going to start the Gay-Straight Alliance Club at school, Brandon. Will you join?" Brandon hesitated before speaking.

"I'm not sure, Jen. I don't know if I'll have time with baseball."

"Are you sure that's the only reason? Are you ashamed to be in a club with gay kids?"

"Ashamed is not the word I would use. I'm just not sure I want to put myself out there. It's my senior year, you know, and I don't want my classmates talking about me."

"Brandon Hansen! This is your own brother that you don't want to support. He has to face people talking about him every day and making fun of him, too. How do you think he feels?"

"Look! I want to support Jaden in any way I can, but please just leave me out of any club at school!" Brandon stormed out of the room.

Alice looked at Jenny and said, "Just let him cool down, honey. When he thinks about it, he may change his mind." Alice hated to see how much Brandon was like Donnie when he felt pushed into a corner. Speaking of Donnie, in he walked.

"What's going on? Why the long faces?"

"Nothing to worry about, Donnie. We were just discussing the GSA club. The principal told Jenny that it would be approved for this year." Donnie's face clouded over. The uneasy truce that he and Alice had drawn since before Christmas had continued through the year so far. Alice thought this might be the end of it. But he merely shook his head and went into the living room to read the newspaper.

Chapter 33

One day early in February, Brandon looked up from his lunch in the school cafeteria to see Emily standing before him, her eyes slits, and her mouth contorted. Starting to smile, he thought better of it.

"Hey, what's up?"

"You know what's up! You better keep that bitch of an ex-girlfriend of yours away from me!" Her face was beet-red.

"Wait, what are you talking about?" Brandon was totally flustered.

"Why did you tell her that I'm the reason you broke up with her?"

"I didn't tell her that! I don't know what you're talking about."

"Then why did she get in my face and threaten to beat my ass? She told me I'd better watch my back if she ever saw me walking around school with you."

"Emily, please. It's true we broke up, but I told her I was too busy with baseball to have a relationship. She accused me of wanting to be with you, but why would I say something like that when you won't have anything to do with me?" Brandon seemed so earnest that Emily's face was starting to soften a little.

"Emily, I never stopped wanting to go out with you, but I could see you had moved on, so I tried to as well. But I never felt for Sheila like I do…I mean, like I did for you." Brandon was fumbling his words and the truth slipped out. Then, to Brandon's surprise, Emily's face became a torrent of tears. He stood up and tentatively put his arms around her.

"Oh, Brandon, I just don't know what to do," she sobbed.

"Would it make you feel better if we could go out again?" posed a hopeful Brandon. Emily cried that much harder.

"I was a fool for not giving you a second chance," she said brokenly. "But, no, I had to go out with Juan Carlos, and now…"

"And now, what?"

"You don't understand. I can't talk about it…I don't know who to talk to. I can't talk to my mom." Brandon was puzzled.

"Brandon, I'm pregnant." Brandon sharply inhaled. He was floored. After a moment he asked, "Are you sure?"

"Yes, I haven't had my period for four or five months. At first I thought it was stress, but I've taken three home pregnancy tests, and they all came out positive. I'm sure, Brandon. I'm not stupid."

"Emily, I'll help you through this. You don't have to feel alone."

"I don't deserve your support. I just don't know what I'm going to do."

"Well, one thing you don't have to worry about is Sheila. I'm finding her and setting her straight right after school today. And you and I need to talk some more about this whole situation. Can I meet you today after base-ball practice?" Feeling a little less agitated, Emily nodded.

As soon as the bell rang at the end of the day, Brandon went to Sheila's locker to wait for her. He saw her before she saw him, and he started right in.

"How could you go to Emily and lie to her? What were you thinking? I thought we could part as friends, but I sure don't want to be friends with a liar!"

"I didn't lie to her!" she retorted. "You do want to be with her!"

"I never told you I was breaking up with you to be with her."

"What's the difference?" she said sarcastically.

"It doesn't matter. What does matter is if you lay a hand on her, I'll go straight to the police. You're eighteen, and she's not."

"What's the matter, Brandon? Afraid to fight your own battles?"

"This isn't my battle, Sheila. It's you being an idiot. I'm not going to fight anyone and get suspended my senior year. I'm playing baseball, and I'm finishing the season!" he said emphatically. "You just remember what I said," he shouted and stormed off to baseball practice.

As much as he tried to engross himself in batting and fielding, Brandon's concentration level at practice was poor, at best. His emotions kept flip-flopping from anger at Sheila, to happiness that he might have a chance with Emily again, to overwhelming fear when he thought about her being preg-nant. Pregnant! That's a word he hadn't planned to think about until he was like thirty years old! She must be devastated and scared to death. She doesn't know what to do. He didn't know what to do, either, but he was determined to figure out a plan one way or another.

Baseball practice seemed to last an eternity, when usually it seemed so short. He hurriedly packed up his gear and asked a teammate to drop him off at Emily's. He was nervous about knocking on the door, because he didn't know if he'd be welcome in the house. He had no idea what she had told her mom about him last spring. But that dilemma was resolved when she came outside even before he knocked and indicated that he should get in her car.

She said, "It's too cold to stand outside and talk, and we can't go in and talk in front of my mother, so I thought we'd just go somewhere." It didn't answer the question of what her mother thought about him, but he'd worry about that later. They rode to the Dairy Creme and ordered a drink. Emily seemed calmer, but edgy.

"Tell me what happened, Emily." She began by telling him how hurt she had been when they had the big fight last spring, but that she had been seeing him change prior to that, practically from day to day. He had gone from being sweet and attentive, to mean and volatile in a matter of weeks. She had felt like she always had to be walking on eggshells, because she had no idea what would make him flare up. She had thought about breaking up with him several times, but just couldn't because she cared so much for him. She had just kept hoping he would snap out of it.

"Finally, the day when you hit that guy for no reason, I knew we couldn't go on, but when we broke up, I was a wreck the rest of the school year and all summer. I couldn't quit thinking about you and missing you. My mother made me tell her what was wrong, because all I did was mope around. She even had me talk to this counselor at church. The counselor was really nice, and to make a long story short, eventually persuaded me to date other people. After several failed attempts, I met Juan Carlos. He was a good athlete and seemed really cool. We went out, and he talked me into trying a beer. Somehow, that beer made me feel more at ease, so I would always have a few when we went out." When she got to that part, Emily started to falter in her discourse. She stared into space for a while, and then she turned her gaze on Brandon. Tears began to fall unbidden. Listening to all she had to say, Brandon felt worse and worse. He had known, even at the time, that he had been awful to Emily, but he hadn't seemed to be able to stop. Looking at this sweet girl and knowing again that he was the cause of her misery, was almost more than he could bear. He wanted to take her in his arms and tell her everything would be all right. But he wasn't sure of that himself.

Emily started talking again. "This is the part that's so hard, Brandon. I...I don't know if I can even tell you." He squeezed her hand and gave her an encouraging look.

"Emily, I'm not going to judge you. You can tell me anything."

"You know that party after the football game last fall? The one where you saw Juan Carlos and me together? Well, later I saw that Sheila chick lead you into a bedroom, and I was so upset that I finally said yes to Juan Carlos. That was the first night we were intimate. I had drunk several beers, but I still knew what I was doing. We only did it one more time, and that was a couple of weeks before the Halloween party." Brandon was clinching his fists and trying his best not to let Emily see how upset he had become after hearing this. He knew it had to have happened. After all, she was pregnant. But after hearing the details and knowing she had given in after seeing him with Sheila, made it all he could do to keep his feelings hidden. She went on.

"Every time we went out, he wanted to do it again. At the Halloween party, having sex was all he could think about. He kept asking me to go into a bedroom, and I kept saying no. Finally, he just dragged me away from my friends and had his hands all over me. I was yelling at him to stop, but he wouldn't."

"I heard you! I was worried. I made up an excuse to go to the bathroom and looked for you to see if you were okay, but you weren't around, and everything seemed normal."

"Yeah, one of my friends pulled him off of me, and we went outside to cool off. That's where I told him I was sick of him pawing at me, and I broke up with him."

"I saw you when I was leaving the party, and you looked pissed," agreed Brandon.

"In October, I had missed my period. I thought maybe that it didn't come because of all the stress I had been under. But, when I missed again in November, I freaked and bought the pregnancy tests. I checked a couple of times and again the next month." She heaved a big sigh. "So, now you know it all." She looked so sad.

"Have you told anyone else? How about that counselor at your church?"

"I haven't told anyone but you. Not even my friends. I couldn't tell the counselor, because I didn't know if she would tell my mother. Brandon, I want to get an abortion. Will you help me?"

"Whoa, whoa, wait a minute. Are you sure that's something you want to do? Something you *should* do?"

"I've thought a lot about it. Actually, I've been thinking about it continuously for a couple of months, ever since I found out."

"Don't you think it would be wrong to end a life like that? Could you live with yourself afterwards?"

"I'm mixed up about it, Brandon. I don't really want to have an abortion, but I'm in no position to take care of a baby. My life is just starting. I'm planning to go to college and maybe become a physical therapist. How could I take care of a baby and do that? What kind of life would the baby have?"

"Couldn't you give it up for adoption after it's born?"

"I don't know. I don't know how things like that work. I don't know much of anything except I'd give everything if I weren't pregnant. I do know that if I'm going to have an abortion, I need to do it pretty quick, because soon it'll be too late."

"Are you sure you can't talk to your mother? What would she say if she knew?"

"I don't know what she would say, but I just don't want to stress her like that. She would be so upset with me. She would never dream that I would have sex, let alone get pregnant."

"Can I talk to my mom, then? I know she'd never tell your mother. I know she'd respect my confidence. Maybe she'd be able to think of something that we can't."

"I wish you wouldn't." She paused. "I don't know. Maybe you should. I just don't know what to do." She put her face in her hands and let out a deep sigh.

"Okay, promise me you won't do anything until I talk to her."

"It's not like I know where to run have an abortion, Brandon." She paused. "I didn't mean that to sound catty. I just don't know which way to turn."

Chapter 34

Jaden was working on his homework when he got a text.

"Hey, sup? Want to go mt bike riding sat?"

"I don't have a mt bike."

"U can use my brothers."

"I'll ask my mom." The answer was yes, and Jaden and Nolen made plans to meet at 1:00 Saturday at Nolen's house.

"Guess what, Jen? Nolen and I are going mountain bike riding Saturday."

"You've never done that before."

"I know, but it can't be that hard. Riding a bike is riding a bike, right?"

"Yeah, I guess so," Jen said cautiously. "Anyway, it sounds fun. You'll have to tell me about it."

"I know! The best part is that I get the whole afternoon with him. We had a great time when he came over that Sunday."

"Do you like him, Jaden? I mean *like*, like him?"

"I kinda do, Jen."

"What about Trevor?"

"I don't know. I'm just not sure how I feel. I haven't even talked to him in ages."

Coincidentally, the next day after P.E. class, Jaden was surprised to see Trevor waiting for him at his locker. He and Trevor hadn't been face-to-face for weeks. Trevor looked sheepish.

"How are you, Jaden? I've missed you." Jaden's heart melted.

"I've missed you, too."

"Listen, I've had a lot of time to think. I know you heard what happened with Brian. I didn't intend to do anything with him. It just happened. Maybe because I was stupid and smoked pot again. I sure didn't mean to hurt you. I'm really sorry. You're the one I love. I've been so embarrassed that I didn't know what to say to you. Please forgive me?"

"You're not having anything to do with Brian?"

"No, we haven't talked since...that night."

"I want to trust you. It's just that, I don't know, how can I trust you?"

"Jaden, I screwed up big time. I'm not going to do it again." He started to reach for Jaden, but stopped when he saw a kid walk around the corner.

"Oh, my, the fags are back together," the kid said mockingly.

"Go to hell," snapped Trevor. "Let's get out of here, Jaden." Jaden, who was more than ready, was already heading for the door. When they got outside, they were relieved to see that they hadn't been followed.

"Do you want to get together Saturday, Jaden? I'll even ask off work, so we can spend some time together."

"Saturday would be..." Jaden stopped. In a rush of feelings, he suddenly remembered his plans with Nolen. "What time Saturday?" he asked tentatively.

"It doesn't matter. You decide. If I take off, I'll be free all day." Jaden was silent. "What's the matter, don't you want to see me?"

"It's not that, Trevor." Jaden was flustered and fell silent again.

"Then, what is it?" Trevor was starting to become irritated.

"I can see you in the morning. I have plans in the afternoon. It's not that I don't want to be with you. I just already had these plans."

"Plans? Who with? Ricardo?" Trevor said sarcastically.

"No, I'm going mountain bike riding with a friend I met at Christmas. That's all."

"Since when did you become such an athlete? Mountain bike riding? Really?"

"We're just riding on trails. You don't have to make such a big deal about it," Jaden said sharply. He was beginning to remember the way it had been with Trevor before they broke up.

Making a quick about-face, Trevor said, "I'm sorry, I don't mean to give you a hard time. You know how jealous I can get. I just want things to be like they used to be. If you already have plans in the afternoon, we'll see each other in the morning, okay?"

"Sure, sounds good." Jaden walked home wondering why he felt so weird. He had been hoping for this moment to come, when he and Trevor could get back together, but somehow it felt hollow. He began to realize just how much Nolen had been in his thoughts.

Brandon was looking for an opportunity to talk to his mom about Emily. He felt a little odd talking to her about his ex-girlfriend's pregnancy, but he really hoped she could help somehow. He wanted to be sure to find a time when his dad wasn't home, either. On Wednesday, school let out early, so baseball practice was over earlier, too. He arrived home to find no one there but his mom. Perfect opportunity!

"Mom, I need to talk to you about something." Brandon's tone was so serious that Alice was immediately uneasy. She wondered if he were in some kind of trouble.

"Of course, sweetie. What's going on?"

"Emily and I are talking again."

"That's wonderful, Brandon. I know how upset you've been about her." Brandon made a wry face.

"It's wonderful in one way, but not so good in another. Mom, she's pregnant."

"Pregnant? Oh, Brandon! How could you be so careless?"

"It's not me, Mom. I wish it were."

"Brandon! No, you don't!"

"I know, I know. It's just that I wish that it weren't with anyone else, either." Alice nodded, dumbfounded, and waited for him to go on.

"She hasn't told anyone about it, except me. She's afraid to tell her mother, and she's talking about an abortion. I don't know if that's the right thing, but she really doesn't know what to do. She knows she's not in any position to raise a kid."

"Why won't she tell her mother?"

"She's afraid she'll disappoint her, you know, upset her or something. Ever since her mom divorced her dad years ago, Emily's been her mom's focus and she's felt like she needed to constantly please her."

"Brandon, moms are tougher than you think. Our main goal in life is to help our kids. Can you imagine how I would have felt if Jaden had been successful in his suicide attempt? I had tried to get him to talk to me about what was going on, but he was reluctant and scared. He didn't know how I would feel. How do you think Emily's mother might feel if she found out that Emily was going through such a major trauma, and yet, was afraid to talk to her about it? Kids do things and make decisions every day that might not be what we, as parents, would choose for them, but it doesn't make us love you any less. It's part of growing up. I hope to goodness that Jenny doesn't get pregnant, but it would break my heart if I thought she couldn't come to me and let me help her figure things out. Maybe Emily needs to give her mom a chance." Brandon felt a weight lift off his shoulders. His mom was right. Now, if only he could talk Emily into confiding in her mother. Then, he and Emily wouldn't be carrying this enormous weight alone.

Chapter 35

Jaden woke up Saturday morning feeling guilty. He felt that meeting Trevor in the morning, then, going out with Nolen in the afternoon was somehow being unfaithful. But, unfaithful to whom? He and Trevor weren't really back together again, and he and Nolen weren't together. Nevertheless, he had thought about the kiss on the cheek that Nolen had given him. He had thought about it a lot. He had wondered what it would be like to really kiss him. However, now that Trevor was being nice again, everything was all mixed up.

Before he even got out of bed, Jaden got a text from Trevor.

"I'm sick. Can't make it this morn."

His spirits lifted as he texted back, "So sorry. Feel better. TTYL." He couldn't believe how light-hearted he suddenly felt. He was glad he hadn't mentioned hanging out with Trevor to his mom yet. Now he didn't have anything to explain. He was ready for 1:00 to get there.

When his mom dropped him off, he saw Nolen working on a bike in the garage.

"Hey! Glad you're here. I'm lowering the seat on Ward's bike for you. You didn't fit that great on mine last time."

Jaden grinned and said, "I hope this goes okay. I'm kinda nervous. I've never been off-road before."

"We'll do easy trails today, and as you get used to it, we'll do harder and harder trails." Ward came into the garage.

"Looks like you and your boyfriend are about ready to go." Nolen scowled at his brother.

"Shut up, Ward." He seemed embarrassed. "Why'd you come out here?"

"Take it easy, bro. I just came out to say hi and tell you guys to have a good ride," Ward said in a conciliatory voice. "Don't be so touchy. Besides, you know you want him to be your boyfriend." When Nolen reddened, Jaden wondered if it were true.

Breaking the tension, Jaden said, "Thanks for letting me use your bike. I'll try not to crash it."

"It's been through lots of crashes. Don't worry about it. Where are you guys going, Nolen?"

"We're going to the woods behind Rye Estates. There're lots of trails in there, but nothing that hard. Mostly hills and some curves. Fun stuff for Jaden's first time."

"Oh, yeah, that's cool," Ward nodded in agreement. "Okay, see you when you get back." Ward went back inside.

Nolen said, "Sorry he's such a jerk."

"No problem." And they headed off through the neighborhood toward the woods.

When they got there, Nolen said, "This isn't an official mountain bike area, but the trails are all hard packed. Nothing's marked, because it's all easy. When you get used to being on a trail and to shifting down and up, we'll try something harder." They took off with Nolen in the lead, occasionally yelling tips back to Jaden. After riding for about forty-five minutes, they stopped to take a break and drink some water.

"This is great!" exclaimed Jaden. "We've ridden a long way, but it doesn't even seem like it, because we go up and down and turn so much. I like this lots better than riding on a road! And the scenery is great, not just one street after another."

"I figured you'd like it! Next I'm going to take you to the biggest hill, because up at the top, it's beautiful. It seems like there's always something different up there, and I usually get a good picture. It's where I got that picture of the momma bird feeding her baby."

"You brought your camera?"

"I always have my camera. You never know when there'll be a good photo-op. It's in my backpack."

"Let's go then. I'm rested enough. I want to see that view!"

"Man, you weren't kidding when you said this was the biggest hill!" Jaden was breathing hard.

"Downshift! More!" Nolen had slowed down as it was, but now he figured he'd better stay in low, so Jaden could try to catch up. When Nolen got to the top, he turned around to look and saw Jaden slowly walking his bike up the hill. He laughed. "I guess this was a pretty hard one for a beginner," he admitted.

"Really?" Jaden said sarcastically. But he wasn't upset. Just determined to get in better shape, so he could ride wherever Nolen did. When Jaden arrived at the top, he took a gasp, not for oxygen, but because of the mind-blowing beauty of the view. He had never realized there could be such a view so close to where he lived. It wasn't as high as the mountains where he had gone on vacation before, but it was high enough that it provided a view of the lake that the town was built on and a lot of houses nestled in trees down below. He pointed. "Is that the zip-line park way over there?" He had been paying so much attention to the view that he hadn't noticed Nolen get off his bike and move to stand beside him.

"Yeah," replied Nolen and put his arm casually around Jaden's shoulders. Jaden was unsure of his intent, if any, so he just stood there. The moment passed, and Nolen reached around for his backpack and pulled out his camera. Jaden stepped back so as not to obstruct the view, but Nolen said, "No, stay there. I want to take this picture with you in it." Then he stepped back and snapped.

"Let me see," pressed Jaden.

"No, I'll let you see when I get finished with it. Come on, let's ride some more." They continued riding for an hour or so more, then, headed back to Nolen's house.

"I'd better call to see if Brandon can come get me. That was so much fun! But I know I'm gonna be sore tomorrow. My butt already hurts."

"You'll get used to it. I'm sure you got sore when you first started swimming, right?"

"Mostly winded. It really takes a lot to get in shape for swimming. At first you feel like puking whenever you race, but I can't say that it ever made my butt sore."

Nolen laughed. "True that! Anywho, you'll be doing fine soon. We should go again."

When Brandon arrived to pick up Jaden, the two friends had made plans to bike again soon.

Chapter 36

Devon went over to the Hansen house Sunday afternoon to make snacks for the first GSA meeting, as he and Jenny had planned. Jaden was more than happy to join them. Alice had bought cookie dough, as well as icing, sprinkles, and M&Ms to decorate the cookies. The three were chattering happily, deciding to make various sizes and shapes of cookies, so they could be decorated in different ways.

"What's going on in here?" said Brandon, as he walked through the kitchen.

"We're making cookies for the GSA meeting tomorrow. Are you going to come?" asked Devon. Brandon frowned.

"I have too much on my mind right now to be thinking of stuff like that." He abruptly left the kitchen. Devon raised an eyebrow.

"What was that all about?" Jaden and Jenny looked at each other silently.

Alice said, "Don't mind Brandon. He has a lot on going on right now. He'll come around, I'm sure."

"Yeah, let's don't let Brandon's mood spoil our day," Jenny said practically. "I'm ready to make some cookies!" Since Valentine's Day was right around the corner, they decided to make some of the cookies heart-shaped.

"Let's make some like peace signs," suggested Jaden.

"Great idea, and let's decorate some like equals signs, you know, equality?" said Jenny. "How many people do you think will actually come to the meeting? I'm a little nervous about it."

Devon replied, "I know, right? We're trying so hard to get something started that the school board doesn't want us to have, and what if no one shows up? What if no one cares?" It was a sobering thought that they pondered for a moment.

Jenny, who was always optimistic, broke the silence by saying, "Oh, well, we'll do the best we can with whoever shows up. At least the three of us will be there." They spent the rest of the afternoon decorating and laughing at each other's creations. When they were through Alice helped them put the cookies away in containers that could easily be carried to school the next day.

All weekend Brandon had been trying to find a time to talk to Emily, but she had been tied up until Sunday afternoon. They finally had a chance to get together after church.

"How are you feeling, Emily?" Brandon asked with a watchful eye. She looked so sallow. "Do you feel different than usual?"

"Well, if you want to call puking my guts out in the mornings different, then yes, I do," she said unhappily.

"I feel so bad for you," he replied. "It's not enough what you're going through, but to feel sick, too, is just not fair." She made a wry face.

"I guess it's my own fault. My body's telling me I screwed up." Brandon was indignant.

"It's not your fault! It's Juan Carlos' fault. If he hadn't kept on and kept on, it wouldn't have happened!"

"Brandon, it takes two, you know. It is what it is, and I have to live with it."

"Emily, I talked to my mom." She studied his face. "She thinks you should tell your mom. She says moms are tougher than we think."

"I can't, Brandon. You don't know how my mother is. She would never understand that I had sex at my age. She's old-fashioned, and she would be so upset. I guess if I were old-fashioned, too, I wouldn't be in this position." As her face clouded with tears, Brandon felt as if he had been stabbed with a knife. If only he had never taken those steroids. He would never have treated Emily like he did, they would still be together, and she wouldn't be pregnant. True, he and Emily had been intimate, but it hadn't been the same. They had been in love and used protection. He wanted to say all that to her, but he didn't know the words to use.

Instead he said, "Mom said she would be heart-broken if my sister got pregnant and didn't tell her. She would never want Jenny to feel alone and that she wouldn't be there to help her."

"How would you feel if you had to tell your dad that you got a girl pregnant? Never mind, it doesn't matter anyway. I've decided. I'm going to get an abortion. Will you help me?" The impact of those words left Brandon speechless.

When the time for the GSA meeting arrived, Mr. Anthony was waiting in the auditorium. As soon as the bell rang, people started coming in, and some were already there when Devon and the twins arrived. Within ten minutes there were probably twenty-five people seated all over.

Mr. Anthony stood and said, "Okay, people, don't be shy. Everyone move up to the first few rows, so we can all talk to one another. I know some of you are surprised to see me up here, but I'll be brief. This will not be a club led by an adult. This club is for you. You make the decisions about leadership and in what direction you want the club to go. I know most of you are curious, so I'll give you a little introduction, and then, I'm going to turn the floor over to Jenny Hansen. First, though, you need to be aware that to join the club, your parent must sign a permission slip." Groans were heard from some of the students.

"The main purpose of the club here at Lake Griffin High is to learn about and accept people who may seem different from you or different from what you may be used to. You may be gay, you may be straight, you may have an alternative lifestyle, or you may have special needs. You may be white like Jenny, or you may be black like me, or anything in between. Everyone is welcome! That's what you should stress to your parents. Tell them it's not a club that talks about or explores sexual behavior. Nor will it be a group that has cliques where some people are excluded. You are all in this world together, and hopefully, here at LGHS, you can learn to get along and show the rest of our community that you are the new leaders and that they can learn from you."

Mr. Anthony walked away from the podium to a rousing cheer. Everyone continued clapping and whistling as Jenny walked to the podium.

"Well!" said Jenny. "It looks like Mr. Anthony has gotten us off to a great start! I'm so glad all of you showed up, and I'm super glad that everyone seems to have the same agenda in mind." The group applauded again. She looked at the crowd and noticed many of the kids who had been in the TEAM Club, but there were a good number of others, too. "You can get your permission slips from Mr. Anthony as you leave today, and be sure to turn them in before the next meeting. Our first order of business should be to elect officers and then to decide what we, as a club, might like to do."

Someone stood up and said, "I think you should be the president. You and Devon were the ones who got everything together for this, and it's only right you should be our first president." Murmurs of assent went around the room. Jenny looked questioningly at Mr. Anthony.

He asked for other nominations and when no one spoke he said, "I don't think we need to stand on ceremony here. Everybody who would like Jenny to be first president, raise your hand." The auditorium was flooded with hands. "I think it's unanimous. Jenny, congratulations!" Jenny grinned widely.

"Thank you so much, everybody. I'll try to be the best president ever! Now, do we have nominations for other officers?" By the time the meeting was adjourned, Devon was elected VP, Hannah, the girl in the wheelchair was elected secretary, and Brooke was elected treasurer. A date for the next meeting was set, and everyone was asked to think about service projects that might educate people about diversity. They also had decided to have a party in the spring to recruit new members.

Brooke and Chelsea left the meeting feeling happy and satisfied that their school was finally going to do something to recognize the fact that a lot of kids had no place to go where they could feel safe and accepted. Allowing the GSA to be formed would help a lot.

"Brooke, having this club is going to be the greatest thing ever, but how will you get your parents to sign the permission form?" asked Chelsea. "You've already been elected an officer to a club that I'm sure your parents won't let you join."

"I know, Chelsea. I've been thinking about that. I'm not even going to show the form to them. I'm going to sign it myself or have someone sign it for me. Someone who can fake a signature well. I know my parents would never sign it."

"Aren't you afraid of getting caught?"

"What difference does it make? All that would happen is that I would be kicked out of the club. They probably won't verify all the parents' signatures, anyway."

"I guess you're right. It doesn't sound like a good plan, but it's the only plan." Chelsea smiled. "At least it's not near as serious as me getting caught sneaking into your bedroom at night."

"I know, right? My parents would have a cow if they knew that you've been doing that for a whole month. It's a good thing my bedroom is on the other side of the house from theirs. Their whole attitude makes me so mad, though. We don't do anything wrong. Everybody except us gets to go to a sleep-over or have someone spend the night with them."

Chapter 37

Tuesday in P.E. Jaden asked Trevor, "Why didn't you come to the GSA startup meeting yesterday?"

"I don't know. I guess I just didn't feel like it. I went straight home. How was it?"

"It was really good. Lots of kids came. You're still going to join, aren't you?"

"Yeah, I will. What do you have to do to join?"

"Just get a permission slip. That's it. You can get one from Mr. Anthony. That's who you turn it back in to."

"Are your parents going to sign for you?" asked an incredulous Trevor.

"My mom is. She's cool now and supports me. She's the one who went to the meeting with Jenny to get the club started, you know."

"I guess I didn't know. That's when we…we weren't talking." He paused. "Does your dad know all about us now? Does he know you're going to join this club?"

"I pretty sure neither Mom nor Dad knows about *us*, but they both know about me, now. I believe Dad knows both Jenny and I are joining, but I know he won't sign the paper. Mom says he still has a hard time with the whole thing."

"By the way, how was your bike trip Saturday?" Trevor asked casually, but with purpose, because he had a feeling there was more to it than met the eye. "Who was the guy you went with?"

"His name's Nolen. Remember I told you we met at that Christmas thing?"

"What Christmas thing?"

"Devon's mom took us with her to help people at her job give underprivileged families a meal and Christmas presents. Nolen and Ward's mom works at the same place."

"Ward?"

"Yeah, that's Nolen's twin brother. They go to that magnet school for the arts."

"Did Ward go biking, too?"

"No, he let me use his bike, since I don't have a mountain bike. It was really cool. We went off-road on all these trails and climbed hills and stuff."

"Sounds fun. Maybe I could go with you next time." Jaden tried to think fast.

"Uh, yeah, but, you need a mountain bike. You don't have one, do you?"

"Oh, I could probably come up with one, somewhere. Let me know when you're going again. Hey, do you want a ride home?" Of course Jaden did, and Trevor stopped the Mustang before he reached Jaden's house, so he could give Jaden a slow, meaningful kiss.

Jaden left the car that day feeling very conflicted. Just what he had been wishing for was happening. Trevor was acting like the sweet guy that he had first been attracted to and fallen in love with. Wasn't this exactly what he had been wanting for the past two months? That kiss had aroused all the old passions that he had for Trevor, but... it had seemed anticlimactic. Was it because he was afraid that Trevor's feelings would change again? That he would revert back to the sarcasm and constant bickering that had marred their relationship in the fall? Or, could it be that he was now truly interested in Nolen and wanted to see if there was a chance for that friendship to become a relationship. That perhaps it would become a relationship that was easy, that was based on mutual respect. One that his dad had no knowledge of, nor pre-determined feelings about. He decided to air his thoughts to his old, reliable confidant, his sister, Jenny.

That night after dinner, Jaden walked into Jenny's room where he found her doing math homework.

"Hey, Jay, you having problems with today's math? That's what I'm working on right now."

"I haven't even looked at it yet. I want to talk to you about something."

She shoved her chair back and said, "Shoot."

"Trevor's been making up with me, just like you said he should."

"That's great, Jaden!"

"I don't know, though, Jenny. I thought I really wanted him back, and I guess I do. When we kissed today, it was just like it used to be. But, while Trevor was gone from my life, I got interested in Nolen. He's so much fun and so nice."

"Is he interested in you, too?"

"I'm not sure. Ward was teasing him about liking me. He did kiss me on the cheek once, and he put his arm around my shoulder while we were looking at the view down the hill when we went biking. I don't know how serious he is, though."

"Well, it seems to me that you can have both of them. Be friends with Nolen, but let him know that you're with Trevor."

"That's just it, Jenny. I'm not sure I want to be with Trevor. He really hurt me, and it took a long time before I felt okay again. I don't think I want to take a chance on getting hurt again."

"How would you feel if you didn't have a relationship with either of them? Like, if you broke up with Trevor and then found out that Nolen didn't want to go anywhere with it. Would that bother you?"

"I hadn't really thought of it like that. I guess I don't have to have a relationship with anyone. I can have fun with Nolen and keep things casual with Trevor and just see what happens."

"Yeah, but you know how jealous Trevor is. You'll be taking a chance that he won't consider being just friends."

"You're right about that. I better think about it."

Jenny sat pondering at her desk for a while after Jaden went back to his room. I guess I'm lucky, she thought. I've only been in one relationship before now, if you want to call it that. When Dan and I were going out last year, I really liked him, but when we broke up, I felt like it was the best thing. He's so much older, and we didn't have that much in common. It was sort of a mutual thing when we split. Neither of us felt the hurt that Jaden has gone through over and over. And now I'm in a real relationship that's great. Devon is so perfect for me. He's sweet and kind, and he feels the same way that I do about not wanting people to be bullied or made fun of. And one of the best things is that he and Jaden are best friends. It's hard to believe that my boyfriend is best friends with the person that I'm closest in the whole world to, my twin brother.

As she turned back to her math, she thought about Friday night when Devon would play in the last J.V. basketball game of the year. After the game, he was coming over for pizza with the family and then, they were going to watch movies. Despite her rush of excitement, she felt bad that Jaden couldn't enjoy the same openness with someone he wanted to date. It just wasn't fair.

Friday at lunchtime, Mr. Anthony sought out Jenny to give her an update.

"Hey, Jenny, I thought you might like to know about the permission slips coming in. So far, all the officers and about ten of the others have gotten theirs in. I'd say about half of the people who showed up have returned their slips. Even if no others come in, you have a fine nucleus for a club. You and the other officers need to get together to plan the agenda for the next meeting. If you come up with some ideas, I'll help you refine them." Jenny smiled at the prospect.

"That sounds great, Mr. Anthony. I don't know what we would do without you. Devon is coming over to my house tonight after the basketball game, and we'll start thinking. Maybe one day after school next week, we can schedule an officers' meeting to really plan something."

"Tell me what day you want, and I'll get it on the announcements."

Chapter 38

At the end of the school day, Jaden said, "Hey, Trev, want to go to the basketball game tonight?" Trevor frowned.

"You know I don't like sports."

"Yeah, but it's Devon's last game. Don't you think it'd be fun to go and yell for him?"

"Okay, yeah, I guess it'd be fun. You want to just meet there, or do you want me to pick you up?" Suddenly thinking of his dad, Jaden hesitated.

"Probably just meet me there. That way I don't have to explain anything to my dad. We'll be there around 5:30 to watch them warm up."

A lot of the swim team, including Chelsea along with Brooke, was going to be there, too. At 5:30 when the Hansen family arrived, Jaden and Jenny took it upon themselves to round everyone up to make a cheering section for Devon. When Devon's mom, Mrs. Mulder, got there, they grabbed her and seated her with all the rest. Donnie pursed his lips, but had the good sense to keep his mouth shut.

However, when Trevor showed up, he had to say to Alice, "What's he doing here?"

"You know perfectly well that he's friends with this whole group. If you'll recall, he was on the swim team with many of them." Donnie glared at his wife briefly, then stopped talking and made a point of studiously watching the teams warm up.

When the game started it became clear early on that the J.V. Mustangs were going to win the game, but it was still close enough to be interesting. The big play of the game was in the last quarter. The Mustangs had the ball at their own goal when Devon was suddenly unguarded near the goal. A teammate alley-ooped him the ball, and he made a tremendous effort to step and dunk the ball. He didn't quite get the ball high enough, so it bounced hard off the rim, right into the hands of a low-time fellow player standing near the free-throw line. He wildly threw it back toward the goal, where it unexpectedly fell in as the buzzer was sounding. The Mustangs had already won the game, so it wasn't a crucial goal, but it was the only time that particular player had been in a game all season, and everyone was thrilled. Two players picked him up on their shoulders and ran around the gym with him triumphantly, while he beamed.

After the players shook hands with the other team and went into the locker room to change, Jaden asked, "Mom, can Devon spend the night to-night?"

"Sure, honey. Ask his mom right now." When Jaden walked down to ask Mrs. Mulder, Donnie turned to Alice with an incredulous look.

"Really, Alice? Really? Do you think it's a good idea to have our daughter's boyfriend spend the night at our house?" he whispered through clenched teeth.

"Donnie, he's not just Jenny's boyfriend. He's Jaden's best friend, too, and it's not as though we won't be there." Alice was really getting tired of Donnie's attitude.

"I think you've lost your mind, but you just do whatever you want. That's all you do these days, anyway." Jaden, Jenny, and Devon's conversation was so animated on the way home that they didn't notice the adults' silence.

They stopped to pick up pizza, and as they sat around the dining room table eating, they teased Devon about his attempted dunk. He said he had been working on it all season at practice and had been successful a couple of times. It had just seemed the perfect opportunity that night to try it in a game.

"The best part about it was when Luis got that ball," Devon laughed. "Did you see the look on his face? He was like, what do I do now? He got rid of that ball like it was on fire." Everyone roared. "He made a basket, though. You gotta hand it to him." Even Donnie laughed.

After everything was cleaned up, they traipsed into the living room to put a movie on.

"Where's Brandon tonight? And where did Trevor go so quick after the game?" asked Devon.

"Brandon's out with Emily. They're back together again, and Trevor wanted to stop by the YMCA to pick up his paycheck before they closed," said Jaden. The three kids sat down on the couch with Jenny in the middle, while Donnie and Alice sat on recliners. Jenny snuggled up to Devon, leaning on his shoulder and holding his hand. The movie was long, and Donnie dozed off before it was over. When he awoke, the TV was off, and everyone was yawning and stretching, preparing to go to bed. He roused himself and went to the kitchen for a glass of water. He returned to go through the living room just in time to see Devon and Jenny kissing. It wasn't a long kiss, just a 'you're special to me' kiss. But it was enough to get Donnie riled up again. He directed a steely look at Jenny.

"That's enough! It's late. Say *good night*, and get to bed." Jenny looked puzzled, and then hurt. "Right now!" Donnie spoke loudly and aggressively. Jenny mumbled an apology to Devon and left the room. Donnie turned and pointed a finger at Devon.

"Go to Jaden's room, and don't come out until morning!"

Alice who had overheard, firmly said, "Come to bed, Donnie." Once behind a closed bedroom door, Alice turned to Donnie, but before she could say anything, he jumped in.

"Didn't I tell you it was a bad idea to have a boyfriend spend the night here? There they were, right in the middle of the living room, kissing. For all I know, Devon was going to follow her into her bedroom. God only knows how he was raised."

"You're being ridiculous, Donnie! You know your daughter, and you've known Devon for years. That was nothing but a sweet goodnight kiss, just like it would have been had he dropped her off at the house after a date. The way you think and act has been going on far too long. For years Jaden didn't feel like you loved him, and now you've hurt Jenny's feelings, too. I've known you were a homophobe, but I didn't know you were also a bigot."

"That does it! I've had enough. I'm going to get some things together and go stay at my parents' house for a while. I can't stay here and watch you let our kids do whatever with whoever. What if it leads to pregnancy? AIDS? You think you have it all together now, just because you took a class at the college. Well, you don't know everything! I know how to keep my kids out of trouble, even if it's hard for them to take sometimes. Being strict, so they don't get hurt, is how I prove my love to them." With that he walked to the closet, picked up a suitcase and started packing. In a few minutes he was heading for the door.

"Donnie, don't you think you're being a little melodramatic? And, what do you think your parents are going to say when you knock on their door at this late hour? I don't doubt your love for our kids one bit, but I think your outlook on certain parts of our family dynamics needs an overhaul. Jenny is dating now, and she's a mature young lady who's been raised well. We don't have to worry about her choices. Jaden is gay. That's not going to change. He needs all the support he can get. Brandon has been through some tough times, causing us a lot of grief. But he's still a senior in high school and more tough times are bound to happen, even though he's come around and is doing great right now. All our kids need a father who treats them with respect and loves them unconditionally. Maybe you do need to go away for a while, but don't you think the kids deserve an explanation from the two of us together? And not after you've skulked off in the dead of night?" In spite of his anger, Donnie listened to what Alice was saying and agreed to wait until morning to leave.

Brandon had, indeed, been out with Emily that Friday night. They had ordered dinner at a little mom-and-pop diner and continued to sit and talk long after they finished eating.

"Have you given any more thought to not having an abortion?"

"Brandon, I just don't see any other way. We've been around and around about this." He tried once again.

"You could give it up for adoption."

"But then, my mother would know all about it."

"Emily, your mother needs to realize that things are different from when she grew up. If she knew how often kids have sex in high school, she'd think you were a saint. You've only done it a few times. You're not a bad person. You just made a mistake. I could go with you to talk to her." Emily considered his words.

"You would do that? Even when it's someone else's baby?"

"I told you I would help you through this. I love you, Emily. I'll stand by you all the way." He squeezed her hand. "Let's go talk to your mother right now."

"Now?" Emily had a tortured look on her face. She sat staring into space for a long while. Finally, she gave in, because she was at a loss about what else to do. "Okay, Brandon. Let's do it."

They drove back to Emily's house without talking, both lost in their own thoughts.

When they arrived, Emily asked one more time, "Are you sure you want to do this?"

Brandon got out, went to her side of the car, took her arm, and said, "Let's go before we lose our nerve!"

The next morning was somber in the Hansen house. Alice had gotten up first to ensure that no one left the house before she and Donnie could speak to everyone. Jaden had shuffled out next, with Jenny not far behind, looking somewhat put out.

"What's wrong, Jen?" asked Jaden. Before Jenny could answer, Alice spoke up.

"I think she's a little upset with your father, honey. He spoke out of turn with her last night. Are you okay this morning, Jenny?" She hugged her daughter.

"I'm okay, Mom, but totally embarrassed. No telling what Devon thinks."

Jaden replied, "He didn't say anything to me about anything last night. I'm sure he's fine. What's it all about?" Donnie walked into the room, which silenced the conversation.

"Jaden, go get your brother up; we have something to tell you." Jenny's eyes widened as she looked questioningly at her mom. Hearing the activity, Devon wandered out as Jaden came back with Brandon, who looked sleepy and annoyed.

Brandon said, "I hope this is important. I didn't get much sleep last night!"

"Devon," Alice said gently, "We need a family moment. Would you mind waiting in Jaden's room for a few minutes?" When he left, she said, "Go ahead, Donnie."

"Look, kids. As you probably know, your mother and I haven't been seeing eye to eye on numerous things for several months now. It's not the fault of anybody in this room, but we have decided to separate for a while. It doesn't mean we don't love each other anymore, and it doesn't mean a divorce. It's just a time-out, so we can think things through. I'll be staying at my parents' house, but I'll still come to all your baseball games, Brandon, and your softball games, Jenny."

"Won't that be a long way for you to go to work, Dad?" asked Jenny, who, with a pang of guilt for her anger the night before, had right away forgiven her father for what he had said to her. She hoped that kissing Devon hadn't caused her father to leave.

"It won't be that far, princess, and hopefully, it won't be that long." Jaden, who was positive that his being gay was why his dad was leaving, looked down and said nothing.

Alice took note of his anguished face and said, "Listen to me. None of you are to blame. This is between your father and me, and we will straighten it out."

Brandon, who was already out of sorts, sarcastically said under his breath, "You're not the only one with problems, dear Dad." Donnie didn't hear him and prepared to leave.

As he looked around the kitchen at his family, he realized that his irritability of the night before had vanished, as well as most of his resolve. But, when his eyes settled on Jaden, and then he thought about Devon, he knew he couldn't stay and continue feeling the way he did. Something had to change. As he walked out the door, he didn't look back. He didn't want his family to see the tears on his face.

When Alice got the kids out of the kitchen so she could make breakfast, Brandon remained behind.

"Mom, I need to talk to you. Again." The tone of his voice made Alice instantly turn from the refrigerator to study her son's face. "I finally got Emily to talk to her mom."

"Aren't you relieved, son? Now the two of you don't have to make such a big decision alone."

"She told her mother that she was pregnant, and her mother was really mad. Emily was crying and trying to apologize. I didn't know what to say, so I said that I had been trying to talk Emily out of an abortion. Her mother looked at me with a murderous look. Then she said that abortion was out of the question and that I had better be planning to marry Emily before she started to show. Emily tried to butt in and tell her that I wasn't the father, but I stopped her and told her mother that was exactly what I was planning to do."

"Brandon! You didn't!"

"Here's the thing, Mom. I really love Emily, and if it would help her through this, why shouldn't I marry her?"

"What about college? What about baseball? What about your future? How do you think you can manage all those things if you have a wife and a baby to support? What about Emily's plan for college? Have you thought through all of those things? You can always marry her later when you are out of college and on your way to a career."

"Her mom doesn't want her to have an abortion, but she doesn't want her to be an unwed mother. She was firm on that. I just hope she won't show until after we graduate, and then we can get married. People from school won't know when the baby is born after that."

"Brandon, how far along is she?"

"Four or five months, she thinks."

"She needs to get to the doctor right away for prenatal care. It's been too long already. And, honey, I'm afraid she'll probably start showing any day now."

Brandon took a deep breath, then, slowly continued. "I know it's not what I had planned for the next phase of my life, but I'm sure I can work and go to the community college at the same time."

"Brandon, you can't do this! This is not your problem to fix."

"I can do it, and I'm going to do it, Mom."

"Sweetie, it's not your child," Alice said softly.

"I know, Mom, but I want to do this. I love her." Alice felt like she was in over her head. For the first time in a long time, she wished Donnie were there to give input, even though he would probably be crazed with the situation. Regardless, he might be able to talk some sense into Brandon.

Chapter 39

On the other side of town on that same Saturday morning, Brooke and Chelsea were in a heap of trouble. Brooke had gotten home by her curfew Friday night, but at midnight, Chelsea had gone to Brooke's house and sneaked in her window. They had done that same thing several times in January without getting caught or even having a close call. Friday night they had stayed up talking and fooling around and had both fallen asleep, exhausted, around 3 am. The next morning when Wayne Gorman tapped on Brooke's door to say good morning and cracked it open, he was shocked to see the two girls frantically trying to cover their nakedness.

"Oh, my God! Justine!" he turned away and yelled. "You need to come in here this minute!" His wife appeared in a flash, dressed in a housecoat. She was stunned speechless to find Chelsea in her daughter's bed.

Wayne shouted, "Both of you get dressed and meet your mother and me in the living room!" The girls were visibly shaking as they got dressed, and Brooke was as white as a sheet.

"Oh shit, oh shit, oh shit! We are so screwed." Chelsea was sick with fear and humiliation as they went into the living room.

"Brooke, what were you thinking? Are you thinking at all? I thought we could trust you. I can see now that we should have prevented you from seeing this…this *homosexual* at all. But this…what I saw… is intolerable. I'm getting in touch with the police and having you arrested, Chelsea. Brooke is just a child, and you've taken advantage of her innocence." Chelsea felt the blood drain from her face. Oh my God, he can't do this, she thought frantically! But, could he?

"Arrested?" Brooke wailed. "What are you talking about? You can't do that! We haven't done anything wrong."

"Sorry, but you're very mistaken. You told me that she's eighteen, and you're only fifteen. That makes this rape."

"Rape? Are you crazy? You can't do this! It's insane!" Brooke was becoming hysterical. Even though Chelsea was terrified, she tried to calm Brooke down.

"It's okay, Brooke. I'm going home. Try not to worry about anything." She glared at Mr. Gorman. "I love Brooke, and she loves me. I would never hurt her."

"Don't think words are going to change anything, Chelsea. Now get out of my house, and don't ever come back! I'm going to go to the police station and file a formal complaint." Then he took his wife by the arm and pulled her into the kitchen.

"I hate you!" Brooke screamed at her parents as they left the room.

Before Chelsea left, she whispered to Brooke, "It'll be okay. I'll talk to my parents. They'll know what to do."

When they were alone, Justine tried to talk to her husband. She certainly didn't want Brooke to become one of "them", but still thought it rather unwise to file a police report. She didn't want this to become a public spectacle.

"Why don't we just ground her and not let her see that girl at all?"

"You don't understand, Justine. Homosexuality is a scourge to our nation and to our military, too. When they repealed 'Don't ask, don't tell' the nation was set up for ruin. That Chelsea needs to be put away so that she can't recruit other innocent girls. We had made it clear that we didn't want our daughter influenced in that manner, and she deliberately went after her anyway. I'm going down to the police department after breakfast."

When Wayne left the house, Justine went into Brooke's room and found her crying.

"Mom, you can't let him do this. He's going to ruin Chelsea's life. Chelsea didn't do anything to me. I'm a lesbian, too. I couldn't admit it before, because I knew Dad would do just what he's doing. Chelsea and I love each other."

"Brooke, this is wrong. You're just confused. You'll see. In time you'll fall in love with a boy, and you'll understand then why we're trying to protect you."

"Mom! I'm not confused! Can't you understand that? I was born this way."

"I know you can't see reality right now, but regardless, I'm afraid it's out of my hands. You know how your dad is when he gets something in his mind. He'll follow through until the end."

"If he has Chelsea arrested, I'll never speak to him again. And, I'll leave this house the very first chance I get." Then she turned over in her bed, signaling that she was through talking.

Justine was greatly disturbed by the events of the morning. She wasn't sure what she should do, or even could do. She was sick at the thought of losing Brooke. But even if they kept her under lock and key, if her husband went through with this, they would lose her for all intents and purposes. She needed to think.

By the time Chelsea got home, her forced composure was wrecked. As she entered the kitchen, she saw her parents drinking coffee and totally fell apart.

"Chelsea, good grief! What's wrong?" asked her father. She was sobbing so copiously that she couldn't speak. Her mother jumped up and put her arms around her distraught daughter. She looked across at her husband with a bewildered face. He got up and joined the mother-and-daughter hug and said, "It's okay, baby, whatever it is, we'll take care of it." The two of them murmured soothing comments until Chelsea finally pulled herself together enough to explain what had happened. Although both of her parents were upset that Chelsea had snuck into Brooke's house, that discussion could wait. Ed Harper was too furious to address that issue now.

"Who does this guy think he is? Having you arrested! Did you admit anything to them?"

"No, he didn't even ask us any questions. Just said I raped Brooke."

"Honey, he doesn't have a leg to stand on, then. Don't admit anything to anyone. Brooke won't say anything to him, will she?"

"I doubt it. He'll be lucky if she ever looks at him again. But, Dad, I'm scared. What's going to happen to me?"

"Nothing will happen to you, sweetie. I'll call an attorney first thing Monday. Try to relax and not let your fear run away with you." Her dad was more worried than he let on, though. He couldn't really picture an arrest, but, on the other hand, he wasn't sure what to expect.

At the Hansen house, Jaden, Jenny, and Devon were having a serious discussion in the living room, while Brandon was in the kitchen talking to his mom.

"I know Mom and Dad weren't getting along the greatest, but I never thought Dad would leave," Jenny spoke sadly. "I got mad at him last night when he embarrassed me, but I didn't mean it. I would never want him to leave."

"It's not your fault, Jen. It's me. He's never been able to accept that I'm gay. Mom has started taking my side, and that's why they don't get along. I know that's the reason!" Jaden said emphatically.

"Hold up! Both of you. Didn't you say your mom said it wasn't any-body's fault?" Devon was trying to be supportive and practical at the same time. "Sometimes parents just don't get along. My mom kicked my old man out of the house years ago, because he kept getting drunk. I hardly know him. You can't blame yourselves." Jenny smiled at Devon and slid closer to him on the couch. Devon continued. "Don't worry, your dad will be back. All of us will just have to make sure your mom doesn't get too upset about it. She needs us."

"I hope you're right, Devon," replied Jaden. "I can't think about this any more right now. I'm gonna text Nolen. I need to do something to get my mind off things."

"Good idea. Jenny, want to go for a walk?"

Chapter 40

Wayne Gorman left the police department Saturday morning angry and frustrated. The officer had asked him if he had any definitive proof that a sexual act had occurred, and if he didn't, nothing could be done. Apparently, being in the same bed naked didn't prove anything. When Wayne hedged, he was told to either catch them in the act, or get his daughter to agree to provide information. However, the officer did say he would bring both girls in and take their statements before any decision was made about pursuing the matter further. Wayne said he wanted to be there during the questioning, and he was told that he had a right to be present with his daughter, but not with Chelsea.

When Wayne returned to his house, he called a sullen Brooke into the living room, along with her mother.

"I talked with the police department about you and Chelsea, and they're going to bring each of you in to take formal statements." Brooke shot an alarmed look at her mom. "There's no getting around the fact that I caught the two of you in bed. Whatever he asks you, you *will* tell the absolute truth. You'll get in a lot of trouble if you try to lie to law enforcement. I'll be in the room when the officer questions you, and I'll know if you're lying."

"What kind of person would turn his own daughter in to the police?" Brooke screamed. "You're not my father any more! Go to hell!" Her father slapped her soundly across the face.

"I am your father, and you can't talk to me like that! Go to your room."

"Gladly! But, you can't keep me a prisoner here forever." When Brooke got back in her room, she immediately texted Chelsea what she had found out, in case her father came in to take her phone away. Chelsea warned her not to admit to anything and affirmed that her dad was going to help them. She felt a tiny bit better after that.

On Saturday afternoon, the police department apprised the Harpers, Chelsea's parents, that a complaint had been filed against their daughter. After that call, Ed Harper called his attorney, not wanting to wait until

Monday morning. He told him what had happened and that the girls were being called in to make statements. The attorney agreed with Ed that as long as no one had admitted anything, there wouldn't be much of a case. He told Ed he would be there to represent Chelsea when she was questioned and that he would answer all questions on her behalf.

The weekend passed solemnly for all parties involved. Devon had gone home Saturday afternoon, Nolen was otherwise occupied, and Emily wanted time alone, so the Hansens were just hanging around their house, as were Chelsea and Brooke at their respective houses. Alice was feeling the full weight of Donnie's absence. When he had left for a few days at Thanksgiving, she had known it was temporary. This time it had an open-ended feeling, and it was unnerving.

When Monday came, and everyone was off to school, she tried to stay busy with her usual household tasks, but it just felt different. She was actually looking forward to Brandon's first baseball game Friday night, because she knew Donnie would be there.

The police had called the two families to let them know when the statements would be taken. Monday morning found Ed and Wayne staring each other down in the waiting room of the police station, while the two mothers were avoiding eye contact. They wouldn't have even been there at the same time if Wayne hadn't insisted on arriving an hour early. Now they were all there together, and the hostility was palpable. The two girls, Chelsea with her attorney, had been placed in other areas, away from their parents, and from each other. The Harpers were called in first and found Chelsea and her lawyer already in the room. When they walked in, they could see that she was noticeably shaken. She got up and hugged her parents tightly. The detective informed them that this was not an arrest, and she was not in trouble. This meeting was strictly for fact-finding. He then asked her to tell him her version of what had happened on Saturday night. She looked at her dad who told the detective that he could address all questions to his attorney. The session concluded quickly because no admission of sexual contact was made.

"I guess that wraps it up for now, then," said the detective. He said he would be in touch.

"What's going to happen now, Dad?" Chelsea asked when they were getting in their car.

"I think it's going to be okay, but we'll have to wait until we hear from our lawyer before we know for sure."

"It's so hard for me to believe that people like Brooke's parents are so narrow-minded and evil that they would sooner turn their daughter away than love her for who she is. I'm so thankful for you and Mom. I don't know what I would do without your love and support, and I feel so bad for Brooke. Can they keep us apart?"

"Honey, I'm afraid if that man wants to, he will find a way, and frankly, I think you should stay away from Brooke for a while anyway. Her father will be gunning for you, and I don't want you to give him any ammunition." Chelsea said nothing.

When the Gormans were called in, they, too, found their daughter already in the room. However, unlike Chelsea, Brooke was disgusted by her parents' forcing her to be there and turned as far away from them as she could.

The detective then asked Brooke for her account of what happened Saturday night.

She admitted that against her father's wishes, she had invited Chelsea over and they had stayed up half the night talking. They had fallen asleep and were still sleeping when her father barged into her room the next morning, accusing them of perverted things. When the detective asked if their relationship was of a sexual nature, she emphatically said no.

"Brooke, you tell this man the truth!" snapped her father. "You know you were both naked in bed!"

"The heat was on too high, and we were hot," responded Brooke smugly. Her father looked at the detective.

"You know that's ridiculous. Can't you make her tell the truth?"

"I'm sorry, sir. All I can do is question her. I don't think we have anything here."

"This whole thing is a travesty! That girl raped my daughter, and you know it!" Wayne jumped up and stormed out. Justine meekly followed, as did Brooke, but unlike her father, she had a look of satisfaction on her face.

Chapter 41

In P.E. on Monday Trevor wanted to know what was up with Jaden.

"I thought we might get together this past weekend, but I didn't hear a word from you the whole time. What were you doing?"

"It wasn't such a good weekend for us, Trev. My parents had a big fight after Devon's basketball game, and my dad's moved out for a while." Jaden looked so dejected that Trevor's heart went out to him. He wanted to hug him and try to make him feel better, but the memory of that kid coming around the corner in the locker room still stung.

He just said, "Jaden, I'm so sorry. I know that must be awful for you. Why didn't you text me?"

Feeling guilty because he had texted Nolen instead, Jaden replied, "I just didn't feel like talking or doing anything."

"Well, we definitely need to do something soon. It's been way too long. Maybe we can go bike riding with that friend of yours. My neighbor said I could use his mountain bike any time I want. He said it just sits there."

"Uh… okay. Uh, yeah, that would be cool. I'll get in touch with Nolen."

When Jaden got home that afternoon he didn't know what to say to Nolen, but he knew he had to come up with something. He decided to just text him that a friend of his wanted to go biking with them, and what did he think about it? Nolen thought it would be a lot of fun.

Jaden, on the other hand, thought it might be very stressful instead of fun. What if Trevor acted like they were a couple? What if Nolen didn't want to have anything to do with him if he thought he was with somebody already? He began to wish he had never set the whole thing up.

The next morning, Jaden saw Brooke in the hall and asked her where she'd been the day before.

"My dad's got me virtually on lockdown. Wait 'til I tell you what happened. It's World War III at my house."

"Why? What'd you do?"

"My dad caught Chelsea and me in bed Saturday morning after she had sneaked into my room Friday night. I hate to tell you, because you have every right to say I told you so. You warned us about getting in trouble. Boy, we should have listened! And get this! My father got the police involved, and they questioned us yesterday. That's why I wasn't at school. It was worse than horrible."

"Oh my God, Brooke! What happened when they questioned you? I can't believe this!" Jaden's words came out in a rush.

"They didn't do anything, because we denied that we had sex, so my dad got a restraining order put on Chelsea. We're not allowed to have any contact with each other whatsoever. We're going to have to secretly meet in the library or the bathroom here at school."

"How can they do this? I mean, it's not the dark ages. Being gay isn't illegal!"

"It's because Chelsea is eighteen, and I'm not even sixteen yet. My dad was saying Chelsea raped me! Can you believe that? He's out of his freaking mind!"

"Oh, my God! Now we can't all hang out together anymore? What if you get caught here at school?"

"I'm going to see her anyway. What else can they do to me? I don't really care what my parents do. I'm moving out as soon as I can." Jaden sighed. Brooke's story brought back painful memories of his own life the year before. Why can't our parents just accept and love us for who we are? How many other kids are going through this? This feeling of hopelessness persisted in Jaden's thoughts all day. When he got home from school, Alice took one look at him and was immediately concerned.

"What's wrong, honey? Did something happen at school?"

"No, nothing happened to me. I was just talking to Brooke."

"Did something happen to Brooke?" Jaden's eyes filled with tears.

"Mom, does it ever end? You and Dad separated because of me, and now Brooke's parents are after Chelsea and are being so hard on Brooke that she's going to leave home as soon as she can, sometime this year. All this just because she's gay."

"Oh, sweetie, your dad and I aren't separated because of you. There's been a lot going on in our family."

"I know, Mom, but you have to admit that none of this other stuff would have happened if I weren't gay. He's always been upset about that, and everything else was just the last straw. Maybe I should just leave home, too."

"Don't you ever say that, Jaden! I love you so much, and it would break my heart to lose you. I feel very bad about your friend, but try not to take on her struggles as if they were your own. Just do your best to support her." Alice decided she'd better have a word with Donnie.

———

At Friday night's baseball game, Donnie was already in the stands when Alice, Devon, and the twins arrived. Jenny ran up to hug her dad, while Alice and Donnie gave each other genuine smiles. It hadn't been a long separation, but it seemed like forever.

When everyone got seated, Donnie said, "Brandon and another boy on his team are going to be heavily recruited this year. It wouldn't surprise me if there were scouts at every game." Alice didn't know what to say, so she just smiled weakly. Should she be the one to tell Donnie about Brandon's plan, or should she let Brandon tell him? She had a feeling of dread, but this time, it wasn't about what Donnie might say to Brandon. Instead, a heavy feeling had lingered since Brandon had shared his plan to marry Emily. After considering the matter, she decided Brandon should be the one to tell his dad, but before a baseball game would have been a poor choice, in any case.

The Mustangs came out strong in their first game of the season and won five to one. Brandon went three for four at the plate, with no errors at third base. Donnie was pleased to see Brandon hitting in the number three spot. At the end of the game Donnie and Brandon chatted briefly about the game until Brandon told his dad he had a date and needed to go. The other kids hugged their dad, and Donnie left to go back to his parents' house in Center City.

On the way home, Jenny asked, "When is Dad coming home? I miss him."

"I do, too," voiced Jaden. The silence became awkward, because no one had an answer.

On Monday at lunch, Donnie found himself alone in the break room with one of his co-workers, Justine. They had chatted many times in the past, but had kept it mostly professional. Today, however, Donnie was quiet, just staring at his lunch.

"Hey, Donnie, aren't you hungry today?"

Turning to look at Justine, Donnie said, "Oh, hey, Justine. I was just thinking about my son's baseball game Friday night."

"Don't you have two sons? Which son was it?"

"Yes, I have two and a daughter. This was my older son. He's a senior in high school now and has played baseball all four years. It's a serious time in his life right now, because he loves baseball and is trying to get into college on a baseball scholarship."

"Did everything go okay at the game? You look so pensive."

"Yeah." He paused. "Yes, everything went fine at the game. He played error-free and got three hits. It's just...well, you know how things go when you have kids in high school. Your daughter's a teen, isn't she?"

"Boy, is she ever! " Justine shook her head and sighed.

"Enough said," Donnie replied and changed the subject. They finished their lunches talking about a possible merger that had been mentioned at the last staff meeting.

Chapter 42

Jenny and Devon had met with Mr. Anthony a couple of times to plan the next GSA meeting, and in general, to decide the club's focus for the remaining months of school. At the next meeting they had shared the idea of trying to recruit some kids who were known to be anti-gay or bigoted. The idea was that if they could all get together and do some fun things, both groups would be more inclined to accept the other. The following meeting was to be in the first week of March, and Jenny was trying to get the agenda organized. She had less planning time than usual, because softball had started up, and she had made the team as first baseman. Being on the middle school team for two years had fine-tuned her skills, and her hitting was improving each year.

"Devon, if I could get those mean girls from the softball team to join GSA, then I believe we could get anybody to join."

"No kidding! I remember when you and Jaden got suspended in seventh grade for fighting with them. But, I thought it was because they were calling Jaden names, not you."

"Yeah, originally it was about Jaden, but later, after the season started, they were incredibly horrid to me, too. One time after practice, they even tried to jump me. TEAM Club helped me get past all that, and in eighth grade, although they still didn't like me, they didn't outwardly do anything to me any more."

"Well, if you get them to join, you'll be a miracle worker. They're just out-and-out bullies. Maybe you should lower your goal for recruiting at first."

"I don't know. We'll see."

Before Friday night's baseball game, Alice spoke to Brandon privately.

"Are you going to tell your father about Emily? He should probably know about your plans. This is serious."

"Yeah, I know. I'm going to tell him. I'm just not sure when. I'm still kind of pissed at him for leaving and all, and I'm not sure I'm ready to have a heart-to-heart father-son talk, especially when I know what his reaction will be." His tone was acerbic.

"I understand how you feel, honey, but he was already talking about recruiters at the last game."

"I'll take care of it, Mom. Just give me a little time."

Trevor had been being so nice lately. It was more than Jaden could ever have hoped for. Wouldn't you know? It's almost like he knows he has competition. Why couldn't he have always been this nice and attentive? Jaden was getting more and more worried. The group bike ride was coming up next Sunday. He knew he should probably say something to Trevor about just being friends, but he couldn't bring himself to do it. He didn't know what he was afraid of. Why couldn't he just have told Trevor that Nolen could only go riding on Saturday when Trevor had to work.

Trevor had borrowed a bike rack and had a mountain bike strapped to the back of his Mustang when he went to pick up Jaden on Sunday. For once in his life, Jaden had wished church would last longer, because he was so stressed out about the afternoon bike ride. He tried to act normal on the way to Nolen's house, but he couldn't think of anything to talk about. Thankfully, Trevor was full of chatter about the latest happenings in the play that he and his parents were in.

At a pause in Trevor's discourse, Jaden was able to say, "Yeah, you'll have to let me know the dates of the performances." He couldn't come up with anything more.

After parking the car and helping unload Trevor's bike, Jaden knocked on the door. When Nolen and Ward both answered, Trevor did a double-take.

"Wow, I'd forgotten you said there were two of them!" he joked. The twins grinned and introduced themselves.

"This is my... this is Trevor," said Jaden.

"Glad you could come, Trevor," said Nolen. "Are you ready? Let's get going, guys. I want to show Trevor the view from the hill and some trails that'll be new to both of you."

"Have a good ride. I'm going in to watch the NBA game with Dad."

Jaden knew as long as they were riding, there wouldn't be much conversation, and he could relax a little. He still worried about the stops, though. When they got to the top of the big hill, they got off their bikes to drink water and enjoy the view. Jaden's stomach dropped when Nolen stood beside him and proprietarily put a hand on his shoulder. Trevor didn't say anything, but Jaden saw his eyes turn steely as he stared at them. Jaden knew he would hear about it on the way home.

"Isn't this a cool view? When you're down there, you don't realize how many trees there are and how pretty the town is," remarked Nolen.

"Yeah," responded Trevor. "I never expected to see what I'm seeing," he added in a tone that Jaden was well familiar with. Jaden looked away, so neither could see how flushed his face had become.

"Okay, you guys rested enough? I want to show you some switchback turns." The rest of the ride was fun, and thankfully, uneventful, as far as Jaden was concerned. When they returned to the house, Jaden made an excuse about having some homework to do. He wasn't particularly anxious to face Trevor alone in the car, but he didn't want anything else to happen before they left that might give Trevor ammunition.

When they got in the car, Jaden took a deep breath and thought, here it comes.

"You didn't tell me Nolen was gay."

"I didn't?" Jaden feigned innocence. "I thought sure I told you that. It doesn't really matter, though, does it?" He was trying his best to avoid a confrontation. Trevor was quiet for a beat.

"Probably not," he said slowly, "as long as he keeps his distance. "Were you trying to keep stuff from me?"

"No, not at all," Jaden said too fast. His heart was pounding. He was afraid that any minute Trevor would blow. But he didn't. As they got close to Jaden's house, he realized he had been holding his breath, and he slowly expelled it before reaching over to give Trevor a quick peck. When he walked into his house, he was relieved, thinking that maybe Trevor hadn't gotten upset after all.

Trevor, on the other hand, drove home pensively. He wondered how far Nolen and Jaden had already gone and if it might be too late to salvage his relationship. Jaden had certainly not told him he was in a relationship with Nolen. In fact, he had seemed glad to be back together. He decided he would play it by ear for a time, while he figured things out. Now that there was a chance he might lose Jaden, his old feelings for him had magnified.

Chapter 43

In the break room at lunch on Monday, Donnie found himself talking to Justine again.

"How was the game Friday night?" she asked.

"Lake Griffin won again, easily. I think they'll go the distance this year. I'm pretty sure there were some scouts in the stands."

"Pretty sure? Didn't your son know for sure if scouts were there? Don't the coaches let them know?" Donnie sighed and looked down.

"He might have known, but he didn't tell me. You may as well know that Brandon and I aren't that close at the moment. His mother and I are on a trial separation, and he's not happy about it."

"Oh, Donnie, I'm so sorry. If there's anything I can do, let me know. At the very least I can lend a sympathetic ear.

"Thanks."

"Actually, Ed and I are having a rough time in our relationship, too. Nothing as serious as separation, but I'm very upset with how my husband is treating our daughter."

"What's happening, if you don't mind my asking?"

"I'm a little embarrassed to tell you. My daughter is… she thinks she's a…she's hanging out with a lesbian." Donnie's shock registered on his face.

"I knew I shouldn't have said anything. Just forget it. I know you don't want to hear about stuff like that."

"No, no, Justine! It's not like that. Not at all. It's just that there's a similar problem in my house."

"Your daughter?" She was surprised.

"No, it's my son."

"The baseball player?" Now it was Justine's turn to show her shock.

"Hell, no! Not Brandon. It's my younger son, Jaden. It's been going on for several years now, and I haven't been the best father in the world about it."

"I'm sure you've been better about it than my husband is. It's not just him, though. I'm very upset, too. Maybe you can give me some insight.

"Unfortunately, our situation may be far worse. Jaden tried to commit suicide last spring. I don't think I have much insight to give to anyone."

"Oh, my lord! It means that much to these kids? That they will commit suicide if they can't be with someone?"

"No, Justine, it wasn't just that. There was a lot going on. Jaden became very depressed because he was bullied intolerably at school." He paused for a beat. "I'm ashamed to admit it, but I bullied him at home, too."

"Oh, Donnie, I don't know what to say."

"I know. I felt really bad about it last year. I'm afraid my separation might partially be a result of all that. My wife thinks I still don't accept that Jaden is…that way. Maybe it's true. Plus, my daughter is dating a black boy, and I'm not too happy about that either. My wife thinks I need time to sort things out." Not wanting to dwell on his inadequacies, Donnie asked, "What exactly is your husband doing? How is he treating your daughter?"

"He caught her and her 'girlfriend'," she gestured quotation marks, "naked in bed together, and he tried to have the other girl arrested. Since he didn't have proof that they actually did anything, the police couldn't do anything but talk to the girls. Nothing came of that, so, he's gotten a restraining order against the other girl." Donnie had inwardly grimaced when he heard "naked in bed together", but he didn't say anything.

"I guess your daughter's not too happy about the restraining order. What about school?"

"In school they can't be in the same classes or lunch, and away from school, this girl has to stay a hundred yards away from my little girl. And, no, she's not at all happy. In fact, she told her father that she hates him and plans to leave home as soon as she's able."

"How old is your daughter?"

"She'll be sixteen in a few weeks."

"Well, you better make peace soon. I'm not sure how old you have to be to legally leave, but she can get a job at sixteen, and that's a start."

"Oh, my God! Where would she go? She's only a junior in high school. I think she's just making a threat. Surely she wouldn't leave."

But unbeknownst to her mother, Brooke had already been talking to Chelsea about leaving. When her dad had informed her about the restraining order, Brooke knew that any kind of bond they might have had in the past, had permanently severed. Chelsea, in turn, had talked to her parents about Brooke's leaving home, and they had said she was welcome to live with them until she finished high school, if the restraining order were lifted. Before her father had laid down the law, Brooke had spent lots of time at the Harper house, and they had become quite fond of her. In addition, Ed Harper had no love lost for Wayne Gorman. He couldn't believe what he had done to the two girls and what he had tried to do to Chelsea.

Devon wasn't playing any spring sports, so he decided to watch Jenny's softball practice one day. At the end of practice, Jenny ran over to him smiling from ear to ear.

"Devon! What are you doing here?"

"I wanted to see what the team looked like this year, plus I thought I'd walk you home."

"You're so sweet." He reached for her ball bag, and Jenny put her arm around his waist as they started walking.

"Oh, wait, Jen. Which girls were you thinking about asking to join GSA? Maybe we could ask them together."

"Wow. That'd probably be a good idea. To tell the truth, I've been a little nervous about approaching them after I started thinking about their ganging up on me that time. I really don't want to ask all of them. Maybe just Liz and Erica. They seem to be the group leaders. They're over there, standing behind the dugout." Devon grabbed Jenny's hand, gave her a wink, and headed toward the two girls. As they approached, Liz and Erica stopped talking and stared at them with cold eyes.

"What do you want?" asked Liz, gruffly.

"Yeah, what?" said Erica. "You have to have some big guy come with you to talk to us?" Jenny gulped.

"I was just going to invite the two of you to join our new club at school."

Erica retorted, "Oh, you mean that stupid club with all the fags, dykes, and retards? You must be kidding!" Liz didn't say a word, but appeared uncomfortable. "What makes you think we want to have anything to do with people like that? Are *you* recruiting now, Jennifer?"

"Shut up, Erica," said Liz, suddenly. Erica turned to look at Liz with her eyes and mouth wide open. Clearly she was taken aback. "What the freakin' hell, Liz?"

"You don't have to label everybody!" she shot back. Obviously, Erica was unaware that Liz's cousin, Sadie, whom she adored, was born mentally challenged. Sadie was six years younger than Liz and had always looked up to her, and Liz had never allowed anyone make fun of her or call her names. "You're not so smart yourself."

"Well, excu-u-se me," Erica said and walked away with a scowl. Devon and Jenny just looked at each other with raised eyebrows. Liz started speaking without making eye contact.

"I don't know if I want to join your club, but I might come and check it out. When's the next meeting?"

Jenny told her the date and said, "I hope you'll come."

Liz walked away saying, "Maybe."

"What do you think that was all about?" asked Devon.

"I have no idea. It was weird, but maybe she'll show up. Thanks for helping, Devon."

Brandon was spending as much time as he could with Emily. It was tough with baseball practice and games two or three times a week, but he felt himself falling deeper and deeper in love with her. Even though the steroids had made him act like a jerk to her last year, and he regretted that immensely, after having dated someone else he realized how much he really did care for Emily. He was so glad that they were working things out.

Saturday afternoon he said to her, "I think I'm going to tell my dad about us pretty soon. I'm not really ready to talk to him, but he keeps bringing up college recruiters, and he needs to know that I'm not going to play baseball next year."

"Brandon, are you sure that's what you want to do? I know that's been your lifelong goal. I feel like I'm messing up all your plans. I feel terrible about this."

"Don't feel that way! This is way more important than baseball. Being with you and taking care of the baby is my number one priority now. I'll adjust. It'll be worth it." He didn't feel as confident as he sounded, but he did feel Emily was his priority. Changing the subject he said, "Speaking of the baby, who do you think it will look like?"

"I'm actually really nervous about that. If it's dark like Juan Carlos, my mother will freak. She'll think I've slept with every boy around."

"She knows you better than that!"

"In case you haven't noticed, I'm pregnant. She thought she knew me better than that, too."

"At least I have dark hair like Juan Carlos. If the baby has dark hair and light skin, we should be okay. How have you been feeling lately? Any better?"

"Not yet. I'm so tired of getting sick to my stomach. Will it ever end?"

"Mom said it usually gets better after two or three months, but sometimes it can last the whole pregnancy."

"Oh my God, I hope not!"

"Hang in there, baby. We'll make it through this." As Brandon hugged her, Emily buried her face in his chest and thought I hope so.

Chapter 44

Jaden and Nolen had been trying to spend most Saturdays together. One morning, Nolen unexpectedly arrived at Jaden's house, spilling over with excitement.

"Hey, Jaden! Our parents are throwing Ward and me a big sixteenth birthday party! We want you and Jenny and Devon, Brooke and Chelsea to come, and Brandon, too, if he wants to be there."

"Cool!"

"Oh, and what do you think about Trevor coming? I've only met him that one time, but he seems like a good guy." Jaden looked down and was slow to reply.

"I'm not sure," he finally said. "He has a lot going on with theater and work. He may not have time."

"You sort of sound like you don't really want him to come…"

"It's not that, Nolen. It's just that I like you a lot."

"Okay, yeah…I like you a lot, too."

"Well, but, I don't know how to say it, but, here goes. Trevor and I used to be in a relationship, but we broke up before Christmas."

"Yeah, I kind of wondered about that. But you get along, right? I mean you had fun together when we went riding."

"Yeah, but Trevor's kind of possessive about me. There was some tension on the bike ride, even though it was fun."

"Why would he be possessive? I don't understand."

"Well, Trevor sort of thinks we're still together. But, we're not!" he said emphatically. "Actually, I'd like to see how things might go with you and me, that is, if you would go out with me."

"I'd love that! I wasn't sure how you felt about me. But, you need to make it clear to him that that you guys are over. Maybe we should hold off on inviting him to the party 'til you talk to him."

"Yeah, that's probably best, and, Nolen, I *will* make it clear that we're not together anymore." Jaden spoke with determination, but was uneasy about the outcome. Changing the subject, Jaden asked, "What are we going to do at the party?"

"We'll just hang out and eat and have cake, mostly, but my dad says he has a big surprise for Ward and me."

"Wonder what it is?"

"I don't know. We've been trying to figure it out ever since he told us. It's bound to be fun, though, if my dad planned it." The two friends spent the rest of the morning with Nolen showing Jaden how to use his camera and how to set up a good shot.

When Nolen left, Jaden found Jenny and told her about the party. She immediately texted Devon, who was glad to be included.

When Jaden told Brandon about it, Brandon asked, "Do you think Emily could go, too? I know we'd both want to go."

"I'm sure that would be okay. I'll ask Nolen, though."

Tuesday in P.E. Jaden told Trevor he had something to talk to him about, and asked if he could stop by his house after work that night.

"Sure, but what's up? You look so serious," Trevor asked apprehensively.

"I don't want to talk about anything here at school where we have no privacy." Jaden was in no hurry to start the conversation, but he had put the ball in motion.

Chapter 45

Trevor's knock on the door at 6:15 was answered by Alice, who greeted him with a big smile.

"Hi, Trevor, are you hungry? We'll be sitting down to eat in about twenty minutes." Jaden who had trailed his mom to the door shook his head almost imperceptibly.

Seeing that, Trevor replied, "No, Mrs. Hansen, thank you. I'm just getting off work and need to get home. I just wanted to see Jaden for a minute." Alice smiled and headed back to the kitchen.

"Let's go to my room," Jaden suggested. Trevor noticed Jaden was having trouble making eye contact.

"Jaden, what's this all about? I'm getting a bad vibe about it."

"It's not bad, Trev. It's just that, I don't know how to say it. I think, uh, that maybe we should just be friends for a while." There, he said it. It was out in the open. Trevor's jaw dropped.

"Have I done something wrong? I told you how sorry I was for acting like an idiot. Oh, wait. I know. It's Nolen, isn't it? Just tell me the truth, Jaden. Are you with him now?"

"No, I'm not with Nolen. But, I do like him a lot, and I pretty sure he likes me. I just want to be able to do things with him and not feel like I'm being unfaithful to you. I just want to see what happens." Trevor's first impulse had been to get very angry and storm out of the house.

"I can't believe you're doing this! We've been through so much together!"

"You started it! You smoked pot! You went out with Brian! And, even though you were always so moody, I still hung in there, Trevor! But, you cheated on me and broke my heart."

"We just planned to spend the evening together, Jaden! It wasn't a date. Nothing really happened with Brian and me!"

"Do you expect me to believe that? People saw you at the lake."

But as Trevor listened and Jaden's words sank in, he knew when he had come on to Brian, it was because his relationship with Jaden was getting old. It had been great the first year, but they had kind of outgrown each other without realizing it. Jaden wasn't in theater anymore, so they didn't have that tie. They were just growing apart. It was very sad, but not devastating.

"I guess maybe you're right, Jaden. I know we weren't getting along very well for a quite a while. But this really hurts! I'm gonna go. See you." Trevor's eyes filled with tears, and he took a deep breath. As he walked out, Jaden felt a flush of relief tinged by a wave of melancholy. It had been good, and it wasn't easy to break up with your "first".

They couldn't make eye contact the next day in P.E., but time did its thing, and conversation became less stilted as the week wore on. By the end of the second week, they were talking almost like friends again.

"I saw Ricardo in the hall the other day," Trevor offered. "I guess I never did really get to know him before. We talked for a while, and I think he's really nice." Jaden felt a pang of remorse. Even though he wanted to move forward with Nolen, Trevor had been his first love, and it was hard to let go.

"You always thought something was going on with us, but it wasn't. He's just a nice guy."

"Yeah, he is. And cute! I'm picking him up on Saturday, and we're going to hang out."

"Cool!" said Jaden, but he felt like Trevor was getting over him way too quickly. Jealousy threatened to take over until he thought of Nolen. He once again realized that breaking up had been the right thing to do and immediately felt better.

The Saturday of the party was approaching, and Nolen and Ward were getting more excited. Not only would they be turning sixteen and getting their driver's licenses, but they were greatly intrigued by the surprise promised by their dad. With Jaden's okay, Nolen had decided to invite Trevor and Ricardo, too. Brandon and Emily were both expected to be there. Nolen hadn't invited anyone from his school, because he had never been very close to the kids there. Ever since he had started being friends with Jaden, he had seemed to bond with Jaden's group. Ward had only invited two people, his best friend and his girlfriend, Val.

All the guests had been told to arrive before noon and had started showing up around 11:00. Mrs. Crenshaw had laid out a spread of sandwiches, chips, potato salad, and a cooler with drinks. She told them to go ahead and help themselves, because at 12:30, the boys' dad was to begin his surprise. By the time they finished eating, Mr. Crenshaw had arrived in a fifteen-passenger van. They all loaded up and headed out. Mr. Crenshaw would give them no idea of where they were going, and they made guess after guess trying to get him to tell. After about thirty minutes, he pulled off the main road onto a dirt road that led back to a huge pasture. At least it looked like a pasture, but the group was astounded to see two airplanes sitting on the grass. One was a normal looking small aircraft, but the other was a shiny yellow bi-plane with a huge radial engine on the front. In the back, the aircraft leaned on a small tail-wheel. It only had two seats, and they were one behind the other with an open canopy.

"Dad!" exclaimed Ward. "I've always wanted to ride in a Stearman! Are we going up? Is this the surprise?"

Nolen exclaimed, "Me, too!" He looked at Jaden. "Dad knows I've always liked WWII aircraft. I have lots of pictures of them. This kind was used as a military trainer for the Air Force and Navy during the second world war." Mr. Crenshaw, who was a private pilot, smiled widely.

"Yes, boys, these two planes belong to my flying club friends, and they've agreed to take you all up for a ride. The other plane is a Cherokee Six, so five of you can ride in it at the same time. If you want to go up in the Stearman, you will have to go one at a time." The Crenshaw twins rushed their dad and enveloped him in a bear hug. "And none of you have to worry about what your parents will say. I've spoken to all of them, and every one gave their permission for you to go up."

"Where's the airport?" Jenny asked naively.

"You're standing on it, young lady," replied Mr. Crenshaw, laughing. "This is a grass runway. It looks different, but it works the same way." At that point all the kids ran over to examine the two airplanes. Most of them had never flown on any airplane, and their eyes were wide, but Ricardo was blown away. He slowly walked around the Stearman, lightly rubbing his hand on the fuselage. He was clearly in awe of such a beautiful machine.

"What do you think, Ricardo?" asked Nolen. "Isn't she a beaut?" Suddenly aware that the others were watching him, Ricardo reddened and looked down.

"My papa, he has picture of this. Back in Texas he ride on one, just one time. His boss, he spray the field in one. He take my papa up. He always say it was chance of the lifetime."

Mr. Crenshaw said, "Well, Ricardo, your dad was thrilled when he found out you were going to ride in one, too." Ricardo's eyes shone with gratitude and excitement. Except for the Crenshaw twins and Ricardo, the others all wanted to ride in the Cherokee. While they were deciding who would ride first, a car drove up and two men got out and walked over.

"I can't tell you guys how much I appreciate your giving the kids rides today," said Mr. Crenshaw, as he shook hands with the men.

"It's our pleasure, Jim. You never can tell when you might spark the interest of some future aviator," replied Jerry, one of the pilots.

Bill, the other pilot, agreed and said, "It's just as much fun for us to take them up, as it is for them to go. I love to fly every opportunity I get. Shall we get started? I'm flying the Cherokee. Who wants to go first?" It was decided that Trevor, Brandon, Emily, Jenny, and Devon would go. Jaden wanted to watch Nolen fly in the Stearman, so he opted to wait.

Jim said, "Okay, boys, who's first?"

"You go first, Ward. I want to watch you down here with Jaden." Ward enthusiastically jumped into the front seat of the airplane. He was thrilled when Jim gave him a leather helmet with a headset built in, so he and Jim could talk during the flight. When Jim fired up that radial engine, the ones on the ground covered their ears. After the big airplane taxied over to the departure end of the runway, Jim increased the RPMs and checked out the mags and control surfaces. Finally, it started rolling down the runway, slowly, then, speeding up until it finally lifted off like a lumbering giant.

"Wow! That was awesome," observed Nolen. "I can't wait to go up!" The other plane had loaded as soon as the Stearman took off, and it, too, was now taxiing to the end of the runway. They had a full load of passengers, but the Cherokee still took off with a shorter roll than the Stearman had. The ones on the ground were excitedly waiting their own turns, and they watched each of the airplanes until they were out of sight. Before long, though, they saw the Stearman approaching from the direction it had taken off, then passing over their heads, and finally turning back toward them as it descended. When it finished its landing roll, it spun around and taxied back toward the expectant group. Nolen was next, and as he bounded aboard the plane, Ward was already talking non-stop about the thrill of flying.

"We've ridden with Dad before, but it's not at all the same as having the wind blow in your face. You can hold your arms outside the plane, too. It's hard to do that when your turning, because of the G forces, Jim said. When we were on the other side of town, Jim did some forty-five degree turns, and that's when I could hardly lift my arm off the side of the plane. You're going to love it, Ricardo." Ricardo looked nervous as Ward was talking, but he nodded his head forcefully.

The Stearman was out of sight again, and the Cherokee was a dot in the distance. As it approached, they noticed it did the same thing that the Stearman had done. It passed over them, then, turned to come back to land. The kids tumbled out and headed toward the others. Emily was looking a little green.

Chelsea asked, "Emily, are you all right? Emily smiled ruefully and admitted that she had thrown up a little while they were up there.

"It was okay, though. There was a barf bag in the seat pocket," explained practical Jenny. "No harm done." She continued. "Can you believe we could see our house almost as soon as we climbed to 1500 feet? We went all over town and over the lake. The cars looked pretty small, and we saw a boat on the lake, too. I could even see a tiny wake behind it. That was so much fun!" Devon remained quiet. He, too, had gotten a little sick, but had fought it off and was trying not to let anyone know.

It was finally Jaden and the others' turn, and after the last group loaded in the Cherokee and took off, the Stearman was headed in with its second passenger. As it landed, Ricardo gulped and a wave of fear crossed his face. Trevor went over and nudged him.

"You can do this, buddy. You're gonna love it!" Ricardo gathered his nerve and climbed up into the big plane.

When both planes had landed for the last time and all the passengers had unloaded, everyone crowded around the two pilots telling them how much fun it had been and how much they had appreciated the flights. Ricardo was beaming, but didn't say much. Brandon excitedly spoke to everyone.

"I know what I want to do with my life now. I want to be a pilot! I got to sit in the co-pilot seat, and Bill let me handle the controls." He grinned at Bill. "He showed me how to use the rudders and yoke at the same time to turn the airplane. I want to take flying lessons as soon as I figure out a way to afford it! Bill even said he would take me up from time to time until I can start lessons." They said their good-byes to the pilots and headed back to the Crenshaw house for ice cream and cake.

On the way back to the house everyone was interrupting each other to tell what exciting thing they had seen on the ground or had gotten to do in the cockpit. Each had his own version that seemingly was a little better than anyone else's. After a few minutes, Brandon quit talking and just listened. He was contemplating what it might be like to be a professional pilot. Something to really think about.

"This cake is delicious," said Jaden. "Plus, I think this is probably the best birthday party I've ever been to. It's like we all got presents, not just the birthday boys!"

"I know," added Chelsea. "Who knew going up in a little airplane would be so much fun?"

"It's been great," chimed in Brooke. Then, in a low voice that only Chelsea could hear, said, "It's worth whatever trouble I get into if my parents find out that you were here, too." She suddenly looked grim. The others continued enjoying cake and chatting, while Chelsea and Brooke stepped back from the group a little in order to talk.

"When are you going to talk to your parents about that emancipation thing?" asked Chelsea. "It'll be so great if you can live at my house!"

"I guess I can go ahead and tell them, even before I turn sixteen. You know, sort of prepare them for what's coming. That was really cool of your dad to set me up with that lawyer, Blair Lockett. She gave me some really good advice. I need to get started writing that paper on why I need to be free and away from my parents."

While Brooke and Chelsea were talking, Nolen grabbed Jaden's hand and dragged him into his bedroom.

"I know it's my birthday," he said. "But I have something for you, too." He went to his desk and came back with a framed picture of Jaden standing on the trail with the view at the top of the hill behind him. Nolen had signed the photograph and put the date of their first outing together on it. Seeing the picture helped put Jaden's conflicted emotions about Trevor to rest. Impulsively, he embraced Nolen, and they shared their first kiss.

Chapter 46

On Monday Donnie had just started eating his sandwich in the breakroom when Justine walked in looking distraught.

"What's the matter?" he asked. His brows furrowed with concern.

"It's Brooke. Her dad got into another confrontation with her in her bedroom this past weekend. Wayne actually slapped her in the face. I heard it and raced in there. His eyes looked wild, and I was afraid he was going to hit her again, so I stepped in between them. In that moment he seemed to get himself together again and told her she was grounded to her room until further notice. He walked out and slammed her door. She opened it and yelled after him, 'It doesn't matter what you try to do to me. I'm petitioning for emancipation as soon as I turn sixteen, and you can't stop me!' Wayne didn't even seem to care, but I begged her to reconsider. She wouldn't even talk to me. Her face had turned red where he had slapped her, and she had started crying." Justine's words were near panic, almost shrill.

"Whoa, now. Calm down. What exactly does emancipation mean?"

"It means she can legally move out and not be under our care and direction anymore," she wailed.

"Hold on, Justine. Where would she live? How could she support herself? Would she keep going to school? I can't believe she could get a legal order unless all those questions were answered."

"Donnie, she's already talked to a lawyer! She told her if she had a job and could support herself, she would have a good chance of its being granted."

"What did your husband say about it after he calmed down?"

"Well, he never really did calm down. He's infuriated. One minute he says he'll fight her all the way, and the next, he says to let her do it. He says she'll fall flat on her face and be begging to come back home. I don't know what's going to happen. I just don't want to lose my baby."

Donnie spent the rest of the day worrying and comparing Justine's dilemma with his own family's problems. He felt that, in a way, he had lost all his children in the separation. But, at least he saw them on a regular basis, and pretty soon Brandon would be in college and things were bound to get better. He would be out of the house and able to think for himself. Donnie was sure that he and Brandon would become close again.

"Mom, I think I may tell Dad about Emily pretty soon, and that I'm going to go to community college part-time and won't be playing baseball. He's all about the baseball recruiters that come to our games, and it wouldn't surprise me if he tried to talk to one of them. He needs to know what's going on." Alice was very pleased about his statement, although she didn't let on. She was still hoping that Donnie might talk some sense into Brandon about college. There was too much at stake concerning his future to just give up on the idea.

"Honey, I think that's probably the right thing to do. He's bound to find out eventually, anyway, so it might as well be now."

"Hard as it is to believe, we're getting down to the end of the season. The tournament is coming up in a few weeks." He turned his head in order to keep his mom from seeing the disappointment that suddenly clouded his face, because he knew that too soon he would be playing baseball for the last time.

Emily was more than seven months along, give or take, and was beginning to show more than a little. She was extremely embarrassed about it and had been wearing looser clothes that would hide it as long as possible.

"Brandon, I'm not going to be able to hide it much longer. Big sweaters and bulky clothes only do so much, plus, it's getting warmer every day." Her dismay was apparent to Brandon, and he struggled to find the right words to say.

"Emily, you are the most beautiful girl I have ever met, and your being pregnant doesn't change that one bit!" She smiled at him.

"I'm so glad you feel that way. But, I think people are already whispering behind my back. Why can't I be like those other girls who get pregnant and act like it's the most natural thing in the world?"

"It is the most natural thing in the world. But I'm sure your feelings come from your mother and how you were raised." He was quiet for a beat.

"Do you want to go ahead and get married now? Then your mother would be fine, and who cares what those other people think?"

"Oh, Brandon, you're so sweet. I'm not sure I want to have a shotgun wedding, though, just to satisfy my mother."

"It wouldn't be a shotgun wedding!" Brandon insisted. "I love you more than I ever could have imagined loving anyone. You're the first thing I think of in the morning and the last thing at night. I adore you, and I want to be the father of your baby for the sole reason that it will be part of you. I can't get enough of you." He pulled her into a long embrace.

"Hey, I think I felt the baby kick me through your stomach," Brandon grinned.

"He really has been kicking a lot lately. I'm sure it'll be a boy, and he'll play soccer or football." Then she grimaced, remembering that soccer was Juan Carlos' favorite sport. Brandon kissed her tenderly and told her everything would be all right.

Chapter 47

Mr. Anthony and Jenny had gotten together to plan the next GSA meeting. Now that it was about to start, Jenny wondered if Liz would actually show up. As she surveyed the students coming into the auditorium, she didn't spot her right away. But there she was in the back of the room on the left side, sitting with her arms crossed in front of her and not talking with anyone. Jenny hoped her mind wouldn't be as closed as her posture seemed to suggest.

Jenny welcomed everyone, then, asked by a show of hands, how many people had been able to get someone else to come to the meeting today. Hands flew up in various parts of the audience, and Jenny believed she counted around eight.

"Not bad, for a first effort," she said. "Would anyone care to let the group know what reasons people gave for not coming?"

Hannah said, "Some people said they didn't want to be part of, and I'll rephrase what they said, a group of people like us. But, several said they didn't want to have to have their parents sign a permission slip to join." Others nodded or spoke agreement.

A boy stood up and said, "I'm one of those that doesn't want to have my parents sign, but I decided I would at least come to this meeting. I'd really like to be a part of a group that accepts everyone and doesn't make fun of anybody. It gets old having people talk behind your back all the time. But I could never let my parents know that I feel like I'm not like other kids and that they make fun of me. They've spent my entire life forcing me into groups that I have no interest in and don't feel comfortable in either. I've always had to hide how I really feel. When all that stuff was in the paper about this club, my parents told me how glad they were that I was normal, and they didn't have to worry about stuff like this."

Jenny replied, "It's awful when our parents think we're not normal. It's also horrible that the school board feels so negative about our club." She did a double take when she saw Liz stand up to speak.

"This is my first meeting, and I'm not so sure I agree with everything everyone is saying. I've never let anyone push me around or make fun of me, so I don't feel like I need this club." Jenny, with raised eyebrows, looked at Devon, who just smiled back at her. "But my little cousin has had that kind of problem, and I'm willing to look into a club that might prevent stuff like that from happening to her." There was a smattering of applause. She asked, "What's your plan for this club?" Devon decided to answer her.

"Our first plan of action is to try to get lots of people to take a look at the club like you have. Then if we can get them to come to a meeting, meet people, and start doing fun things with us, I'm sure their whole attitude will change. We're going to have a party next month and we want people like you, and anybody else you know, to come and have a good time."

"I guess I could do that. I'm sure I could get some others to come, too." Everyone agreed to do a big push to get people to come to the party. They began talking amongst themselves about fun party ideas. Liz was mingling and talking with others as they left the meeting.

"Can you believe Liz spoke up like that?" Jenny asked Devon as they were leaving. "She sounds like she actually could be a help."

"Jenny, we've been looking at her the same way other people look at Jaden. We judged her without finding out what kind of person she really is, just like people judge Jaden. If everybody always picked on her cousin, it might have made her grow up mean."

"How did I ever find such a smart boyfriend? I'm so lucky to have you in my life. I love you, Devon Mulder."

Over the next few days Justine seemed more and more upset at work. One day she rushed into the break-room to give Donnie some news.

"Brooke's been working a month at the YMCA where that friend of hers, Trevor, works. She told us she was saving all her money so she could move out. When she said that, Wayne slapped her again."

"Oh, Justine! That's terrible! Has he always been so violent?"

"Not for a long time. When he was younger he had anger management issues, but in the military they made him see a psychologist, and he got it under control. This thing with Brooke seems to be a trigger, though. He can't seem to reign it in."

"Are you and your husband really going to let her move out and burn bridges, rather than just let her hang out with whoever she wants? Somehow, that just doesn't make sense."

"I don't know that either of us has a grip on what we're doing. I'm mostly concerned that if she moved out, she'd be able to see Chelsea any time she wants. That girl's the cause of all of this. But Wayne won't even talk about it with me. I don't want to lose my daughter, but he might be right to stand firm on this."

"Justine, are you listening to yourself? You need to do whatever it takes to get your husband to back down so that you don't lose your daughter." Justine merely shrugged helplessly and said nothing.

Brandon had made his mind up to talk to his dad after Friday night's game. In the past they had almost always gone out after the game, but he had refused over and over since his dad had left home. This time he would accept. He had lots to talk about.

As usual, Donnie was already in the stands when the rest of the Hansen family arrived. Before the game started, Donnie had noticed a couple of men wearing jackets that said "State" talking to the head coach and then heading to the scorer's box with clipboards. He knew they had to be scouts, and he smiled in anticipation. The match-up wasn't disappointing. Brandon had a heck of a game with no errors. He hit the opposing pitcher like he owned him and finished with three hits, a walk and no errors. Even at that, the game was close and finished four to three with the Mustangs on top.

"Hey, Dad, I'd like to go get something to eat tonight," said Brandon. Donnie felt great hearing that. He talked all the way to the restaurant about how well Brandon had done and what a great future he had. Brandon was uncomfortably quiet. After they had gotten situated at their booth and ordered, he impatiently waited for his dad to stop enthusing about the game so that he could get a word in. Finally, he interrupted.

"Dad, I have something to talk to you about." The seriousness of his tone made Donnie stop what he was doing and stare. He leaned back in the booth and waited. "I'm going to marry Emily at the end of the month. She's pregnant, and I love her very much." Donnie was stunned. He couldn't speak for a minute and when he finally did, he stuttered.

"Wha-what? Pregnant? When? How? Brandon, how could you have been so careless?"

"I'm not the father, but I want to marry her and help her raise the baby."

"You're not the father? Then, what about baseball? What about college? I saw scouts in the stands tonight, and I know they had their eyes on you! Have you lost your mind? Does your mother know?"

"Mom knows. I've been trying to wait for the right time to tell you."

"Son, there is no right time to tell me that you're scrapping all your plans for college and a future. Not only could you get a baseball scholarship, but who knows? Maybe the pros would pick you up. This has been our dream, ever since you were seven years old!"

"I'm sorry to ruin *your* dream, Dad," he said sarcastically, "but this is *my* life. I love Emily! I'd do anything for her."

"Baseball is all you've ever talked about, thought about. At one point the only reason you agreed to go to college was so that you could play baseball. We moved you to third base in high school so you could concentrate and get great at one position. We've planned for this your whole life, Brandon! And you're not even the father? Are you crazy?"

"You know, I sort of thought you might understand, Dad. But, wrong again. You really don't know me, do you? You never understood Jaden, and you were always on his back. I guess the only reason I thought you ever understood me was because we had the same interests. But, you never change, do you? If it's not your way, then what we think doesn't matter." Brandon got up, left the booth, and left his dad sitting there stunned and wondering how everything could have gone so wrong.

Chapter 48

Brandon and Emily decided to announce their engagement to everyone, but not actually get married until the end of May. They figured if they announced the upcoming wedding, it wouldn't matter that she was showing. When they told Emily's mother, she snorted her disapproval, but shrugged her shoulders, so they spread the word. Jaden and Jenny couldn't believe Brandon was actually going to get married, but they were both all for whatever would make him happy. They remembered how bad it had been for him when he and Emily had broken up.

Donnie just shook his head when he heard that the date was set. After Brandon's announcement that awful night, he felt like everything had changed. He had no say-so with his kids, and his wife didn't want him. He knew that he had drifted so far from his former life that he wasn't sure he was the same person anymore. He realized, though, that the person he was now was just going through the motions and not really living.

Alice wasn't sure what to think about the marriage. Of course she wanted her son's wedding to be a big deal, but Brandon and Emily were just going to have a notary pronounce the vows with only the mothers there. That would be about as far from a big deal as she could imagine, but, under the circumstances, a big deal would be inappropriate anyway.

Emily's friends at school were very supportive and were planning baby showers for her. After the engagement had been announced, Emily had decided that what the other girls thought didn't matter any more. Once she relaxed, she found that they were actually friendly, asking about her due date and if she knew the sex of the baby.

Brandon's friends were typical high school boys. They made teasing comments about the action he must have been getting, and how he would have perpetual access now. Brandon felt awkward, but tried to rib good-naturedly back with them. His best friend, Dan, was the only one who cast any doubts on the whole thing. He knew the history of Brandon and Emily's former breakup, as well as having made the assumption that Emily had been intimate with Juan Carlos.

"Dude, you need to be honest with yourself. You know it's possible Juan Carlos is the father. Are you sure you would want to raise someone else's kid?" Brandon looked troubled. Should he confide in Dan about everything? Dan was his best friend and had kept him out of trouble several times. He decided it would be the right thing to do.

"I know for a fact that he's the father, Dan. Emily and I haven't...you know, we haven't done anything since we've been back together. I don't care if he is. I love her."

"Wow. That's a big deal, bro. Are you fully aware of what you're up against? What if Juan Carlos comes in and tries to make trouble? What if he figures out it's his kid and wants to do something about it? He does have rights, you know."

"I hadn't really thought about that part. I guess we'd figure something out."

"You know it's gonna look like him. You can't hide Hispanic genes."

"I don't know, Dan. I hope it looks enough like me not to raise suspicions, but I just don't know." Brandon left Dan feeling very unsettled.

Now that more time had passed, Trevor seemed to be making efforts to be better friends with Jaden. They weren't hanging out much, but the few times the whole group got together, he was especially nice. Jaden worried a little, because he and Nolen were getting closer, and he didn't want Trevor to think that he could win him back, but at the same time, he wasn't totally sure he wanted to lose Trevor altogether. He tried to think of a non-confrontational way to talk to him about it.

"Trevor, how's your life-guarding going? You sure are working a lot of hours every week."

"It's going good. It's my choice to work all those hours, because I'm saving money to get a really good system in my car. Plus, it never hurts to have some extra cash in case you might want to buy a special present for someone." Jaden gulped, but kept going.

"Have you met anyone special at the Y, or are you and Ricardo getting serious?"

"As a matter of fact, I've wanted to talk to you about that. Ever since that day we went up in the airplane, Ricardo and I have been seeing each other. He's such a cool guy, and he's so hot!" He smiled at his play on words. "You remember how jealous I was when I thought you two were interested in each other. Well, we started doing a lot of stuff together, and one thing led to another, if you know what I mean!" A churning feeling in the pit of his stomach made Jaden realized he had mixed feelings. This couldn't be better, as far as Trevor's being with Ricardo, but he still felt a little funny when he thought of Trevor and Ricardo together. Surely he wasn't jealous.

"Wow, that's great, Trev," he said somewhat uneasily. "You couldn't find a nicer guy. I'm happy for you both. You need to bring him whenever we all do stuff. Plus, I want you to get to know Nolen better, too. He's an awesome photographer, a great biker, and just fun to be with." Once again, thinking of Nolen made him feel better.

At his parents' house, Donnie had settled into the routine of coming home, reading the paper, eating dinner, and going to bed. They only place he ever went was to Brandon's baseball games and Jenny's softball games, when they weren't too early. And anyway, the joy of going to baseball games had changed drastically since the conversation with the son. Baseball season was almost over, in any case. One Saturday, his dad, Donald, Sr. decided to approach Donnie.

"I've noticed you sinking lower and lower into yourself, son. I realize that things aren't hunky-dory with Alice, but I don't see you over there try-ing to make things right. Don't you think you should be talking to her and working things out? I know you still love her, and you must miss the kids like crazy."

"Dad, I don't even know what I'm doing anymore. My kids think I don't care about them, and Alice seems like she's moved on past me, what with her college class, ladies groups, and school board meetings. And, now, Brandon isn't even going to college to play baseball! Instead, he's marrying a pregnant girl whose baby isn't even his."

"Quit your belly-aching, son. Life is not an easy ride. You're a grown man with a family to take care of. Didn't I always teach you not to give up? To go hard after something that you want bad enough? I know you want your family. I know you love your kids. Try to think outside the box. Instead of crying to your mother and me about everything that's gone wrong for you, try to think of what you can do to help your family with *their* problems. They need you. Things didn't go so well when you tried to change all of them, so why don't you try to change yourself, instead?" Donnie sat stunned as his dad's words sank in. I have been a fool, he thought. I miss Alice so much, and I do love the kids. How could I have been so hardheaded?

"What do you think I should do, Dad? I do want to make things right."

"You might try to go home where you belong and beg everyone's forgiveness, for a start. Then, talk to Jaden. I know you have a hard time with his being gay, but what's that got to do with you? You didn't make him gay, and you can't change him from being gay. He needs your love and support. Life is hard enough in the outside world. He needs both his parents. And, Jenny, bless her heart. When Devon was just Jaden's friend, you thought he was great. But now that he's Jenny's boyfriend, color suddenly matters. You shouldn't care if he's bright blue as long as he's a good person and makes Jenny happy. Jeez! As far as Brandon goes, don't give him grief about what must have been an incredibly hard decision for him to make. You know how he loves baseball! Give him credit for being so devoted to Emily. Maybe you can think of some way that he could still go to college, and maybe still play baseball, even with the new obligations. Did that even enter your mind, son?"

Chapter 49

Devon had become the softball team's biggest fan. He attended every game, and his cheering was very noticeable in the primarily small crowds. He cheered for Jenny, but he also cheered for Liz and her friends. At the GSA meeting he had made up his mind to figure out how to crack Liz's hard, exterior shell, because he appreciated the fact that she was giving the club a chance. He knew that she had taken an emotional risk to show up at the club where her last year's nemesis was president. With that in mind, he just started yelling for her at bat. The first time, she stepped out of the box and looked into the stands, trying to figure out who it was. The second time the trace of a smile appeared on her face. When she heard Devon cheering for her friends as well, she softened and went over to Jenny when she was in the on-deck circle and gave her an encouraging slap on the shoulders.

"Come on, Jenny. Get a hit up there!" Jenny's eyes widened, and then glowed with pleasure. When the game was over, Jenny spoke of her astonishment to Devon.

He replied, "You know, I think deep down all of us want the same thing. We want to be treated with respect. I think always trying to defend her cousin from others' ridicule made Liz distrustful of everyone. Her eyes seem to be opening." Jenny and Devon hugged with happiness.

It was the end of April, and both the softball and baseball seasons were winding down. Before the district tournament final baseball game, Donnie had called Alice and asked if he could take the whole family, including Devon, out to eat after the game. He said he had something important to talk to everyone about. Alice told him she would make the arrangements. He had done some deep thinking and had come up with, what he thought, was a workable plan.

The Lake Griffin Mustangs had played a phenomenal season and were touted to be district winners and to go to the state tournament. Scouts were in the stands, but not allowed to speak to any players until the season was over. For one of the teams that night, the season would end. The seniors on the Mustangs did not want it to be them. They played their hearts out and came out on top once again! After the game Brandon was among the most celebratory. Unlike a lot of the players, he had known if they didn't win, it would be his last baseball game forever. He hugged every player, then, joined the team as they dumped the Gatorade cooler on Coach Cushing. As the coach dismissed them, the team spilled up into the stands, hugging friends, family, and girlfriends. Donnie watched and enjoyed every moment of his son's triumph. He remembered how he had felt when his team in high school had been headed to state tournament. Even though he wouldn't deny his son all the excitement and fanfare, he was still a little impatient, because he felt he had something really mind-boggling to share.

The moment finally came when they all piled into the vehicles and headed to the diner. As soon as they were seated and had ordered, Donnie asked for everyone's attention. As everyone was looking at him expectantly, Brandon's phone rang.

"Brandon, you've got to come to the hospital!" It was Emily's mother. "Emily's had a severe headache all day. When she got a bad pain in her stomach and starting throwing up, I got really scared. I called the doctor who told me to call an ambulance. He met us at the hospital and after examining Emily, he said she has preeclampsia and told us the baby's starting to be in distress. They're going to induce labor. You better get here! I knew nothing good could come of this whole fiasco. This is what you and Emily get for having premarital sex. Now we'll all pay, Brandon. We'll all pay." The line clicked dead. Brandon felt his face go clammy.

"Honey, what's wrong?" asked Alice.

"That was Mrs. Davidson, Emily's mother. I've got to go to the hospital! Emily's in trouble, and they're going to induce labor." Donnie stood up and spoke forcefully.

"We'll go with you, son. I don't want you waiting alone. You and Emily will need our support." Brandon looked stunned at his dad's words for a second, then, eyes filled with tears of appreciation, he headed for the door.

When the group arrived at the hospital, they found Emily's mother, alone in the waiting room, looking both stricken and angry.

"What's happened? Where's Emily?" Brandon practically shouted.

"Well, Brandon, now it's worse." Her tone was accusatory. "The baby's heartbeat became faint, and they're doing an emergency C-section. She's in surgery now." She sat down and stared at the floor. Alice went over and put her arm around her shoulders, trying to comfort her, in spite of her obvious hostility toward Brandon. Brandon, with tears in his eyes, walked out of the room. He didn't want to cry like a baby in front of his whole family. Donnie followed him.

"Brandon, wait. I want to talk to you."

"I don't need to hear it, Dad. I know you're against Emily and me getting married, but I have too much on my mind to talk about it right now. What if something happens to Emily and the baby? They're all I care about."

"I know you're scared, son. I just want you to know that I'm here for you. I've been so wrong, and I'll do whatever I can for you. We can talk about all that later. In the meantime, remember that Emily is young and healthy, and the doctors are good here. She and the baby will come out of this just fine." No longer trying to hide his tears, Brandon turned toward his dad, and it suddenly felt so good to have his dad's comforting arms around him as they hugged for a long time.

The air in the waiting room was saturated with tension. The silence allowed the ticking of the clock to be heard as it counted off second after second, minute after minute. Would the waiting never end? Alice tried to maintain an air of calm for Emily's mother, but she was nervous and had no idea how it would all turn out. Jenny and Devon had been quietly gripping each other's hands the whole time they had been waiting. Jenny finally spoke in a low voice.

"This is so weird. It seems like we just found out Brandon and Emily were getting married, and now, they're going to have a baby any minute. I sure hope this turns out okay."

"I know, Jen. I hope nothing like this happens to us, you know, if we get married some day. I know it's way too soon to think about that, but I love you so much." Jenny's eyes shone with happy tears as she looked at Devon's face.

"I love you, too."

"Enough of this mush," said Jaden. He managed a smile. "We need to focus our energy on Emily and the baby. I'm also worried about Brandon. I know he's upset. He and Dad have been gone a long time." Finally, at that very moment, Brandon and Donnie burst through the door, grinning from ear to ear, followed by the doctor.

"The doctor just told us that Emily and the baby are doing fine!" said a jubilant Brandon. The obstetrician sat down beside Emily's mother and told her that her daughter was fine and the baby was doing well in spite of being born prematurely.

"Tell us, Brandon! Is it a boy or a girl?" Jenny couldn't hold back.

"It's a girl, and I can't wait to see her!" Brandon said proudly, just as if she were his own flesh and blood.

The doctor, addressing the whole excited group, said that Emily would be out of the recovery room shortly and that family could visit for a few minutes, two at a time. He said that because the baby was premature, she would have to spend most of her first day in the NICU for precautionary observation, but would be brought into Emily's room to nurse every few hours.

As the doctor got up to leave, he said, " A nurse will be in to tell you when Emily and the baby are ready for visitors, but remember, just a few minutes each."

Emily's mother looked at Donnie and Alice and said, "Brandon and I will go first then, you can go meet your granddaughter." Donnie and Alice exchanged an uneasy glance. How would this woman feel if she knew it was not Brandon's baby?

After fitfully waiting for what seemed like forever, the family was told Emily was ready for brief visits. When Mrs. Davidson and Brandon got to her room, Brandon rushed to Emily's side and gave her a tender kiss on the cheek. Then he looked at the tiny bundle nursing at her breast.

"Oh, oh, my God! Oh, Emily! Look at her. She's so beautiful," he said. Emily's mother was staring coldly. Her voice had a hard edge.

"Look at all the hair that child has. And her skin is so dark. I guess that will lighten up in a few days, right? I've heard that sometimes the trauma of birth affects their skin. Is that what it is, Emily? Birth trauma?" She stared at Emily. Brandon and Emily saw confusion on her face. Brandon thought, this is wrong. I need to step up and be a man and a father. No one, not even her mother, should treat my Emily this way. He decided to speak up.

"Mrs. Davidson, there's something..." Emily quickly tried to shush him.

"No, Brandon!"

"She needs to know, Emily. I won't have her questioning you this way. It can't be avoided now."

"I need to know what? What, dear Brandon, do I need to know?" Mrs. Davidson spoke sharply.

"Mrs. Davidson, I love Emily with all my heart, and I'm going to marry her as planned. I will raise her daughter as if she were my own..."

"What do you mean, as if she were your own, Brandon?" Mrs. Davidson's voice was tight. She glared at him.

"Don't look at him like that, Mother. It's not his fault. He's been nothing but sweet, supportive, and loving."

"So whose baby is this, Emily? Dark skin and dark eyes. How could you do this, Emily? How many boys have you slept with? What kind of boys? You're nothing but a tramp, and I want no part of this." Emily began crying as her mother stormed out.

Chapter 50

Jaden excitedly texted Nolen. "I'm an uncle. Baby came early. A girl!"
"Cool! Have u seen her?"
"Not yet. Brandon's in there w her mom."
"I like kids. U ever thnk u cld be a dad?"
"Idk. I like kids, too, tho."

Mrs. Davidson didn't return to the waiting room. She left Emily's room and headed straight for the exit. Brandon hurried back to the door of the waiting room and motioned for his mom to step outside.

"Mom, Emily's very upset. Her mom called her a tramp and left furious. I told her the truth about the baby."

"Brandon, I'm so proud of you. You're a courageous person, and you did the right thing. You and Emily can't live a lie, nor should you have to. I'll go in to see her. You go into the waiting room and talk to your dad." Brandon explained to Donnie what had happened, and Donnie decided this was the time to speak. He called the others over.

"I didn't get a chance to talk to you at the restaurant, but I want to do it now. What I was going to say was that I know I've been a pitiful father lately, and I guess it took being away from you for a while to see that and to realize how much I miss you. I love you all so much, and I hope you'll accept my apology. I don't know what gets into me sometimes, but I was wrong, and I'm so sorry. Devon, I apologize to you, too. You don't deserve how I acted." He looked back at his children and said, "I'll be begging your mother's forgiveness for everything." It had all been spilling out quickly, and he stopped to take a breath. "Brandon, I don't want you to miss out on college and baseball, so I have a suggestion. If you can get a scholarship close to home, Emily and the baby can live with us, and our family will support them and take care of them while you're away. You can come home as often as possible when it's not baseball season, and when it is, we'll all be at the home games."

Jenny hugged her dad and said, "That would be so great, Dad. I would love to take care of my little niece! Wouldn't you, Devon?"

As he nodded, Jaden jumped in, "Me, too! And Nolen and I were just talking about how we love little kids. We can all help!" Brandon sat down, eyes glistening with tears.

"You guys would all do that to help me and Emily? Even after I wouldn't join your club, Jay? And, Dad, I can't begin to tell you how much I've missed having you at home. I was ready for you to leave at first, because I was so mad. It seemed like you weren't interested in anything about me that didn't have to do with baseball. But, you really knew how much I would miss playing. I'm so grateful to at least have the chance. I can't wait to tell Emily. But who knows if I'll get a scholarship?"

Donnie replied, "You just keep playing the same good baseball that you have been playing, and the rest will fall into place. Now if it's okay with you, I'd like to go find your mother and welcome Emily and the baby into our family."

Emily and the baby moved in with the Hansens when they left the hospital. They decided to name the baby, Jeannette, after Brandon's great-grandmother. Emily had hoped that her mother had just been upset and exasperated when she had seen the baby, but her mother let her know quickly that she was no longer welcome in her house. Brandon and Emily quietly said their vows at the end of baseball season without Emily's mother present.

"Brandon, I knew she probably would feel this way, but I guess I sort of hoped I'd be wrong. She wouldn't even listen when I tried to explain to her that it wasn't like it seemed. It doesn't feel right that she doesn't want me around. It makes me so sad. Your parents are so sweet and understanding, but…don't get me wrong, I just don't feel comfortable in your house. You, me, and baby Jeannette are all crowded into your room, where there's barely enough room for just your stuff. I hardly know your family at all, and I can't imagine how I'll feel when you go off to college."

"I know it's hard, Emily, but we can make it together. You'll feel comfortable in time, I know you will! I love you so much."

Lake Griffin High Mustangs had finished as runners-up in the state baseball tournament, and Brandon had been offered two baseball scholarships. One of them was to State University that was three hundred miles away. The other was to Todd College, a smaller college that was only an hour and a half away, but had courses in aviation science. The fact that he could major in business and minor in aviation science was the icing on the cake.

Chapter 51

After the restraining order had been placed on Chelsea, Brooke and her father had practically no relationship at all, other than occasional shouting matches.

He started a conversation one Saturday by saying, "Brooke, I want you to start helping more around the house, and I want you to get rid of that sour attitude. All you do is stay in your room, and when you do come out, you have a nasty expression on your face."

"Why should I help around here? It's like I'm a prisoner. All I can do is go to school and come back home."

"Your mother needs help. And you're not a prisoner, but you're going to learn that I mean business when I make a decision for your own good."

"You're not in the military anymore, and you can't make me do anything!" Wayne, in a burst of anger, slapped his daughter again and grabbed her by the shoulders.

"Why can't you leave me alone?" screamed Brooke.

Her father roared back, "Don't you yell at me, young lady! You can stay in your room forever, for all I care!" He shoved her back roughly.

"Mom, do something! Are you going to let him ruin my life like this?" Her mother, who had felt powerless during the fray, began to cry.

She said, "Brooke, please just listen to him. If you'll change your attitude, everything will be fine again. You'll make lots of other friends."

Her face still burning from the slap, Brooke answered, "What do you care, right, Mother? You always agree with him! You don't stop him, and you don't care about how I feel. That's it! I'm leaving!" She went to her room and began throwing things into a suitcase. She called her friend Zoe, who had always been sympathetic to Chelsea and her, and asked if she could stay at her house for a while. They decided to tell Zoe's parents that Brooke's mother and father had been called away suddenly on a family emergency.

Brooke left that afternoon and walked over to Zoe's house with her suitcase. She went to school from her house on Monday, and after first period, she was called to the office, where she found her father and the school resource officer waiting.

Wayne said, "Don't think you can just run away, Brooke! And, it's not going to do you any good anyway. You still can't see Chelsea! This officer is going to escort you home after school today. And every day, if need be."

Without looking at her father, Brooke said, "Whatever."

This went on for a week, and Saturday, Brooke left again. This time her father hunted her down at Zoe's house.

"I hate you!" yelled Brooke, standing on Zoe's front porch. "Why do you make me come home just so you can slap me around?" Zoe's mom, thinking Brooke was back at their house with her parents' permission, heard the conversation and stuck her head out to see if she could intervene. Wayne became infuriated and threatened to call the police on Zoe's parents for harboring his daughter. He practically dragged Brooke home. On the way home, he became more and more angry.

When they got there, he erupted, "I can't believe you embarrassed me like that, and I'm sick of you smarting off to me! You think you're grown and can go and do whatever you want. Then, go ahead and be grown! I'm not going to be responsible for your stupid decisions anymore! I'll even lift the restraining order. See how well you can make it on your own! Get out of my sight! Just get out!"

She moved in with the Harpers two weeks before graduation.

"I sure wish I was graduating this year with you, Chelsea. I can't stand the idea of you going off to college in the fall, while I'm stuck here in high school, and in this town."

"I know you're bitter, Brooke, but at least we're together now. And you know my parents love you and are thrilled that you'll be here next year."

"Yeah, but what if my father decides to make me go back home?"

"Well, you need to keep working with that lawyer until you're finally granted emancipation. It shouldn't be too much longer, should it?"

"Oh, who knows? She keeps telling me that it's a process."

The two girls settled into a comfortable life, as Brooke tried to wipe out the memory of her father's words and actions. Besides, the Harpers were glad to have Brooke stay with them. Their little nest wouldn't feel so empty when Chelsea left for college at the end of the summer.

Graduation had finally arrived! It was to be the next day, and while all the other seniors were out of school spending a couple of days hanging out with each other, having parties, and celebrating, Brandon and Emily were changing diapers and trying to get some sleep at night. Jeannette was a good baby, but hadn't started sleeping through the night yet.

Emily overheard Brandon talking on the phone to Dan.

"Dude, you're kidding! You stayed on the lake all afternoon yesterday? Wish I could have been there."

When he hung up, Emily quietly said, "I'm sorry, Brandon. If it weren't for Jeannette and me, you'd be out there having fun with all your friends. If I hadn't been so stupid, I'd be out there, too." Brandon grabbed her shoulders.

"Don't even say that, Emily. I love you, and I love our life together."

"You know it's not how it should be, though. Tomorrow is graduation, and we both should be celebrating with our friends, instead of taking care of a baby. You'll get to go to college, but I don't have my career in physical therapy to look forward to. I don't think I'll even walk in the ceremony tomorrow night." Still holding her shoulders, Brandon looked deeply into her eyes.

"This part of our lives will be over in an instant. Yeah, sometimes it's hard not to be able to do what the others do, but we have a wonderful baby who will be with us and love us and bring us joy for years to come after graduation. You are going to walk tomorrow night, and Mom will hold Jeannette, and we'll be able to tell our child later in her life that she saw her parents graduate. When she starts school, I'll be through with college, and you can go back to school, too."

"Brandon, I love you so much. You always make me feel better."

At the graduation ceremony the following night, it was hard to tell which member of the Hansen family was the proudest. Brandon's heart was pounding with joy, as he watched his *wife,* Emily Hansen, receive her diploma. Jaden and Jenny cheered and clapped until they were hoarse, and their hands were sore.

Although Alice was elated that Brandon had grown up so much and was graduating, she was overjoyed, as well, at the change that seemed to have come over her husband. The year before, Donnie had made promises that he didn't keep, but when he moved back home from his parents' house a few weeks ago, he had seemed truly changed. They had talked late into the night many times about his innermost feelings and what had precipitated his change for the better. He made a point of telling Alice how he had felt when he had heard about Justine Gorman's family problems and how that had helped him look at his own. Alice felt good about the talks, because Donnie had never before confided his deepest feelings to her. Life finally seemed to be on the right track.

Epilogue

During the summer, Brandon had to report to Todd College for conditioning three days a week, but the rest of the time he was home with Emily and the baby. On the days he was home, he had a part-time job at the airport where he learned to fuel aircraft and was afforded the opportunity to question and learn from the resident mechanic, as well as the pilots that kept their planes there. Bill, the owner of the Cherokee Six took him up again several times, as he had promised.

Emily loved the days that Brandon was home, but although she was extremely grateful for the Hansens' help and support, she felt very lonely when he was gone. The whole family continued to be loving and tried their best to make her feel at home, but she still felt like she was living with strangers. She worried about what it would be like when Brandon was away at school full-time, and she'd be there virtually alone.

Chelsea and Brooke knew their peaceful life would be interrupted at the end of the summer when Chelsea went off to State University. Even though it would only be a year until Brooke could join her there, and Chelsea would be home for many weekends and holidays, sometimes, Brooke felt uneasy. When she had gone with Chelsea to her mid-summer orientation, there had been an informal get-together where she had noticed several cute girls that she just knew were lesbians. Chelsea had assured her that she had no worries, but Brooke had been sure that a couple of them had been flirting with Chelsea. After all she had done to be with her, she knew she wouldn't be able to face losing her.

Jaden couldn't help but feel that this was the best summer of his life. The previous summer had definitely been the worst, but now he and Nolen were tight, and they spent a lot of time with Jenny and Devon, Trevor and Ricardo, and Chelsea and Brooke. Jenny, Devon, Jaden and Nolen undertook the duty of taking care of baby Jeannette very seriously. It gave them all a chance to have a first-hand view of the responsibilities of caring for a child. After a summer of changing diapers, Jenny and Devon were convinced that, for them, babies should be put off for a long, long time. They decided that the full force of their effort should be school, the GSA and working for equality for all. Jaden and Nolen knew they didn't have to worry, because babies would never be unplanned for them, but they were glad to get a taste of what it might be like. Who knew what the future might hold? But now, it was time to think about school again. They all felt that the next school year would be full of promise.